Letters to Cassie

by

JOAN LOVESTRAND FARLEY

Published by hope*books
2217 Matthews Township Pkwy
Suite D302
Matthews, NC 28105
www.hopebooks.com

hope*books is a division of hope*media

Printed in the United States of America

First paperback edition.
Paperback ISBN: 979-8-89185-208-2
Hardcover ISBN: 979-8-89185-129-0
Ebook ISBN: 979-8-89185-130-6
Library of Congress Number: 2024948855

Scripture taken from The King James Version (KJV) are in the public domain and has been used in reverence to those who spent their lives translating the Word.

"My father died when I was ten. His last words to me were in his suicide note. Joan's book gives the grieving child something I wish I had in that unspeakably dark time – a fictional parent who finds a creative way to bring godly comfort to the darkest days of her daughter's life. In a world that struggles to those in grief, this story is a rare gift."

–KAT SILVERGLATE
Founder of The Ridiculous Hour Foundation, Inc.

"Letters to Cassie is a beautiful story of a young woman entering her senior year of high school with courage and hope. Her mother, who passed when she was a junior, left her a series of letters that gives her comfort, encouragement, wisdom, and direction. Within the pages, the reader will also find creative ideas for handling challenging situations in a teenager's life. It's a great book for mothers and daughters to read together. Then, take the time to discuss the choices, emotions, and decisions Cassie made as a follower of Christ."

– LAURA LEE LEATHERS
Freelance Writer, Author & Speaker

"Growing up can be hard! And growing into godly womanhood in a world full of distractions and discouragements is even harder. In Letters to Cassie, Christian teens will find a fictional friend who navigates the challenges of becoming God's girl. This engaging and relatable story gives hope and help to real girls who want to live for the Lord today."

–JENNY MARKLE
Pastor's wife and Mother of six

Joan Farley's many years as a pastor's wife, Christian educator, and missionary have given her unique insights into children, teens, and young adults. I have had the privilege to work with Joan for seven years as we sought to help young people trust Christ as Savior and help church leaders and teachers disciple children and youth. Joan has been so intent on helping young people that she has also developed and written Christian curriculum for others to use. Joan has had the opportunity not just to work with adolescents, but also to train individuals so they can work with young people.

Letters to Cassie shares Joan's desire to influence teen girls when heartache enters their lives. She desires them to see the majesty of God's Word and Who Jesus Christ can be to them. The reader will want to follow Cassie as she seeks to complete 'The Nine Challenges' her mom has left for her senior high daughter. The book would be helpful to Christian teen girls because it sees things through their eyes and its format makes it very readable for them.

—CHARLES SARTOR
BA, MS, and Specialist in Pastoral Ministry, and Christian
Education Leadership
45 years as pastor, educator, and missionary

I enjoyed reading about Cassie and her family! I loved getting to know the different characters and their personalities and their reactions to different circumstances. I appreciated Mrs. Farley adding so many every-day struggles for girls and then showing how they can be overcome through God and His word. I definitely recommend this book to girls wanting to strengthen their walk with the Lord! It was my honor to read Letters to Cassie by Mrs. Joan Farley.

—MAKENNA ALVERSON
college student and pastor's daughter

To all the girls
I have watched grow into maturity and are now raising
children of their own. You have inspired these pages.

CHAPTER 1

Gone.

Like a tornado, my world turned upside down. No, it was worse than that. A nuclear bomb demolished my protected life and left behind devastation where there used to be beauty and joy. Only two months ago, Mom was a beacon of light in my world. Now, only shadows, sadness, and darkness remain.

Sitting cross-legged in front of her tombstone, my curly red hair forms a curtain over my face and brushes my knees. I clench my fists as my body trembles, tears cascading down my cheeks. Minutes pass, but I can't stop. My mind forms thoughts my lips can't say. Finally, the gulping sobs slow. I raise my head and lift my hand to the cloudless Minneapolis sky.

"Why, God? Why? Why did you take her? I may be a senior now, but I still need her." I rest my head on my knees. Anger mixes with sorrow as rivers stream down my cheeks. I whisper a final plea. "Help me. Please."

She was my world, my confidence. She was there with a listening ear, hugs, and encouragement when I needed someone. She believed in me. She'd tell me God had great things planned for me. Even in pain, she knew what to say to help me. Our family struggles so much now that Mom's hopeful voice has disappeared. I start to bawl again. My head aches. Tears fall, painting small polka dots on my blue jeans. A low moan escapes when I try to stop. My heart feels like a stone. When the tears finally stop, I lean back on the cool grass and look up at the varying greens of the trees. How can the world be so bright when I'm so sad? July's brilliant days mock my sorrow. The sky should be raining tears, too, instead of warming me with its bright sunshine.

I listen to the rustling leaves of the grand oaks lining the narrow lanes that drown out the distant hum of city traffic. The smell of freshly mown grass mixes with a hint of rose scent on the gentle breeze. Curious, I sit up. Turning my head, I see the rose bushes lining the lane. I hadn't noticed them on the way in. Soft footsteps approach, and I sigh, knowing my sister's steady presence will help.

Alexandra's soft hand touches my shoulder. "Cassie, it's time to go. We promised Dad we'd be home for supper." She extends her hand to pull me to my feet.

I shake my head. I'm not ready to leave.

She sits down beside me and wraps an arm around my shoulders. "I miss her too, Cassie." Her voice sounds broken like she's been crying too. She hands me one of her tissues.

After I wipe my eyes and blow my nose, I stuff the tissue in my jeans pocket. We sit together, staring at the tombstone before us: "Carol Angela Nelson, September 23, 1979–May 5, 2024." Leaning against Alex, I see her wipe the tears running down her cheeks.

People never guess we're sisters, me with my freckles and curly red hair and her with clear skin and long, straight blond hair. When our family was together, people knew I took after Mom, and Alex was a blond version of Dad. But now, no one will see our relationship. I'm 5'7", but she's got Dad's height. At 5'11", she should have taken up basketball. Or modeling, since she also has that perfect model figure. Me? I'm just a beanpole. But with Mom here, I was happy with my unmistakable resemblance to her. Now she's gone.

Finally, I work up the courage to ask the question I've been asking myself all day: "Is it wrong to ask God 'why?'"

She frowns. After a long minute, she shakes her head. "After all, Jesus asked God 'why' on the cross. I think He felt deserted by His Father. Do you feel abandoned?"

"Not by Mom. She couldn't help it. But by God. Why would He let her die when she was such a good mom to us? I prayed for her healing, but she died anyway. I just want her back." Sobs bubble to the surface again. I try to contain them, but soon we're both crying.

Alex recovers first. "Sometimes the grief comes at the worst times. I don't know if I should run away so I can cry or choke back the tears and pretend things are okay." She turns to look at me and then at the tombstone. "Mom is happy and free of pain, but I miss her so much." She gets to her feet. "Come on. We need to go."

Slowly, I stand. Then I notice the two long-stemmed white roses Alex retrieves from the ground beside her. "You remembered," I exclaim, reaching to take one. "I didn't see them earlier, and I was afraid you forgot." I nod toward the simple, white marble vase where one rose stands tall. "Dad's already been here today."

Alex leans over to look at the single rose. "Dad still loves you, Mom," she says, her voice cracking with emotion. "And I do, too," she adds, inserting her flower.

"Me too, Mom." I gently kiss the rose, inhale its calming fragrance, and add it to the other two.

Ten minutes later, Alex drives the car into our driveway.

"Dad, we're home," Alex calls as she opens the door.

Removing my shoes, I glance around. Mom's favorite CD is playing, and the dining room table is set with Grandma's old china. Mom loved getting it out when it was just our family. I sniff the air. I think I smell brownies.

We walk into the kitchen just as Dad opens the oven to pull out a roasted chicken and places it on the counter. He picks up the tongs and places the baked potatoes on a plate. "Girls, would you put these things on the table?"

I lift the chicken from the counter and inhale the herb-scented steam. Setting it down on the dining room table, I notice the candles and the white rose centerpiece. "Wow, Dad. You outdid yourself tonight."

"Well, easy family favorites are good for marking significant events. Even though she's not here, this is still the day we got married." Tears glisten in his eyes.

Alex lights the candles, and we sit in our places. Mom's empty seat still crushes me.

Dad prays, and we fill our plates. Forks and knives ding against the plates as we begin to eat. How many times have we eaten this same meal together over the years? Even though the food tastes so good, enjoying it without Mom feels wrong.

"It's hard for me to talk about your mom without crying, but I need to try. I want my memories to stay fresh and for you to hear them." Dad puts down his fork and clears his throat. "Did I ever tell you about how we met?"

"Only a million times." My mouth eases into a half-grin.

"Well, you're about to hear it for the millionth and first time, then." Once he starts talking, the light comes back into his eyes, and he can't stop. He tells us about the first time he noticed her at a youth group bonfire. The way the light caught her face and made it glow. The way he couldn't take his eyes off her and how they spent hours together studying and enjoying youth group activities.

He continues. "We wanted to get married right out of high school, but our parents asked us to wait until we knew what direction we were headed. So, instead, we went to college together. Finally, when I could tell my parents I was going to be a math teacher, they gave me their blessing to go ahead and ask her to marry me. I could hardly wait."

Dad's misty eyes turn to the wedding photo on the buffet beside us. Then he smiles while tears travel down his cheeks. "It was hot that July, but July 5th made sense since everyone gets the Fourth off. The breezes off the lake made it more tolerable."

His memories continue. "We wanted children, but your mom didn't get pregnant right away. Then Alex came along – the light of our eyes until..." He stops to look at me. "You followed four years later. We would have loved to have more, but we were grateful for both of you. Look at you now. Both of you graduating next year. I couldn't be more pleased."

Dad stops and looks at Alex and then at me. "You two are done eating, and I still have half my plate. I could say more, but I want to hear your stories, too."

I hope Alex doesn't steal my memories.

"I remember," she begins. A gentle smile extends to her eyes as she talks about her first piano lessons from Mom, her feet swinging in midair while Mom taught her. Then, Mom held her hand as they walked together to school on that first day of kindergarten. Her highlight of school days was opening the door after school to find Mom waiting with an afternoon snack and a listening ear as she talked about her day. She stops to catch her breath, and I reach for her hand as she struggles to continue.

She recalls the bedtime stories Mom read, feeling safe and secure in her arms. She'd tell Mom her heartaches, and Mom would pray with her. "She always knew what to say to help me. I know I would not be me without her." Her voice catches, and a single tear travels down her cheek. "I miss her so much."

Alex and Dad look at me. I open my mouth, but the words stick in my throat. Tears well in my eyes and then tumble down my cheeks. Yes, I have good memories. But today, all I feel is the dark emptiness of her absence. She'll never sit with us at this table again. She'll never pray with me. Sing to me. Tuck a stray curl behind my ear. Send me off to school in the morning. Or kiss my cheek good night.

"I can't." I shove my chair back from the table and rush out, taking the stairs two at a time. I plop face down on my bed, my ragged breaths mix with deep groans as tears stream down my cheeks.

When my tears subside, I sit up and reach for the photo of Mom on my bedside table. Her French braid has relaxed, and a few loose, auburn curls outline her face. The sapphire necklace, a gift from Dad last year, makes her blue eyes shine. It's how I remember her—happy, relaxed, and carefree before cancer reduced her to skin and bones.

A rustle in the hall brings me back to the present. Alex walks in, sits on the bed, and puts her hand on my shoulder. "Hey. We have brownies à la mode. Want some?"

I nod, wipe my tears, kiss the photo before replacing it on the table, and follow her.

"Sorry, kiddo. I wouldn't have asked you to share if I'd known it was too hard." Dad's arms open to enfold me in a warm hug. "You can tell your stories when you're ready."

"I know," I mumble into his shoulder. "I just hate that God took her when I still need her."

Dad's arms hug me a little tighter. "I have something that might help." He lets go of me and steps over to the bookshelf. He pulls a pink envelope out of his Bible and hands it to me. "I've been praying about when to give this to you."

"What is this? How long have you had it?" I stare at the pink envelope where my name is written in Mom's familiar handwriting.

"She wrote it shortly after Christmas," he tells me, "but she asked me to give you time to grieve before I gave it to you."

A memory flashes through my mind. I went into Mom's room to say goodnight, and she quickly put her Bible on top of what she was writing. I figured it was personal, but now I recognize the pink stationery.

I stare at it, wondering what she wrote. I carefully set it beside my spoon as Alex returns from the kitchen. The warm chocolate brownies, icy vanilla ice cream, hot fudge, and cool whipped cream are a delectable dessert. It was one of Mom's favorites and mine, too. I feel guilty enjoying it without her.

Dad turns to me as I scrape the last bit out of the bowl. "Go ahead. I know you want to read that. Alex and I'll clean up."

I grab the letter and dash up the stairs to my room. I dig around the bedside table drawer for my tiny scissors. After slitting the top open, I carefully lift out the page.

> *My dear Cassie,*
>
> *Even though I'm anxious to see Jesus, I don't want to leave you. It's your senior year, and you're on the brink of adulthood. I want to experience your joys and sorrows and watch you graduate, but I won't be around.*
>
> *As I prayed for you, an idea came to me. Even though I can't be here, I can help you through this year by giving you nine challenges. Each is something I wanted to teach you myself this year. If you get stuck on any of them, you have your dad, sister, and Aunt Sandi to help you.*
>
> *So here's the first one: Use your quiet time to build your relationship with God, not just as something to check off your "To Do" list. You already have a habit of spending a few minutes with God every day. It's time to move beyond habit to getting to know Him better. Since you keep a journal, use it to write down the things God is teaching you.*
>
> *Some of my challenges can be completed quickly, while others will continue the whole year. You decide when you have enough of a handle on one to ask your dad for the next one. When you complete all nine, Dad has a special surprise for you. I hope that you will finish all nine of them within a year.*
>
> *I love you, Cassie. Thank you for doing this. It makes leaving you a tiny bit easier.*
>
> > *Love you to heaven and back,*
> > *Mom*

"I love you to heaven and back, too, Mom," I whisper.

Wow. Nine letters from Mom. But nine? What will they be?

She knew me better than anyone. Would she challenge me or encourage me? Will they be hard or easy? And what will the surprise be?

Well, at least I know about this one. She's right. I sometimes want to check my quiet time off my list instead of building my relationship with God. Will I ever be satisfied enough with my devotions to feel ready to ask for the next challenge? And what will that one be?

The bedroom door opens, and our black Siamese, Starlight, shoots by Alex's feet and jumps up on my bed. Nestling beside me, she starts to purr. I rub the white diamond shape on her forehead, and her purring increases to a low rumble.

"Is Dad okay?" I ask Alex, looking up at her.

"Yup, he is. I think he's doing better than I am, even though it may be harder for him. After all, he spent more years with her than we did."

"Yeah. But we knew her our whole lives." My shoulders slump as I think of the year ahead of me without her.

She nods and sits down, facing me on the bed while I tuck Mom's letter back into the envelope and slip it inside my Bible.

"Are you okay?" Alex motions toward the letter.

"Yeah. Did you know about this?"

"No, but yesterday Dad gave me a video she made before she died, but I'm not ready to watch it yet."

I reach for her hands, and she pulls her feet up onto the bed, sitting cross-legged and facing me. Starlight moves into the space between our joined hands, stretches, and settles in, purring once again. "Can you pray with me?" I ask.

Alex prays. Although she's choking on some of her words, she asks God to be the comfort we all need, especially Dad, on this first anniversary without Mom. She squeezes my hands, and some of her tears drop on my hand. "God," she prays. "Once again, I submit to Your sovereign will. You will not leave us without comfort. You will be with us in our grief. Amen."

I open my eyes and raise an eyebrow at her. "Submit? What was that all about?"

"I guess I never told you, did I?"

"Told me what?"

"When we found out the cancer treatments weren't working, I got really mad at God. I still needed Mom. I had been praying for her healing. But then I realized that I can't pick and choose what I like about God and His ways. Either He's God, or I'm trying to make myself God." She reaches down to stroke Starlight's long fur. "One night, after a long battle with God, I finally laid down my will and accepted that He knows what is best, even though I don't understand. I still have to do that sometimes, especially on days like today, when it's harder than usual."

She leans in to hug me. Starlight meows, and we laugh.

Alex gets up to climb into her bed, and I grab Mom's picture off the side table again. As I think of Mom's happiness in heaven, a tiny bit of the hurt eases. Kissing the glass, I place it gently back on the table. After I turn off the light beside me, Alex's muffled sobs reach my ears. When will the pain go away? I'm tired of being sad.

In a voice just above a whisper, I begin to recite Psalm 23. "The Lord is my shepherd."

Alex hears me and joins in, her voice breaking. When we reach the end, she says, "Thanks, sis. I needed that."

I turn on my side. Tomorrow, the first challenge begins. I wonder how long it will take me to ask for the next one.

CHAPTER 2

When I open my eyes the following day, my watch reads 5:55. Turning off the six o'clock alarm, I ease out of bed. Alex sleeps on, her long blond hair strewn like rays of sunshine against the dark green pillowcase. Grabbing my Bible and my journal, I ease open the door.

Usually, I read at night since I have so little time in the morning before the bus comes. And it's nice to have Scripture on my mind as I close my eyes at night. But on this glorious Saturday, I have the whole morning free, and I'm anxious to get started on Mom's challenge.

Hot coffee awaits me in the programmed machine, and I pour myself a cup and add a smidgen of sugar and a lot of cream. Light streams through the window onto my favorite chair in the living room. Setting down the steaming cup beside me on the end table, I open my Bible to where I was last reading in the book of Philippians.

How do I do this? How do I make this more about my relationship with God than a habit? I grab my journal and jot down things I notice in my reading.

"Good morning, sweetheart." Dad's voice startles me out of my reverie.

"Good morning, Dad." I look up and smile.

He bends over to kiss my bedhead and continues into the kitchen.

The clock chimes. Almost an hour has passed. How did that happen? But what did I learn? How did I improve my relationship with God? Do I know Him any better than when I started?

I bow my head to pray, confessing that I have a long way to go in getting to know my God.

A day later, my eyes scan the high school Sunday school class for Gemma, my best friend. Near the front of the room, the Winter twins, Titus and Timothy, hold a small group spellbound with one of their stories. Laughter erupts from the group. I choose a seat on the opposite side of the room where it's quieter, and I can watch for my friend.

Minutes later, tiny Gemma saunters in, her black hair swinging around her. I wave, and she rushes to join me.

Across the room, I see Titus slouching in his chair, and I don't know if he's bored or tired. Even though I've known them a long time, it's hard to tell the twins apart. Usually, Titus looks like a young seminary professor with a sports jacket, bow tie, and dress shoes. But Timothy wears a nice shirt, trousers, and sneakers. If they didn't dress differently, I'd have a tough time.

Lily and Sophia walk in and take a seat behind Titus and Timothy. Titus, I think, sits up straight and turns around to talk to them. That's different, I think to myself. Usually, Timothy is the first one to talk.

Seventeen students and Declan's wife, Hope, occupy the seats in our room, but some are on vacation. Everyone else already has their Bibles open. I catch up and pay attention.

Pastor Declan talks about how we can have more friends by being friendly. That's so hard for me. Does God give me a pass on this because He made me shy? Or am I using my shyness as an excuse? Besides, do I need more friends? Isn't Gemma enough?

I remember Mom's challenge. What does having human friends have to do with knowing God? And will one of her challenges be about friends?

After class, everyone starts for the door to the worship service, but I remain seated and wait to talk to Pastor Declan. My jaw tightens as the room clears. Gemma looks at me, and I nod to our youth pastor. Understanding my motion, she gives me a one-armed hug as she heads out. "Catch ya later."

Glued to my chair with my stomach churning, I feel the enormous room closing in on me. I chicken out and decide to leave, but then he notices me.

"What can I do for you, Cassie?" Grabbing a chair, he swings his leg over the seat and folds his arms on the back, waiting for me to say something. Hope pulls up a chair, and joins us.

I clear my throat. "Um, I wanted to ask about something," I tell him about Mom's challenge. "I know it's only been one day. But I feel lost. I'm not sure how to make my Bible and prayer time more meaningful. I thought I was doing fine the way things were, but now I realize there's more to knowing God than just spending a few minutes reading the Bible."

"You make my heart glad, Cassie." A big grin spreads across his face. "What a great problem to have." He turns to face Hope. "We were just talking about Bible reading this morning and how to help all of you with it." She nods.

"Tell you what. I planned to wait until school started to teach it, but since you've asked, I'll teach that lesson in two weeks. Next week I'll announce it. I'll add a little mystery to make them curious, so don't tell."

"I won't."

He slaps his thigh and stands. "We're going to be late for the worship service if we don't go."

I find Alex and Dad in the auditorium and sit beside them. Should I ask one of them for help? No. For now, I'll keep trying myself. I decide to ask Dad or Alex if Pastor Declan's teaching doesn't help me enough.

The quiet house that afternoon beckons me to dig out my journal. When Alex gets home from her date with her wonderful boyfriend Jon, she may want to talk, so if I'm going to write, it better be now.

As I turn Mom's photo to face me, this week's activities parade through my mind. I'm paying more attention to my relationship with God instead of just checking off an item on my daily list. But I still feel lost.

God was as real to Mom as her children were, and He was her best friend. He's my friend, too, but it's hard for me to imagine Him as my best friend when I can't see His smile or frown, touch His robe or His hand, or look into His eyes to see if He approves. I can read His words from thousands of years ago, but they weren't addressed specifically to me. How do I manage this challenge?

I pull out my journal and a pink pen.

Dear Lord,

I'm trying—I really am. I want You to be close to me like You were to Mom. You were her best friend, but I don't understand how she got there. Other than reading the Bible and praying, what am I supposed to do? I hope Pastor

Declan can help me. Otherwise, I don't know if I'll ever be ready to ask for the next challenge.

I keep writing, filling the page with my musings about summer, spending time with Alex, and the hours spent with Gemma. Sadness blasts through my heart with the force of a runaway freight train. A single tear drops on my page, and I brush it away.

Lord, help me, please. I want You to be my best friend.
Amen.

CHAPTER 3

The last two weeks have sped by, but I'm still no closer to understanding how to make my Bible time more focused on a relationship than a habit. I'm spending more time in prayer and reading, but is there more to it than that? Hopefully, Pastor Declan will help today.

At church, we pull in next to the Winter family's vehicle. As soon as Dad stops the car, I jump out and run to catch up with Natalie and the twins.

"Any idea what our topic is?" I ask, breathless. A half smile crosses my face since I'm in on the secret.

"No, even though I've been trying to figure it out," Natalie replies as she links her arm through mine. "Pastor Declan said it could make a difference for us for the rest of our lives."

Opening the door, the laughter and chatter around us embrace me like a warm hug. I love this group. I'll miss seeing them if I go away to college. Of course, I already know the twins and Gemma plan to attend college elsewhere. Where will I end up?

Natalie's face lights up with a sly smile. "I know. He's going to talk about getting married. That would make a difference for the rest of our lives."

"You're joking, right?" I punch her lightly in the arm.

"Of course, I'm joking. The way he talks, sometimes you'd think we need to be thirty years old before we get married. I'm not waiting that long. I'm finding a guy sooner than thirty."

"Well, Pastor Declan was almost thirty when he got married," Timothy says as he sits beside us. "I guess since it worked for him, he assumes it will work well for others too."

Gemma sits down to listen for a minute before adding, "Not me. I'm getting married as soon as I finish college." With a toss of her head and defiance written across her face, Gemma sounds like she can control the universe. "Well," she continues, "I suppose that depends on finding a godly guy, and that might be hard. But I'm praying and expecting God to answer in the affirmative."

Gemma and I move to the second row and find seats behind the Winter siblings. The rows of chairs fill with chatting teens. Pastor Declan and Hope are quietly praying in the corner. When they finish, he grabs his guitar and walks toward us.

"Anyone figure out our topic?" Declan asks as he sets his guitar beside him.

Guesses start flying from all over the room. Investing in the stock market? Choosing a college? Getting married? Choosing a career?

"Those are all things that can change your future," Pastor Declan agrees. "You are right about that. But I'm looking at something that applies to all of us. Not everyone here will go to college. Some of you might not get married. While we sing, keep thinking."

He stands and leads us through a chorus and a favorite hymn. Then, with his guitar hanging loosely from the neck strap, he prays, "Father God, You are the most important being in this room today. We want all that we say or do to honor You. Help us approach this important topic to learn what You want us to know. Amen."

He opens his eyes and looks intently around the circle at each of us. "Turn in your Bibles to Psalm 119."

"Oh no," Timothy grumbles. 'We're going to miss the worship service."

We chuckle together, knowing he won't teach all of that very long psalm.

Even Pastor Declan smiles. "While you are turning, let's talk about the coming school year. How many of you already have plans or goals you are considering for the coming year?"

Titus is the only one who raises his hand.

"That figures," Gemma whispers next to me. "He's always thinking ahead."

Pastor Declan smiles at us. "Our topic this morning might play into your plans if you have those. But even if you don't have a plan other than getting through the year, I hope this discussion will benefit you for the rest of your life. Let's talk about reading and studying the Word of God.

He puts down his guitar and opens his Bible. 'Some of you already read your Bibles regularly, but I'm not sure if it's benefiting you as much as it could. So today, I want to show you one simple Bible study method that might help you. I'm challenging all of you to try this method this year. It's a method I learned when I was about your age, and periodically, I go back to it because I find it helpful."

'If we read the Bible to check it off our 'to do' list, that's dangerous. If we read the Bible but then walk away and forget what we read, we distance ourselves from the One who loves us most. I don't want any of you to do that.

God wants you to know Him, and I want you to see you grow in your relationship with Him. Next summer, I hope you can look back and see that you are closer to God now than before."

I lean in, soaking up every word. Sometimes, I read the words instead of listening to what God is teaching me. But I want the Holy Spirit to change me. I know now that there's a difference between reading and growing closer to God.

Beside me, Gemma is taking notes. I get out my notebook to join her. Maybe we can hold each other accountable.

Pastor Declan assigns verses. "Timothy, would you read Psalm 119:11? Gemma, you can read verse 28 in the same psalm. Titus, would you read verse 98?" He assigns more verses before he stops.

"When you read the verse I assigned, look for one thing: What does this psalm say that the Word of God will do for you? The psalmist may have used words like statutes, commands, or something else to refer to God's Word. We'll make a list on the board."

As the class reads, Pastor Declan's list grows. The Bible keeps us from sinning, shame, and covetousness. It gives us strength, wisdom, and delight.

Declan adds more until a long list appears. "This is the power of God's Word. Do you see why I want you to learn how to read and respond to the Bible so it changes you? If we read without letting it change us, we endanger our own and others' souls. If we don't read it, we miss out on one of the great treasures and resources for living the Christian life.

"I put Scripture passages on the tables on the other side of the room. Each sheet of paper is different. Go ahead and move, and I'll explain the rest when you get there."

Chairs scrape as everyone picks up a chair to take to the tables on the other side of the room. When everyone quiets down again, Pastor Declan continues.

"Each of you has a small box of colored pencils and a list for color coding your Scripture passage. Anytime you see something that is a sin, underline it in black. If you see a characteristic of God, underline it in red. If you read that He is almighty, that's red. Underline a promise in blue. If you find a condition attached to that promise, underline that in purple. If you see a warning, underline it in orange. A command you need to obey? Underline that in green. I've left you an explanation sheet there to help you as you read. If you need to use an additional color for something else, add it.

"In addition to reading and underlining, look for one thing that stands out to you. If you read before you leave for school in the morning, don't just read and underline. Instead, ask the Lord, 'What one thing do You want me to pay attention to today? A promise? A command? Something about the character of God? You will probably find multiple things to underline. On the bottom is the question you need to answer when you finish your underlining: What one thing do I need for today?'"

Hope wanders the room while Declan continues. "When you finish, put down your pencil. Then, you may open your Bible and read something while you wait for the others or keep quiet. Maybe you will want to pray about what you found. We want to give everyone as much time as they need, so please, no talking. Go ahead. Start reading and underlining."

Even the loudmouths in our group are quiet as we begin. Pencils tap and scratch as we work. Across the table from me, Titus draws in a long sigh and picks up a black pencil. It seems he's found something significant. I keep picking up different colored pencils and underlining until I finish. Now, I have a multicolored page.

Which of these underlined sections is most important for me today? Aren't they all? But I think I know which one I need the most. I pick up a pink pencil and draw a box around it. Then, I write the answer to the question at the bottom of the page.

When I finish, I open my worn Bible. Now that I've read the passage, I want to see its context. Is there anything else that I need to notice before Pastor Declan calls us back together again?

Before long, the pencils stop moving. Pastor Declan stands to his feet to return to the podium. "Have any of you done anything like this before?" he asks.

Throughout the room, heads shake. Only one person nods.

"Good. Then I'm glad we've had a chance to do this together. If you decide to do this on your own, you'll need a Bible you don't mind writing in. Sometimes, I grabbed an inexpensive paperback Bible when I wanted to do this because it helps if you don't have a lot of other writing already there. The other writing can distract you from what God may want for you right now. So, first impressions? Tell the group what passage you had and what you thought of this exercise."

Gemma's hand goes up first. "I was amazed. I have the passage in John 10 about the Good Shepherd. I thought I knew this passage, but by doing this, I saw Jesus's relationship with his Father, so I added a color. I wanted to keep

Jesus separate from God the Father, so I made the color for Jesus yellow."

She starts to say more, but Pastor Declan interrupts. "Gemma, did the colors help?"

"They did. Adding the yellow made it clear to me that this passage wasn't only about Jesus and His relationship with us but also His relationship with His Father. In the past, I have been so focused on His relationship to me that I missed some of the other things. Doing it on a clean sheet of paper helped too because then I wasn't pulled in by my comments in the margins of my Bible."

Across the room, Jacob raises his hand. "I have Matthew 6:25-32. I have read these verses before, but the colors helped me pay attention. It was almost like I could hear Jesus speaking to the crowd."

Timothy's hand is waving. "I have I Timothy 4, where Paul tells Timothy not to let anyone despise him because he is young. We memorized that verse, so I knew it, but I was surprised at how many other commands Paul gave Timothy in that section. But I have a question. If Paul commanded Timothy to do something, does that apply to us, too? Because he has a lot of commands here, like..."

He starts to say more, but Pastor Declan puts up his hand to stop him. "We could spend an entire lesson on each of these passages. But today, that is not what we are doing. This morning, I want to see if this method will help you pay better attention to what you are reading. From what you have said so far, I think it does that. Do you agree?"

My yes joins a murmur of yeses in the room, and heads nod. Everyone seems engaged. Sometimes, a few kids make it obvious they're bored and can't wait to leave. Not today.

Pastor Declan wanders through the room, looking over our shoulders at our papers. "Take some time to pray about this until the summer ends. When school starts, I will ask you to commit to Bible study. It does not have to be this method.

'I will ask three questions. One. Will you commit to a time of daily devotions? Two. What will you do in your daily devotions? Three. How do you want to be held accountable?"

Natalie raises her hand. 'Pastor Declan? What if I'm afraid to commit because I think I'll fail?"

'Don't beat yourself up if you miss a day or two." Pastor Declan looks around at the whole group of us. 'Just get back to doing it again. Having an accountability partner will help. Knowing your friend will ask you about it will make you less likely to give up. And some of you may want to ask someone in your family to hold you accountable."

Yeah. Dad and Alex would do that for me, but so would Gemma.

Pastor Declan checks his watch. We only have a few more minutes.

Peter, another youth, raises his hand.

'Pastor Declan," Peter says when the pastor doesn't acknowledge him.

'Yes, Peter?"

'I usually have my devotions using my cell phone. When I first returned from camp, I tried using my Bible, and my dad purposely interrupted me or told me to do something. So, I started using my cell phone. Sometimes, he complains about how much time I'm looking at my phone, but at least he doesn't try to stop me. How can I do something like this on my phone?"

'Good question, Peter. Who else uses a digital device more often than a paper Bible?" A few raise their hands.

"Look for apps you can use. You can highlight in different colors if you download a digital Bible. You can even export verses and parts of verses into another document to keep track of the things you learned. Put your heads together. I think you can figure out a good solution that will allow you to do this exercise digitally. I'm old school. I like the feel and weight of a paper Bible."

After surveying the room, his eyes settle on Titus. "Would you lead us, Titus, in a closing prayer?"

I love listening to Titus when he prays. He opens his heart, even when it's public.

"Wasn't that fun?" Gemma asks. "It was like Scripture began to make more sense to me. I am definitely doing it this year. In fact, I don't think I'll wait until school starts." She turns toward me. "What about you?"

"I am too," I tell her about Mom's letter.

For a minute, Gemma's stern expression makes me wonder if I've said something wrong. "Your mom left you nine letters, and you're only now telling me? That's amazing."

I stand and gather my things. "Yeah, it is. I guess I haven't seen you much lately, so that's why I didn't tell you."

"Earth to Cassie." She points her finger at me, and her dark eyes look up at me. "There are such things as phones, you know. And texting."

Tears well in my eyes. "I know." One tear slides down my cheek. "It's been hard since Mom died, and I haven't felt much like talking."

She reaches out and gives me a side hug. "Sorry. I know it's been hard. But I want you to know I'm here. I'm still your best friend, right?"

"You are." I hug her back, and we walk together toward the auditorium.

CHAPTER 4

Since I started color-coding my Bible, a whole new world has opened to me. Sometimes, I can hardly wait to start and see what God has for me. The tricky thing is figuring out what one thing I should notice the most. Then, the next day, when I go back and look at what I wrote down for the one thing that stood out, I realize I forgot to pay attention to it throughout the day.

Am I any closer to having a relationship instead of a habit? A well of joy bubbles up in me. I am! I still have a long way to go to have the kind of relationship I want, but this is working. I'm obeying more of Jesus' commands. I'm seeing more fruit of the Spirit in my life. I am slowly changing.

Last night, Alex said, "Cassie, I don't know what's different about you, but you seem much more at peace than you were a month ago." So I told her about Mom's challenge and Pastor Declan's Bible study method. She wants to do it too. Even though she'll be away soon at college, we can still hold each other accountable.

Does this mean I'm ready to ask for the next one? I'm getting closer. On a post-it note, I write my one thing for tomorrow: Don't let your heart be afraid. (John 14:27) It joins the other colorful notes on the wall by my bed. Eventually, I'll have to figure out another place to keep these.

I don't know why I'm fearful so much of the time. It's been worse with Mom gone. So tomorrow, I'll keep reminding myself that Jesus doesn't want me to be afraid. Soon, I'll ask for a new challenge.

Gray clouds hang heavy in the sky when Dad drops me off for the first day of cross-country practice the next morning. As I run across the field to join the team, I sigh with relief that the rain hasn't started. I love running, but every year, the group is different from the previous year, so my nerves get to me. Arriving at the field out of breath, I take a quick look around. Am I the last one? I check my watch. At least I'm not late. I finger the post-it note in the pocket of my shorts that I pulled off the wall, reminding myself that Jesus does not want me to be afraid.

Coach Jamison looks up as I join the group. "Welcome, everyone, to a new year of cross-country, and a special welcome to the incoming freshmen."

We clap to welcome them. Our group is larger this year.

Scanning the whole group, Coach grins. His gaze returns to his notes. "Before we start today, I want to discuss my expectations as your coach. If we are going to do well, you need to follow these. If you don't, you're telling me you don't want to be part of the team. That's fine. Go find something else to do. But while I'm your coach, I expect these things of you.

"First, keep your grades up. That's the case for all the sports here at Central High School. If you start to fail any of your classes, you will be suspended from the team until your grades improve. Don't let that happen."

A gust of wind flaps the pages of Coach's clipboard and forces him to raise his voice so we can hear. "Two. Run at least five times a week. Three. Get a good night's sleep every night, but especially the night before races. Be home and preferably in bed by ten o'clock. This is a curfew. I don't want to hear that you were partying late the night before a race." His long stare drills the intended meaning into us.

Under his gaze, a new guy fidgets. "Uh, coach. Does that mean we can party every night except before races?" The boys around him chuckle, but Coach's stare silences them.

"Four. Eat right. I'll share some ideas on what to eat leading up to a race. Five. Encourage each other. We are not competing against each other. We are competing together to win as a team. The more you encourage each other, the better our team will do. Finally, be at every practice and race. This is important. Your teammates need to know that they can count on you."

Peter starts to whisper something to me, but I shush him. I need to hear this and don't want to get into trouble.

Coach flips the page on his clipboard. "I'll also speak with each of you about setting goals. Today's run will give us a baseline. Set a goal of how much you think you can improve during the season."

My mind goes to last year. I improved, but my goals were cautious. Mom had just been diagnosed with an aggressive cancer, and I ran to clear my head of the grief of losing her, not to get faster. Running helped me cope, and it helped me to be with other people who liked to run. Maybe this year, I can be more of an asset to this team.

Coach's sharp eyes rest on me like he's trying to make a point. "I expect improvement. Today, we'll find out where our team is right now. As the weeks progress, think about how much you can improve. By the end of the season, everyone should be faster."

Coach lays his clipboard on the grass, blows a short whistle, and shouts, "Are you ready to run?"

"Yes," we yell back. Forming a big circle, we reach our hands toward the center, but with the guys' and the girls' teams together, we're too many to touch each other. "Go, Falcons!" we all shout, lifting our hands to the sky.

Shuffling toward the starting line, I see a girl wearing an orange headscarf watching us. Who is she? Why is she here? Her eyes follow our star, Malcolm, as he darts over to talk with Coach, and I understand. Who wouldn't want to watch Malcolm run? He runs like a gazelle – smooth, fast and surefooted. Is there more than his running that interests her? He is good-looking. Who is she? How does she know him?

As we wait for Coach's command, my feet dance in my shoes, eager to get the miles behind me. And I'm off. We all are.

As we jostle for position, I feel joy spread through me. Running is so fun at first. I feel like a deer bounding through the meadow, heading toward the well-worn path in the woods. When I reach the woods, my breaths are deep and strong. The middle mile is hard. You're away from the beginning, but the end is not in sight. Slowing down, I keep pace with the guy in front of me, reserving some energy to sprint toward the finish. Two guys pass me, and I pick up my pace a little. So does the guy in front of me. When I see the finish line, I force my legs faster by pumping my arms, hoping to pass at least one person. I've never been the fastest on our team, but I need to be faster than last year. Fire descends into my lungs. I have to finish better than my starting time last year. After all, I've been running all summer.

Crossing the finish line, I fall into a heap on the ground, panting and holding my side. Fast, aching breaths assure me that I did well. As my breaths slow, the burn eases, and I relax, massaging my sore calves. As a senior, I want to be on the starting lineup. I think I'll make it, but I'm not sure. Coach won't announce it for a couple of weeks, just in case someone who typically does well had a bad day today.

Shoes stop near me, and I look up. "Hey, Peter," I say. "How did you do today?"

"Pretty good. I was ahead of you, but not by much. I think you're one of the fastest girls this year."

"You're kidding, right?"

"Nope. I was surprised he ran us together. Last year, we ran separately." A grin teases the corners of his mouth. "Maybe he thinks the guys will motivate the girls to run faster."

Jumping to my feet, I punch his arm. Not hard. Just enough to let him know he's a goofball. "Well, watch out then. If you were only just ahead of me, maybe I'll be faster than you this year."

"Not a chance."

A whistle's sharp tone cuts through our teasing, and we stroll over to join the rest of the group.

Coach waits until we've formed a half-circle around him. "You did great today. I think we're going to have a good team this year. Take a handout, and I'll see you at the next practice." He looks at me. "Cassie, can you stay a minute? I need to talk with you."

I nod. While everyone else grabs the handout from Coach and heads to the locker rooms, I stare down at my shoes, wiping clammy hands on my shorts. What did I do? Why does he want to talk to me?

Coach hands me a copy of the list of expectations. "I was impressed with your time today. You were the first of the girls to finish."

"I was?" I had no idea.

"I always thought you were holding back. Last year, I understood, but I'm hoping you will push yourself this year so that you can see how well you can do. You don't expect to be the first one across the finish line, so you hold back. Today, you didn't know you were first because the boys ran with the girls. You don't need to hide, Cassie. It's okay to shine."

I drop my eyes and fidget with the edges of my t-shirt. How did he know that's what I was doing? Does everyone know?

"Now that I know you can do better, I'll look for it. From now on, I expect you to be at the front of the pack. Maybe not the first of the girls' team like today since Ava wasn't here, but certainly leading the way. You're a senior. It's time to reach for the stars."

Drops of rain begin to fall as I run toward the locker room. Thoughts tumble around in my head. The fastest? Lead the way? Those are words I never thought I'd hear. Can I? But what if I fail? It's more comfortable in the middle, where people don't notice me. If I win in an actual race, people will start to expect things from me. What have I gotten myself into? Then I remember: "Don't let your heart be afraid."

"Help me, Jesus," I whisper.

CHAPTER 5

As I emerge from the gym, our silver car, Mia the Kia, rolls to a stop in front of me. Dad leans across the passenger seat and opens the door.

Dodging the raindrops, I jump in and buckle my seat belt. "I thought you were going to let me walk home."

"I was. Until I saw the rain. It looks like it 'll be pouring down in a few minutes."

And almost like a prophet, the wind chooses that moment to punch the bottoms of the clouds open, spilling buckets of rain down on our car. The slow swipes of the car's wipers turn to quick taps, keeping the windshield clear as Dad drives through deepening puddles. As we pull into the driveway, I'm grateful for our attached garage, so we won't have to run through the downpour.

Dad opens the door to the house. "I'll put the kettle on for tea."

"After I change out of my sweaty clothes, I'll join you."

A few minutes later, Dad hands me the box of tea bags. I smell the Earl Grey in the steam rising from his cup. I choose an Indian chai blend and dip the bag into a mug of hot water. "Dad?"

He continues to swirl his tea bag. "Yes?"

"How will I know when I'm ready for Mom's next challenge?" I reach into the fridge for some milk to add to my tea. "I know that getting to know Jesus will take a lifetime, so how do I know if I'm on the right track so that I'm ready to add another challenge?"

He pulls out a chair to sit at the old oak kitchen table, and I sit down across from him. He looks at me with a faraway look in his eyes. "Mom wanted you to decide when you were ready."

I thought he might say that. I take a deep breath. "Then, I think I'm ready."

A dimple forms on his left cheek. "Can you tell me how the last month has gone? You haven't said much."

So, I launch into an explanation of what I've learned so far – about spending more time reading, Pastor Declan's teaching, and Alex's teaming up with me for accountability. "I know I still have a lot to learn." Relaxing against the back of my chair, I put the mug to my lips and sip the hot liquid. "But Mom was right. God is not something to check off your to-do list. He's Someone to know. And I'm starting to get to know Him better. He is more real to me today than He was a month ago."

"Well, that's what matters." Dad sets his cup on the table. "I'll be right back with the next one."

While he's gone, I wonder. What will it be?

When he returns with another pink envelope, he hands it to me. "I hope you're keeping these."

"Of course!" I clutch the envelope to my chest like it's a long-lost puppy and scamper up the stairs to my room.

The rain pattering on the roof has stopped, but the mist keeps the sunlight away. My dark bedroom and my expectant heart beg for more light, so I open the curtains, switch on the bedside lamp, and sit on my bed to read.

> *My dear Cassie,*
>
> *So you feel ready for another challenge. I'm glad. The first one is the most important to me because I want you to be as sure of God's love and care for you as you were of mine. People may fail you, but God never will. If you can keep growing closer and closer to God, He will keep you through all the mountains and valleys of your life. He will be your guide and your closest friend. I know you well, Cassie. So this one is going to be harder for you.*

I stop reading. She shouldn't have warned me. Now I don't want to keep going, but I want to know what she says. I take a deep breath and continue.

> *I want you to find someone to mentor.*

What? How can I do that? First, I don't know anyone who wants a mentor. Second, even if I knew someone who wanted to be mentored, they wouldn't want me.

> *I can almost hear what you are thinking right now. You don't want to do this. You don't think you have any-thing to offer. But you do, Cassie. As a senior, many younger girls look up to you. I've watched you interact with your youth group. You have something to give them. If nothing else, you can tell them what you've learned through these weeks of seeking God.*

Seeking God. She's right. That's exactly what I've been doing. But everyone at church got the same lesson I did from Pastor Declan. I don't think I could help anyone. Mom's handwriting pulls me back into her letter, and I keep reading.

God has at least one girl for you to bless by taking her under your wing – someone who could benefit from being mentored by you. When you find her, commit to her for this school year. You may find that you will learn as much from her as she does from you. God has designed His body to work that way.

Mentoring you and Alex has been one of the greatest joys of my life. But the other women and girls who have looked to me for wisdom, prayer, or friendship have blessed me beyond what I imagined. When I began to say "yes" to those little tugs from God to reach out to someone, I had no idea I would benefit as much as I did. I want you to receive the blessings God gives when we give of ourselves to others.

I know you'd rather stay hidden and watch from the sidelines. But God has so much more for you than that. It's time to spread your wings and get ready to soar.

I love you to heaven and back.

> *Mom*

How, Mom? How do I do this?

I tuck the letter back into the envelope and slide it between the cover and pages of my journal. Little did I know that God was already working behind the scenes.

CHAPTER 6

When I get to church the following Sunday, my eyes scan the youth room for Gemma. Near the front of the room, the twins hold a small group spellbound once again with one of their stories. Laughter erupts from the group. I sit on the opposite side of the room to think and watch for my friend.

"Cassie, may I speak with you a moment after class?" Pastor Declan's voice interrupts my thoughts.

"Uh, sure," I stammer.

Minutes later, Gemma saunters in, her black hair swinging around her. I wave, and she rushes to join me. "Did Pastor Declan talk to you yet?" she asks.

"All he said was that he wanted to talk to me after class. What's it about?"

"Probably the same thing he asked me, but we'll talk later." Just like that, she switches gears and focuses on Pastor Declan. The rest of the group finds their seats, but the chatter continues. Why doesn't she want to tell me?

I look around the room and count seventeen students, not including me. Where is the Smith family today? Bible pages rustle around me, and I realize I didn't hear Declan announce the passage. I better catch up and pay attention.

After class, the students bunch at the door on their way out, greeting each other with fist bumps, but I stay glued to my seat, waiting for Pastor Declan. Tightness grips my jaw as I wonder what he wants.

Gemma gives me a one-armed hug and stands to leave. "Catch ya later."

My stomach churns. The enormous room is starting to close in on me. What did I do? But I guess he talked to Gemma, too, so maybe it doesn't have to do with me. Maybe it's about being a senior.

Pastor Declan picks up his Bible from the podium, walks over, and sits down. "Cassie," he begins. "I want to ask you something. You don't have to answer right away, but I need to know before the end of the month." He stops. Is he waiting for me to say something?

Hope joins us, and he continues. "This year, I decided to form small groups in our class. My teaching time will be shorter to allow discussion at the end. We'll divide into small groups to discuss some questions from the lessons. I don't know if you've noticed, but only a few people participate when I lead discussions from the front. I know some people like you are hesitant to speak in front of the group, so I'm trying this. Everyone will benefit by contributing more. So, would you be a small group leader?"

He pauses. Can he see my apprehension? My stomach does a few flips and gurgles. Me? Lead a group? How could I possibly do that? Some days, it's hard for me to even come, especially if I know Gemma won't be here.

He goes on. "You're a senior now. The other girls look up to you. I know it's more comfortable for you to hang out with Gemma, but I've asked her to do this, too, and she agreed. I wouldn't put you in the same group, and I think the other girls will find it strange if you're the only senior who is not a leader. Think about it. Ask God to give you the courage to do this because I think you're ready. Any questions I can answer to help you decide?"

Inside, my objections rise to the surface. What if I can't lead? What if someone runs right over me? What if they don't like me as their leader? What if the group doesn't want to discuss the questions but wants to talk about other things? Before I think about this, I need to know something. Willing my voice to sound normal, I ask, "Are there any other requirements besides leading the discussion during class?"

"That's the main one, of course. I also want you to commit to praying for your group. I hope a bond will form, and you will find joy in leading. But no one knows if that will happen."

I can pray for people, but lead? I stutter out my worst fear. "What if I really can't do it? I feel like I can't right now, but what if it's true? What if I can't lead a group discussion?"

Hope smiles at me as though she understands my fear. Pastor Declan studies my face and goes on. "I'll help you. On youth group nights, I'll gather the four of you to ask how things went on Sunday. Then I'll give you tips on how to do better. It's a learning experience for all of you, but I think you can do it."

He may think so, but I don't. I've never done anything like this before. At school, group leaders are always voluntary, and I never volunteer. "I appreciate that, Pastor Declan. I really do, but I wish you would ask someone else. It sounds, though, like the other seniors have already agreed."

"They have." He smiles. "I waited to ask you until the end because if the others had not agreed, there would be no point in asking. I didn't want to worry you unnecessarily. We won't start this until school starts, so you have time to think about it."

He turns to go. "Pray about it, okay, and talk with your dad. I think he'll be able to help you."

I nod and follow him and Hope out of the room toward the auditorium. I hope Gemma didn't tell him she thought I could do this. If she did, I'll. I stop to think. What would I do to my best friend for believing in me? Nothing. But maybe I could threaten.

How will I pay attention during worship today with this request hovering over me? I guess I'll pray and ask God to lead me whenever it distracts me, and then I'll turn my mind back to what's happening.

I do know one thing: God cares. He cares about how scared I am. He cares about the other girls in our group. He will show me what to do.

As the instruments begin to play, the warmth of my dad's arm on the seat behind me offers comfort and safety. As I lean into his solid strength, my worry subsides. "Father, help me," I pray. It's all I can manage right now, but I know He hears me.

Days have passed, and I still haven't come to a decision. I don't even want to think about it. Dad's been busy with work, and I haven't asked Alex either. Between work, practicing the piano and voice, and spending time with Jon, I don't see her much. So, I don't think of it when she's home. But when I'm alone, and it's quiet, I get nervous about it again. Tonight, she's off with Jon again. I'm happy for her, but I wish she were home a little more.

Dad and I are eating supper when he turns to look at me. "Cassie, you've been troubled lately. Want to talk about it?"

I'm glad he noticed. I don't know if I would have brought it up myself. "Yeah." I sigh and look down at my plate. "On Sunday, Pastor Declan asked me to be a discussion leader for a group of girls in Sunday school. You know how hard it is for me to do anything like that. It scares me to even think about it."

"What scares you most about it?" Scooping up some mashed potatoes with his chicken, he fills his mouth and turns his eyes toward me, waiting for an answer.

"What if I can't do it? I mean, what if I'm not a good leader?" I feel uneasy as I talk about it. Sometimes, I hate how insecure I am. It gets in the way of doing things.

"Why did he ask you to do it? Did he tell you?" His brow furrows as he looks at me. I guess he genuinely wants to know.

This is Dad. Asking questions to help me define why I'm feeling the way I am. He's good at that. Even though he thinks in numbers, he's a good counselor, especially for Alex and me. Mom was better, but he's pretty good too.

"Because I'm a senior. He says the other girls look up to me. It's hard for me to believe that. I would rather disappear than lead."

"Is there anyone else in the group you think the girls look up to more than you?"

"Gemma. But she's going to be a leader too. I'll never be like Gemma. She's so charismatic. She could make anyone like her."

For a few minutes, he's quiet. I can tell he's thinking about how to help me. "Maybe you could ask him to give you the younger ones. That way, you'd feel more at ease."

"That's it," I exclaim. I can't believe I didn't think of that. That would make all the difference in the world. The Juniors scare me, but the younger ones don't. "I'll ask him on Sunday. If he'd do that for me, then maybe I can do it."

Leaning back in his chair, he grins. "Next time, don't take so long to talk to me. I don't want to invade your privacy, but it troubles me when I see you bothered."

"Okay, Dad. Thanks." I get up, kiss him on the cheek, and clear the table.

Dad picks up the leftover mashed potatoes and puts them on the counter. "And didn't you say Mom wanted you to mentor someone this year? Wouldn't this be a way to do that? It sounds like God has gone ahead of you to give you an easy way to make that happen—if you're willing to mentor and not just lead a discussion."

I rinse the plates and put them in the dishwasher. "You're right. Maybe this can lead to mentoring." But if leading a discussion feels like pulling my insides out and showing them to the world, how will I ever be able to mentor someone? And what does that even look like?

CHAPTER 8

It's Sunday again—a glorious day. Sometimes, I wonder how God could create such a beautiful world for us. It's that kind of day when God seems to shout, "I'm alive! I made all this! I made you too!" The leaves shimmer in the breeze against a bright blue sky on these beautiful late summer days. The days are hot, but the nights are cooler. It all makes me feel more alive.

I look around for Gemma, but I don't see her. I hurry to our room to talk with Pastor Declan before class begins.

"Hi, Cassie," he says.

"Um, hi. Do you have a few minutes?" I struggle to get the words out.

"Sure do. Have you thought more about what I asked?" His voice is gentle, and he's always been kind to me. I don't think I could talk with one of those hard-nosed adults who always have something to say and not enough time to listen.

"I did. Honestly? It scares me. But Dad said I should ask you something. Could I have the younger girls in my group and let Gemma take the older ones? I think I'd be okay leading the younger ones. Some Juniors are almost as old as I am, and they might be better at being leaders than I would. Gemma would be a better leader for them." I glance sideways at him, afraid he'll think I'm a coward. Or even worse, that I know how to run the youth group better than he does.

"That's a great idea, Cassie." A smile from him helps me relax a little. "Hope and I had this conversation this morning. She thought it would be better to divide the group like that, too. I'm glad we're thinking the same way."

My shoulders relax, and I start to breathe again. It's going to be okay. I can be a big sister to the younger ones. I already think of some of them that way, like Natalie.

After class, Pastor Declan pulls us seniors aside, and Hope joins us. "Here are your groups." He hands each of us a slip of paper with names, phone numbers, and birthdates. "I decided to divide by age. For the guys, that means Timothy gets the sophomores and juniors, and Titus gets the first-year students. Gemma will take the junior girls, and Cassie has the first- and second-year students. I'll text everyone this week to let them know which group they are in. After I do that, reach out to your group. Any questions?"

He looks around at us. I already knew my group, but the others study their lists.

Soon, Timothy and Titus head for the door. Gemma follows. When she realizes I'm not with her, she stops and turns around, and I motion for her to wait.

"Pastor Declan, this is going to be hard for me."

"I know. But it's time for you to fight your fears. Don't let fear rule your actions. Take courage, Cassie. Courage is not being free of fear but doing what needs to be done even if you are afraid. Be strong. I believe, and so do you, that this will be good for you."

I look down and shake my head, my stomach still tight.

Hope puts her arm around me. "Cassie. You can do this."

Pastor Declan looks at his watch. "We'll be praying for you, Cassie."

"Thanks."

Gemma opens the door, and we walk toward the auditorium together. "What was that about? Still scared?"

"Uh-huh."

"Give it a week or two, Cassie. You can do this. Don't let your insecurity win this one."

"Fine for you to say. You don't even know what it feels like."

"I know. But I know what fear feels like. Don't you think I get scared too?

I don't argue with her. But it's probably ten times worse for me than for her. I see my family sitting in their usual place, and I slide in next to Alex. Letting the music slide over my soul, I relax. I'll read some of Joshua this afternoon. I need to see how he handled fear.

That afternoon, I'm wondering what it will be like to lead a group. Even though it is only three girls, the idea of leading brings up other thoughts. As a rising senior, I should know what I plan to do after high school, but I don't.

"Who are you, anyway?" my insecurity growls. Sometimes, only minutes later, it roars, "You'll never amount to anything." When I remember to shout back with truths from the Bible, I can fight those feelings. Otherwise, I believe it, shrink into a corner, and hide from the world. I hid a lot last year. I was hoping I could hide this year, too. I'm not ready to come out of my shell or become an adult.

Sleep will overtake me soon, but I pull out my journal to write before it does. Then, across the top, I put my question.

Who am I?

I've been asking myself this all summer. Really, who am I?

My pen slides easily across the page.

I'm a nobody. If there were an award for the best "nobody," maybe I would get that. No, that's not true. You can't give an award to someone you don't see. I doubt anyone would notice me even in a crowd with other nobodies. They watch the popular kids and ignore other ordinary people. Why would anyone want to notice me anyway? I don't have musical talent like Gemma. I'm not a star athlete like Maya. I get good grades, but I'll never be valedictorian. I'm not gorgeous like my sister. I'm just an average nobody.

Maybe Alex is right. She says I work hard at disappearing. But it's because I'm so scared. I write more.

I'm scared. Scared they won't like me. Scared I'll never measure up. Scared I'll look stupid. Everything is so scary. It's easier when no one notices I'm here. But then my heart breaks because I want to be seen and part of things.

Mom really got me. Of all the people in the world, she understood what being me was like. Now she's gone. Tears stain my page as I write.

Why, God? Why did you take her? She was too young to die. I'm too young for her to be gone.

Sometimes, I wish the ground would open and swallow me. It's not that I want to die. Well, yes, sometimes I do, but not because I hate life. I'm just scared to go on without Mom.

So, who am I? I'm not sure. Lord, let this be a year when You show me who I really am and what You want me to do with my life.

CHAPTER 9

Raindrops spatter the windshield as we drive to church the following Sunday. On the edge of the road, trees shiver in the cold, and dots of orange, yellow, and red trumpet fall's pending arrival. Rainy days usually dampen my mood, but jitters dominate my senses today. Since getting up this morning, I've been singing 'It Is Well' to remind myself that God will get me through today.

Dad hears me humming and smiles. "Are you feeling good about today?" he asks.

'I'm terrified," I confide. 'But I know God is asking me to do this, and it will get better after today."

Before he can ask any more questions, I pull the hood of my jacket over my head, ready to jump from the car. But before he shuts down the ignition, he grabs my hand. 'Let me pray with you."

He prays, claiming Isaiah 41:10. It rolls off his tongue with such confidence that my faith soars. The butterflies in my stomach may never still, but God will keep His promises. He will be with me. He will strengthen me. He'll help me. I'll be okay. I will not let my insecurity win today.

When he finishes, I dash through the drizzle to the front door. In the lobby, I hang my drenched jacket. Nearby, the pastor's children swirl around their mom, hanging up jackets and asking questions. Bella holds up her arms to be carried, and Mrs. Fuller picks her up.

"May I take Moriah to her class for you?" I ask, and she nods in agreement. Babysitting them so much this summer has given me a deep love for them. I know Mrs. Fuller can handle it, but it will distract me for a few minutes.

Five-year-old Moriah skips ahead of me to her room. "Hi, teacher!" she says as she spots my aunt at the door. Aunt Sandi, Mom's younger sister, is so good with children even though she doesn't have any of her own. Ever since she came back from Indonesia to help with Mom's care, she's been like a second mother to me.

Signing her in, I confide to Aunt Sandi. "Pray for me. We are starting our small groups today, and my nerves are showing." I hold out my shaking hand.

She grabs it and pulls me in for a hug. Then she stands back to look up into my eyes. "It's scary to do new things. When I first went to Indonesia, I hardly slept for a month until I got used to all the new sights and sounds. But when I returned to help your mom, I cried about leaving all those precious people. It will be the same for you. Your group will become very special to you. God doesn't ask us to do something without giving us what we need. We need to trust Him, even when it's scary."

As I turn to leave, Gemma rounds the corner and pulls on my arm.

"What's the hurry?" I ask.

"We're late."

I check my watch. My detour to see Aunt Sandi took longer than I realized.

When we open the door, singing spills out. As we make our way to our seats, Pastor Declan starts talking about David's mighty men. "Their loyalty and friendship made them willing to die for one another. According to Jesus, that's the kind of friendship we ought to have for one other."

Would I be willing to risk my life for anyone in this class? Gemma? Of course. Pastor Declan? Not that he'd need help from me, but yeah. Hope? Yes. But what about the others? I don't know. Maybe by the end of the year, I'll be able to say "yes" to everyone in our class, especially those in my group.

Fifteen minutes before the hour is over, we divide into groups. Inside my Bible is the list of questions I'm supposed to ask today. My stomach churns as I face my group of three. Natalie and Emily are freshmen, and Olivia is a sophomore. I send up a silent prayer. "Lord, help me bridge the gap that is here. Natalie and Emily are already close. Help me to lead this group toward being one cohesive group – even adding others in if they join us later."

I clear my throat and decide to be honest. "Leading this group is taking me out of my comfort zone. Have any of you ever heard me answer a question in class?"

Their heads shake in unison.

"Well, it was hard to agree to do it, but I'm glad I did." I take a sip from my bottle of water and then put my shaking hands in my lap, willing my voice not to give away my nervousness. "As Pastor Declan mentioned when he split us up, today's assignment is to get to know each other better. He gave me a list of questions as suggestions. Each one of us can choose one to ask." I put the list in the center of the table so we can all see it.

Olivia leans in. "I don't see my question on that list. I want to ask, 'Have you ever kissed a guy?'"

Natalie and Emily burst into loud laughter, and the girls from Gemma's group turn to look at us.

My stomach lurches. This is why I was afraid. Olivia likes to make people laugh, and I often laugh with her, but how do I handle this?

I clear my throat, and they settle down. "I don't think that's the kind of question Pastor Declan has in mind. How about I start?" I choose my favorite question on the list. "What three words would your best friend use to describe you?"

Olivia jumps in. "That's easy. My best friend would probably say I'm funny, fun, and ready to do anything. But even though she's my best friend, she doesn't see the real me inside. Nobody does. Not my best friend. Not my mom. And especially not my boyfriend."

I nod. "I know what you mean. We all have parts of us we like to keep hidden. Who's next?"

Emily twirls her long blond hair around her finger and sighs. "Can Natalie just answer the question since she's right here? I mean, I might not get it right."

I thought one of them might say that, so I'm prepared. "Well, that's part of the fun. It will be interesting for Natalie to see what you think she would say. Go ahead and try."

Natalie looks at Emily as though trying to read her mind. "Emily would probably say I'm shy, athletic, and scared of spiders. Am I right?"

Emily gives a sideways grin. "Yup. Though I might have said, 'Scared of spiders and snakes.'"

I smile at her. "I don't like those either, though I wouldn't say I'm scared of them. They're just creepy. And what do you think Natalie would say about you?"

Emily rests her chin on her hand. "She would say I'm shy, patient, and studious." She turns to look at Natalie. "Am I right?"

Natalie nods. Then she leans toward us and whispers, "But I would add that Emily is godly."

Emily's face turns a shade pinker as a soft smile steals across her face.

"Why are you whispering?" Olivia asks.

Natalie leans forward and whispers again. "Because Emily gets embarrassed when I say she's godly."

"Because I'm not." Emily shakes her head and puts her face in her hands. "If you could see inside of me, you'd know it's not true. I need God's grace and mercy all the time."

Interesting. If Natalie thinks Emily is godly, God may have chosen Em for something unique.

When Emily looks up again, the others turn to look at me. I look briefly over at Gemma and wonder how she would answer the question. "I think Gemma would say I'm quiet, studious, and fun. I'll have to ask her later and find out."

Olivia chooses the second question. "If someone gave you $1,000, what would you do with it?" But then, Pastor Declan stands to his feet. "Time's up. I'm glad you're enjoying this. We'll keep breaking into small groups for the discussion of our lesson, but today, I just wanted you to get better acquainted." He closes in prayer, and chairs scrape as we disperse from the tables to head for the door.

Today was a good start. I already know more about my group than I would have known in a year if we hadn't done this. I'll keep my list of "Who are you?" questions handy in case we finish that day's discussion questions with time to spare.

That night, I call Gemma. "How did your group go?"

"It was wonderful," she gushes. "I got to know them

better from those few minutes than I did all year. I'm glad we're doing this."

We talk a few minutes. It doesn't surprise me that she loved it. And she doesn't understand why new things are hard for me. I don't even know what I'm doing next year. The other seniors all have college plans next year. I don't know when, where, or if I should go.

How I miss Mom. I pull the pink envelope out of my Bible to reread her challenge. A jolt of understanding hits me. Isn't leading my little discussion group like mentoring? Or at least, will it lead to that? If I care about these girls and give them my real self—someone still growing in Christ—isn't that mentoring? I look up "mentor" on my phone: "Someone who influences and helps someone else over a period of time." That's what I hope to do. So, Pastor Declan's request answered Mom's prayer for me.

Peace envelops me as I lay down to sleep. Even though she's gone, God is working to answer Mom's prayers for me. That's incredible. That's my amazing God.

CHAPTER 10

The warm summer days fly by, and September lurks around the corner. I text my three girls every week to see how they're doing and get their prayer requests. The following Sunday afternoon, Natalie texts me.

Hey, I was wondering. Since you're our discussion group leader now, can you do me a favor? I'm struggling to be consistent in my quiet time. Timothy suggested I ask you to hold me accountable. Would you do that?

I find a big smiley face emoji and text back. Of course.

So, not only do I have a discussion group, but I'm also becoming Natalie's mentor.

I turn from the small suitcase I filled with the stacks of clothing and shoes Alex asked me to pack. Tears threaten to overwhelm me. I will not cry. Not now. But the emptiness of my heart aches to have her stay. Our house will be sadder without her.

The chime of the doorbell interrupts my thoughts. Alex grabs her big suitcase and lugs it down the stairs. I pick up the carry-on case and a bulging shopping bag and follow her. Putting down her suitcase, Alex slings open the door and hugs Jon. 'I've missed you."

He grins as he hugs her back. 'It's only been a few days, and we talk every night."

'I know, but you're better in person."

Alex breaks off the hug and runs back upstairs. Jon picks up the suitcase, and I follow him out the door to the car. Mock grunting, I lift the suitcase into the trunk and shove the shopping bag into a corner. "So why aren't you two engaged yet?" Alex would kill me for asking, but I want to know.

He turns, his mouth open at the question.

Reaching out, I tap him on the arm. "Hey. I've never seen you at a loss for words. Obviously, you two love each other, so what's the holdup?"

He nods and closes the trunk. "We do love each other. But engagement will add pressure. My friends don't understand why we're not sleeping together, but we're waiting for marriage. If we're engaged, they will pressure me even more."

"Does Alex know this? When I asked her, she said, 'That's Jon's decision.'"

"She does, but I know she would love to be married already. And there's still something holding me back."

"You're kidding, right? You two were made for each other."

He scowls at me and walks back to the house. I shouldn't have said anything. It's their decision. What does he mean?

Alex emerges with her hanging things, and Jon takes some of them from her and lays them in the back seat. When all of Alex's things are in the car, Dad calls us into a huddle for prayer. Tears glisten in his eyes when he finishes.

Jon gives me a brief hug and whispers in my ear. "Pray for me, okay?"

I nod.

Alex grabs me in a fierce bear hug. "I'm so glad your cross-country team will be at my school this fall. I'll see you then. Or before. If we come home for a visit." I head back upstairs and check my phone.

Natalie: *Thank you. BTW, I love what your mom did for you in your first challenge. I want to get to know God better too!!! Please keep telling us about her challenges.*

I send back a thumbs up.

CHAPTER 11

Goosebumps spread across my skin as I walk into homeroom on the first day of school. Who will be in my homeroom? Will I still spend much of the day alone? Part of me wants a good friend, but after getting hurt last year, I don't want that to happen again. Sliding into my desk, I look around and wait. A girl across the room meets my eyes and waves. She's one of the popular kids, so I'm surprised she'd notice me. I give a half-hearted wave back and keep looking. Most faces are familiar.

As I glance around the room, I spot a girl I've never seen. Her dark eyes sparkle with mischief, and her mouth curves into a small smile. The blue hijab around her head accentuates her thin, dark face, the perfect complement to her navy blue harem pants and white long-sleeved top.

When the announcements end, I get up and pick up my backpack. As I sling it over my shoulder, it bumps the new girl.

"Oh, no. I'm sorry." Reaching out to touch her shoulder, I ask, "Are you okay?"

She nods.

"I'm Cassie. Are you new here?"

"Yasmin. Is it obvious?" Her forehead furrows with worry.

"Not really," I reassure her. "But after three years here,

I recognize most of the seniors. I don't remember seeing you."

"I thought maybe it was because I'm Muslim." Yasmin points to her head covering.

Shaking my head, I smile, and we join the jostling crowds in the hall as everyone hurries to their next class. Students shout hellos to each other as they pass, but I keep my head down. I see the gray girl approaching us in the corner of my vision. I call her that because she often wears gray, and her gray eyes look like a cloudy day. I deliberately turn my head toward Yasmin so she can't make eye contact.

Yasmin almost collides with a guy who is texting as he walks. "Good thing he's not behind the wheel of a car," Yasmin smirks.

Something is familiar about her. Is she the girl I've seen watching the cross-country practices? She sees me studying her.

"What?" she asks as we step around a boy digging his phone out of his backpack.

"Did I see you at the cross-country practice?"

"You might have. I went to watch Malcolm run. He's my next-door neighbor and was the first to notice me when we arrived. He's fast, isn't he?"

I nod. "And good-looking."

"And he's Muslim, so we have that in common too."

Well, that's one riddle solved. We arrive at the choir room, and I stop to say goodbye. "I'm sorry we can't talk more. I really want to get to know you, but this is my next class. See you tomorrow in homeroom, okay?"

"This is your class?" A bright smile spreads over her face. "I'm in choir too. Where do the altos sit?" Yasmin surveys the arc of chairs on the risers.

"Over here. I'm an alto, too."

One by one, other students file in and sit down. Finally, Maya arrives, surrounded by other girls. Her bright smile stands out against her dark skin. Athletic, stunning, and blessed with a magnetic personality, clusters of friends follow her around school. I tentatively raise my hand to see if she notices me, and she grins as she walks over. "I can't stay, you know. I belong with the high and mighty sopranos. So sorry you get stuck with the lowly altos." She winks at us.

I try to think of a comeback, but I can't. I'm not quick like her. "I want to introduce you to Yasmin. She's new here this year."

"Hi, Yasmin. Glad to meet you." She looks her over and asks, "Any chance you play basketball?"

"I do."

"Guard or forward?" Maya stands back and mimes a perfect free throw.

Yasmin smiles, recognizing the motion. "Usually guard."

"Great. Then I guess I'll be seeing you on the basketball court." Maya gives us a thumbs-up and heads back to her seat in the soprano section. Her long cornrow braids swing as she walks.

I met Maya a few days after I found out that Mom's cancer was terminal. Lonely, scared, and wanting a friend, I never expected Maya to notice me. But after school one day, she found me and promised to pray for me. I invited her to youth group, and soon we were friends, even though I may be one of the least popular girls in the school. She's been such a blessing.

"Find a seat, everyone," Mr. Clark calls out. "If you're new, find the section where you think you belong, and I'll listen to you later to make sure you are in the right place."

He passes out music and starts us on vocal exercises. "La, la, la, la, la" fills the room. We spend the hour going through the new pieces. My sight-reading skills are rusty, and I'm not the only one. Sometimes, Mr. Clark grimaces and stops us. By the end of the third piece, I'm exhausted.

Mr. Clark looks over his new choir. "We have a lot of work to do if we are going to be ready for the December concert or participate in any state competitions. If you need to take pieces home to work on, check them out with me. Talk to me if you want to sing a solo or be in a small group. However, new choir members need to stay today so I can listen to you. I'll give you a late pass for your next class. Class dismissed."

Yasmin groans. "I hope he doesn't keep me too long. I hate being late for class."

I giggle. I hate that too. Yet another thing we have in common. It's like God is deliberately putting us together.

"Bye, Yasmin. Gotta go. Catch ya later." I run to catch up with Maya. I edge through the crowd and fall into step beside her as we walk down the tiled hall.

"Now that youth group is starting again this fall, can you come?" I ask.

"You bet! I wouldn't miss it for the world!"

"Wonderful! I'll see you later."

How can two people who are so different become good friends? I'm so ordinary. Hardly anyone sees me, but she stands out in any crowd. Literally. Six feet tall with a magnetic smile that lights her dark eyes. What I like best about her is her deep faith in Jesus. I'm glad I found that out right away. And her laugh. Her laughter sounds like music.

At the entrance to the classroom, I stop as Maya keeps walking down the hall, surrounded by her groupies. Watching her go, I remember being jealous of Maya's ability to draw a crowd. Then I found out how much pressure it adds to her life and realized invisibility has some advantages. At least I don't have to keep guarding myself against fake friends.

Someone bumps my side, and I turn to see Natalie grinning at me. "I'm so glad I got to see you today." She gestures at the churning mob of students around us. "This place is a madhouse. But I wanted to ask you to pray that I would find someone who needs me to be her friend."

She runs off, and I send up a quick prayer for her. Does Yasmin need a friend? Maybe I should be praying the same thing for myself. It's interesting how God works. Natalie asked me to help her, but she's helping me too.

"Hey Cassie!" a classmate calls out as she passes. I'm going to miss it here. I finally have a few friends, and soon I will have to start all over, making new ones.

"You're here too?" I hear an unknown voice behind me. I turn. There's Yasmin, looking ever so pleased with herself at finding me again. "How many more classes will we have together?" she asks.

"Well, from here, I go to calculus," I say as we find two empty desks beside each other.

"Calculus! You must be smart. Once I finished geome-try, I was done with math."

"Not really, but I do like math. It makes sense to me." I wonder why that is. I guess I do take after my dad. He certainly loves math. "Besides," I add, "My dad teaches math at the community college, so I have a built-in tutor at home."

We find empty seats next to each other. Mrs. Davis is leaning against her desk, a copy of "A Tale of Two Cities" in her hand. Of all the teachers I've had so far, she's my favorite. My last year of English. Every class and activity is my last one.

The bell rings, and the class quiets down. I dig into my backpack for my English text and the three-ring binder. Laying them on the desk, I open the binder to the picture I've taped on the inside. My finger traces the outline of my mom's face in the photo of my family on our last vacation at the lake. I'm back there. The wind in my hair. The sun on my face. Mom laughing.

"Cassie?" Mrs. Davis's voice jolts me out of my reverie. "Are you with us?"

Around me, the class jumps into a lively discussion. I need to stop daydreaming to keep my grades up. And since this is my last year, I don't want to waste even one day of this year, not even one moment.

When the bell rings, the class spills out into the hallway again. Yasmin goes left, and I go right to my calculus class. Then it's lunchtime for me. I hate going to lunch on the first day back. I have no idea who else might have lunch at the same time. I'll probably eat alone.

Entering the cafeteria, I look around for Yasmin. Not here. Then, out of the corner of my eye, I see Gemma heading to the cafeteria line. I drop my books on a table and speed toward my homeschool friend.

"Hey, why are you here today? Homeschooling not agreeing with you? Orchestra isn't until tomorrow. And cafeteria food? What is wrong with you anyway?" A sly smile turns up the corners of my mouth.

"All right! Slow down." She looks ready for a date or a fancy dinner party. Black skirt. Red blouse. Dangling gold earrings. Her dark, oval eyes flash with excitement. "I didn't have time to make lunch this morning. I was too worried about my appearance and spent too much time getting ready." Her voice trails off dreamily. She's gazing at Dylan in line ahead of us. His cobalt blue shirt makes him hard to miss.

I lean in, whispering, "He's cute."

Gemma glares, putting her finger to her lips. "Later," she whispers.

Mac and cheese, mashed potatoes, side salads, fish sticks, burgers, onion rings, and other choices line the counter. My stomach rumbles as we wait in line. Mac and cheese, a side salad, chocolate pudding, and a carton of milk won't cost too much. I might even have enough for a snack later on.

Gemma chooses a chef salad and water. That figures. Even with cafeteria food, she makes healthy choices. We pay, pick up our trays, and head back to the table.

Before we start eating, we both bow our heads to say silent prayers to the Lord.

"So, what were you going to say about Dylan?" I ask as I dig into my food.

"I didn't want him to hear us talking about him. He's really cute."

I mumble my agreement and keep eating.

Gemma's eyes follow Dylan as he joins his friends at another table. "Well, he plays the cello like an angel. I like him. Sometimes, I wish he'd notice me and ask me out, but I guess it's better to keep him as a friend. He has his plans for college and the future, and they don't line up with mine. Besides, Dad says I shouldn't think about dating until I'm ready to get married, and I'm certainly not ready for that."

For real? Gemma's dad thinks that way, too? I thought my dad was the only one who was so old-fashioned. My face must be giving my thoughts away because Gemma wags her hand in front of my eyes.

"Earth to Cassie," she says. "What's up? You look like you just discovered a new planet or something."

"Sorry," I mumble. "It's just that my dad says the same thing. I can't believe your dad says that, too."

"Yeah. I guess it makes sense, but I wish he wouldn't. After all, I'm not going to marry the guy just because we go out on a few dates." Gemma pokes her fork into her salad. "I tease him about it because if that had been true for him, he and Mom never would have married. He was only sixteen when they started dating, and they didn't get married until he was 22. He tells me the waiting was agony, and he doesn't want me to wait that long."

"By the way, I met someone new today." That'll get her. She'll think I'm talking about a boy since we're talking about Dylan.

"Oh, do tell!" Gemma says with a gleam in her eye.

"No, it wasn't a boy." Just like I thought, her face deflates like a worn-out balloon. "But Gemma, you'll like her. Her name is Yasmin. She's Muslim. She's in my homeroom, choir, and English Lit classes. I was hoping she would be here at lunch too, but I guess she has lunch during the other hour. I want you to meet her. By the way, why are you here today? It's not an orchestra day."

"I had a meeting with the head of the Music Department. He knows someone who helps musical talent find the right school. He thinks I'm good enough to get a scholarship at Juilliard, but if that doesn't work, I could probably get a full scholarship at another school."

"Seriously? That's great. What did you say?"

"I told him I'd do an audition, but I needed some time to think about it." Gemma motions air quotes with her fingers. "That's my code for 'I need to pray about it.' You know me, Cassie. I really like playing the violin, and everyone says I'm really good, but..."

"You are!" I exclaim, but my mouth is full, and it doesn't sound right.

"Watch it!" Gemma laughs. "You know what your mom always said when you talked with food in your mouth."

I carefully swallow my food, take a drink of water, clear my throat, and say with my mother's pretend Irish brogue, "The erudite who speaks with a full mouth is a 'mouth fool.'" I start to giggle at the memory, and we double over with laughter. How many times did she say that, and we'd all laugh till our bellies hurt? Then my eyes fill with tears, and I wipe them away. When Gemma stops laughing, I say, "Seriously, Gemma, you are really talented."

"But I wanted to go to college with you."

"I know, but I think I'd take it if someone offered me a full scholarship. College is so expensive."

"It threw me. I thought he wanted to talk to me about doing a solo for our next concert. I had no idea I might be good enough for a Juilliard scholarship."

I wish I had a talent like Gemma's. No one's going to pay for my college. If she goes to Juilliard, we won't go to college together. Not wanting her to see the disappointment on my face, I turn my attention to my chocolate pudding, digging into the corners of the plastic container to get the last ounce.

She's my best friend. I want what's best for her. My disappointment settles into the background as I focus on what Juilliard would mean for her. "Well, unless you think you're ready to write that great novel you've been talking about, you probably need more training. I was thinking about taking a year off, but Dad suggested that I go to the community college where he teaches instead. If someone offered me a full scholarship, especially to a quality school like Juilliard, I think I'd see it as God's answer to my prayers and take it."

Gemma finishes her salad and puts down her fork. "I want to be sure it's the right thing. I'd been thinking about Word University. We both were. It would be nice to be surrounded by Christians and have teachers who believe the Bible is true. I'm unsure if homeschooling has prepared my faith for the challenges I'll find at a secular university. It scares me."

I nod. We've had this conversation before. I'm more used to having my ideas challenged than she is, but I would love to go to a Christian college, too. It would be nice to be part of the majority for a change. Sometimes, I get tired of being surrounded by people who tolerate my faith instead of encouraging me in it.

Gemma's dark eyes seem darker today, as if storm clouds have gathered behind them. "It sounds like a breath of fresh air to go to chapel every day and start our classes with prayer. On the other hand, maybe God wants me to be a light in a dark place."

I look into her dark eyes, smiling to hide my swirling emotions. "Gemma, God will show you. Just lean on Him. For me, it's even harder. It would be nice to have one great talent like you do. I have no clue what's next for me."

"Any more ideas on what your future holds?"

"None. I like to write, but it takes me forever to do it well, so journalism is out. I like math, but I don't know that I want to major in it, especially if it leads me to a career where I sit at a computer all day. To be honest, there's only one thing I'm sure of."

"What's that?"

"I want to be God's girl. Whatever He has for me, that's what I want." I put my spoon down to look at her. "But He's not telling me what that is."

"Patience, Cassie. God will show you. He takes care of His children."

"I know. But why is it taking so long? It seems like all the seniors know what's next except me."

"Just because they know doesn't mean God showed them anything. You're waiting on God, and that's a good thing. Keep waiting and listening. He'll show you."

On the way to physics, I spot the gray girl in the distance and turn down another hall to go the long way around. I can't deal with her right now.

As I walk into the room, I see Yasmin in the far corner. The desks near her are taken, so I choose one closer to the exit. The faster I can get out of here to get on the bus for home, the better. Hopefully, today's class will be interesting enough that I won't struggle to stay awake.

The ringing bell, signaling the end of class and the end of the day, comes sooner than I thought. At least this first class wasn't bad. I pick up my books and head for the door.

As I pass his desk, Mr. Bannick stops me. "Cassie, I have a question for you."

Dread creeps into my stomach as I wait for him to continue. Students bump me on their way out of the room, and Yasmin passes her hand over my shoulder as she leaves.

"I noticed that physics seems to make sense to you. Could I pair you with one of the students who is having trouble so you can help her learn?"

"Sure, I guess."

"Her name is Yasmin."

"Really?"

"Yes. Do you have a problem with that?"

'Not at all. I'm glad to help. I'm kind of surprised, though. She seems to have the right answers when you call on her."

"She does. But before class, she told me she might need extra help. I think a fellow student might be more helpful than I am. Next week, I'm rearranging the seating order so you can be next to her. That will make it easier for you to work together on problems."

He tells me of some things Yasmin mentioned. They aren't easy, but my affection for math probably helps me.

When I leave, I almost skip down the hall toward the bus. This is amazing. God is certainly working it out for us to spend time together. I think He has a mission for me this year—to be a real friend to Yasmin and show her how much I love Jesus. Wouldn't it be amazing if she began to realize how much God loves her, too?

When I get on the bus, I pull my phone from my pocket to text.

Hey group, I met a new friend today. We have several classes together, and she seems like a lot of fun. I hope I have a chance to tell her about Jesus.

Have you met any new friends this year? Have you had a chance to share your faith in Jesus with them? Maybe we can talk about this on Sunday.

Olivia responds right away. *Pray for my friend, Serenity. She's going through a hard time right now. I'll tell you more on Sunday.*

Emily sends a smiley face.

Natalie writes. *I'm praying that God will send me a special friend. Yes, let's talk about our friends on Sunday.*

I breathe a sigh of relief. These girls are making their way into my heart. By the end of the year, they may seem like sisters to me. Natalie already does.

The next day, Yasmin saves me a seat in choir.

'I hear you're going to be my student tutor for physics." Today, a yellow hijab frames her dark, oval face. She could easily be on the cover of a fashion magazine, but she seems unaware of her beauty.

When we leave choir, people stare and comment as we walk by. Some mention her beauty, but some remarks are mean. "Another Muslim. It's disgusting," one of the popular boys mumbles, loud enough for us to hear.

'Does it bother you to hear comments like that?" I ask after we walk away from him.

"Of course." Yasmin's mouth turns down into a scowl. Words can hurt. And some people know how to get under the skin of others.

When we find our seats in English class, she pulls out a pen and paper and opens Dickens to where we left off yesterday. The shrill sound of the bell breaks into my thoughts and spurs me to find my place in my book as Mrs. Davis steps out from her desk to begin teaching.

After a few days, school settles into a routine. Up at 6:00 a.m. Out the door at 6:45. Classes all day. Cross-country practice after school. Then supper, homework, and bed. Bible and prayer time just before I turn out the light.

"Pajama-mama lover," a guy hisses behind me as I head to lunch. I spin around, only to see a group of guys behind me. They laugh, knowing I have no idea who spoke.

Gemma's bento box, violin, and backpack sit on a nearby table. As I set my lunch on the table and my backpack on the floor, Julia and Sophia plop down on the bench across from me. Gemma returns from the restroom a moment later.

"Hey, girls, I have a question." Gemma holds a baby carrot in between her fingers. "I'm recording my audition for Juilliard in the orchestra room this afternoon. Can you come? I think I'll do better with an audience."

"Really?" Julia's dark eyes shine. "I'd love to. I love hearing you play your violin."

"Me too." Sophia nods as she takes another bite of her sandwich.

Before asking my question, I dip my carrot in the ranch dressing. "Gemma, can I ask Yasmin to join us? I'd like her to meet you."

"Sure. Having someone there I don't know will make me work even harder. I'd love to invite hundreds of people, but we wouldn't all fit in the orchestra room."

Julia laughs. "We'd be so squashed in there that you'd have to stand on someone's shoulders to play."

Taking care to swallow before I join in the laughter, I marvel again at Gemma's ease with people. I'd be terrified to play in front of my teacher, let alone others. But it helps her. Go figure.

Before physics starts, I ask Yasmin if she can join us, and she agrees. "So long as I make the late bus."

After school, our footfalls echo through quiet halls at the back of the school building as Yasmin and I make our way to the orchestra room. A few students wander the halls – some to catch the bus and others to after-school activities. Violin music lures me into the room, where five chairs form a semicircle near the door. Maya, Julia, and Sophia are already seated. At the grand piano on the other side of the room, Gemma and Mr. Taylor run through some exercises. Mrs. Lu, Gemma's violin teacher, stands off to one side, watching her.

I whisper to Maya. "Did I miss anything?"

Maya tosses her braids and looks at me with a smile that adds sparkle to her dark eyes. "She was playing when I got here. I get the impression they've been at this a while."

Across the room, Mrs. Lu advises her student. "Relax, Gemma," she says. "Your tension is showing in your intonation. Melt into your violin so that the music flows through both of you. Focus more on your feeling than on your technique. Your technique is not the problem. Relax, and try to enjoy yourself."

Gemma's eyes concentrate on the sheet music as her bow flies through the notes. When she finishes the short piece, Mrs. Lu nods. "Better. But there's a piece here in the middle." Mrs. Lu picks up her bow and plays through a section of notes. She stops and repeats the same section. "Do you hear the difference? The first sounded mechanical, even though my technique was the same."

I don't know music like Gemma, but I could hear the difference.

Gemma nods. "Can we try recording this time? My friends are all here. I know what you mean, and I think I can do it this time."

Maya leans over. "Have you heard her play these pieces?"

"No. This is the first time. She said she'll do better with an audience than if she plays alone."

Mr. Taylor rises from the piano bench and goes to the sound booth. "Quiet, please. I'm starting the recording now."

Gemma bows to the five of us, her violin in her left hand and the bow in her right. When she stands, it seems she grows a couple more inches as she lifts her violin to her chin. Clear notes cascade from her violin, swirling around the room and disappearing down the hallway as her fingers press and slide across the neck of the violin. Her bow dances to keep up.

Since she told me what she would be playing today, I listened to others play Paganini's Caprice #10. I think she's just as good as them, so I hope the judges at Juilliard think so, too.

Less than three minutes later, it's over. When Mr. Taylor shuts off the recording, we clap, laugh, hoot, and yell.

"That was fantastic."

"Way to go."

Gemma grins. "Thanks."

"Good enough? Or do you want to try again?" Mr. Taylor waits for her response.

"Can you play it back?" Gemma's confident look is gone. Creases etch her brow, and the corners of her mouth turn down. How can she be worried? It sounded amazing.

He plays it back. As the music fills the room, a smile slowly creeps across Gemma's face. I look at Mrs. Lu. She's smiling too. When the last flourish melts into the air, Gemma announces, "I knew I would do better if I had an audience. Thanks, friends."

"You mean you've recorded it before?" I shouldn't be surprised, but I thought she'd wait until we got here.

"Five times," Mrs. Lu acknowledges. "It's good we did all that work before you got here. A tiny piece in the middle kept tripping her up. But now I think that's a wrap. Do you?"

"I do! Now let's record the other one."

Mrs. Lu studies her. "Before you record your Bach piece again, I have a suggestion. Since this is audio and no one will see you, try moving around as you play. Your playing is often more relaxed and emotional when you move to the music. This piece needs that, especially during the dreamy sequence in the middle."

Gemma nods. Mr. Taylor motions for silence and starts the recording. I grip the edge of my seat, willing her to play as perfectly as possible. I can imagine the Juilliard judges with frowns on their faces and clipboards in their hands, listening for miniature faults I would never hear. Come on, Gemma, I urge. Surprise them all. As the music builds, I feel myself begin to relax.

We watch, mesmerized, as she pulls the bow across her violin and glides through the room. Bach's Sonata #1 spills from her gleaming violin and fills the room with a plaintive, subdued song. Then, it picks up its tempo and finishes with a flourish of restrained happiness. I had no idea she could play like that, and I thought I knew her well. I hear her play a lot at church, but this is far more difficult than anything she plays there. No wonder they wanted her to apply for a scholarship.

When her bow stops at the end of the piece, she analyzes the playback. That slow smile spreads across her face once more. The hesitancy is gone.

Mrs. Lu stands back and clasps her hands on Gemma's shoulders. "Let me know when you hear the results. Call me as soon as you know." Packing up her violin in its case, she heads for the door.

"I will," Gemma promises as she turns to Mr. Taylor to fill out the accompanying paperwork.

Yasmin stretches her arms above her head and turns to me. "She's amazing. You said she plays a lot at your church. Does she do concerts? I might come if I got to hear that again."

"Oh, she doesn't play classical music at church. She usually plays hymns. Some of the arrangements she composed herself."

"How does she play a him? And why is it called a him and not a her? What does that even mean?" Yasmin's face wrinkles in confusion.

"Sorry, Yasmin. That's a church word. I sometimes forget that our church's names for things aren't generally understood." I think about how to explain this strange idea to her. "It sounds like him, h-i-m, but it's spelled differently—h-y-m-n. A hymn, h-y-m-n, is a poem set to music that praises God. Since we sing hymns and other Christian songs in church, we hear those words in our heads when she plays."

"So, it's like listening to an orchestra play a popular song we know?"

"Exactly. While classical music evokes emotions, and it's beautiful to listen to, it doesn't help us praise God as much as songs with words we already know."

"I wish I could play like that." Julia sighs with longing, checks her phone, and stands up quickly. "Please thank Gemma for inviting me and let her know that I'm looking forward to seeing her on Sunday." Picking up her backpack, she heads for the door.

Yasmin watches her leave. "Do all of you go to church on Sundays?"

"We do. You could come too." I smile at her.

She shakes her head. "We're Muslim. We're not super religious, but we do the important Muslim things, like Ramadan. My dad would be upset if I asked to go to church."

I nod and say a quick, silent prayer: "Jesus, help me to show her Your love. Thank You for loving her as much as You love me. Show her that You are the God over all gods."

Gemma saunters out of the room, her step lighter and her smile brighter than ten minutes ago.

"Gemma, you were so great!" Yasmin gushes. "I had no idea you could play like that. You should be proud of yourself."

Gemma smiles. "I have put in a lot of hard work, but God gave me this ability. I can't take credit for my accomplishments. I'm grateful, but I try to watch out for pride. After all, anything could happen to me, and my talent could be gone. So I'm glad God gave me musical ability and that my parents spotted it when I was young and forced me to practice."

After Gemma packs up her things, we walk down the empty halls together. As we arrive, the late buses are loading. Yasmin, Sophia, and Maya get on their buses.

"See you tomorrow," I call as I walk to the parking lot to Gemma's car for a ride home.

That night, I pull out my journal, grab a purple pen and start to write.

Dear Lord,

Today, I heard Gemma record her audition tape for Juilliard. It was beyond what I knew she could do. She is so talented. No wonder Mr. Taylor and Mrs. Lu thought she should apply.

I don't have an amazing talent like hers. But maybe it's because I hold back. I don't like trying new things. Gemma would not have her talent for violin today if she'd never tried playing. Who knows? Maybe I have a talent I haven't tried.

Even though I don't have a great talent like hers, I know You created me for a purpose. I just don't know what that purpose is yet. Lord, please show me and help me be patient as I learn about Your purposes for me.

CHAPTER 13

On Saturday morning, my alarm wakes me with the smooth sound of violins playing Beethoven's Hymn to Joy. I stretch and slowly roll out of bed to shut off the alarm. Three weeks into school, and I already love sleeping in on Saturday mornings. But not today. Today we have a meet.

Heading for the shower, I stop to tap on Dad's door. "I'm awake," he calls out. The hot water helps me limber up, and a cold rinse jolts me to alertness. Brrr. I put on my favorite running pants and the team's t-shirt, tie my still-wet hair into a ponytail, and head downstairs.

Before long, the car's headlights peek through the still, quiet neighborhood. The edges of darkness are lifting on the horizon, but the stars are still bright. A comfortable silence fills the car.

Dad stays in with the other parents in the gym while I head to the locker room to find my teammates. Loud, boisterous voices fill the room. Locker doors clang as everyone looks for places to put their things. The smell of sweat lingers in the air.

"Everyone ready?" Ava's blue eyes look around at our group. As our fastest runner, she's the natural team leader. I beat her a couple of times recently in practice, but now that she knows I can, I doubt she'll let me do it today. "We need to show everyone that the Falcons have some serious runners in their women's cross-country team this year. Are you ready?"

"Ready," we shout in unison before making our way to the staging area.

At the starting line, I scan the crowd for Dad. There he is, close to where we will cross the finish line. He sees me spot him and waves. And there's Yasmin. She waves, too.

The starting gun fires, and we're off. We're packed in, and finding a spot to move around other runners is hard. After jostling and darting around runners, I find my pace and focus on the girl in front of me. I pass her. Now, the next one. I keep reminding myself not to push myself too hard until the end. There she is. Ava. Now, I'll lock in behind her and make sure no one passes us. If I hear someone closing in behind me, I'll pick up my pace so that Ava picks up hers. No one passes, and we are gaining on the runner in front of us. I know where we are, and it's not far to the finish line. I pick up my pace. So does Ava. We are close to an all-out sprint by the time we cross the finish line, side by side. I think she finished ahead of me, but we'll see.

"Great job, Cassie. I think you pushed me more than I would have pushed myself." Doubled over, Ava is heaving, the words coming out between her ragged breaths.

"Thanks." That's all I can say. My heart is beating so hard I think it'll jump out of my chest, and I can hardly get my breath.

When we recover, we walk down the line to cheer on our teammates. "Go, Taylor!" we yell together as we see her nearing the finish line. "You can do this!"

The coaches and referees put their heads together when everyone finishes the course. When the results are announced, Ava placed fourth, and I placed fifth. Our school placed third. We have lots of races between now and the state championships, but we did well today. It would be amazing to win a state title. It seems possible this year. One of the first-year students is a fast runner. She's usually hot on my heels in practice.

Yasmin finds me in the crowd. "Wow! You're fast."

"Thanks. I need to be. The team is counting on me."

Dad joins us and hands me my sweatshirt, which I gratefully pull on. I'm shivering from the sweat on my body and the cold breeze.

"Dad, this is the friend I was telling you about. Yasmin." I motion toward her.

"Nice to meet you," she says with a grin.

"You, too. I've heard good things about you from my daughter."

Yasmin's bright smile lights up her dark eyes. "I can't believe my luck in finding a friend on the first day." Her hip bumps into mine. "We're going to have a great year!"

CHAPTER 14

Pulling into a parking place at church on Wednesday night, I wave at Titus, Tim, and Natalie, who cross in front of me on their way to the youth building. As I climb out of the car, Gemma's family pulls into the spot next to mine.

"Hello, Mr. and Mrs. Lindberg. Hi, Gemma."

Gemma slides out of the back seat. "Where's your dad?"

"He had to work late." Looping my arm around Gemma's slim shoulders, I ask, "How was school today? Any fellow students get into trouble?"

"Oh, Clive bugged me mercilessly until I played with him." Her Labradoodle puppy is her only co-student, but I doubt he understands music theory or civics.

"And how did Starlight do today?" she asks.

"I'm sure she entertained herself quite well all alone." I'm careful to check my backpack before heading out the door. No more repeats of the first year when she stowed away, and I got into trouble for bringing a cat to school.

Laughter erupts as we walk in the door to the youth room. In the center of the room, students cluster around Timothy. I hope he's not telling a story about me. Should I join them? Gemma grabs my arm and pulls me into a seat near the front. Relief. I don't have to think about that anymore. Though I should at least talk to Natalie.

I turn around and spot her two rows back. "Hey, Natalie. How was school today?"

She gets up and comes to sit next to me. "Can I ask you a question?"

"Sure."

"How do you know what to read in the Bible? I was following a YouVersion© program, but I finished it, and there are so many that I don't know how to figure out which one to do next." She pulls out her cell phone to show me.

I interrupt her scrolling. "What's on your heart right now?"

"Too many things. That's my problem."

I understand the feeling. "I don't think we have enough time before youth group starts to figure this out. Wanna talk after?"

Guitar music focuses my attention on the front of the room. Is Maya coming tonight? I haven't seen her yet.

"Welcome, everyone." Looking past us to the door, Pastor Declan smiles, and with two quick strums on his guitar, his strong voice leads us in a worship song.

Behind me, Maya's strong soprano lifts my spirits as she walks down the center aisle to the empty seat next to me. She loops her arm around my shoulders while belting out her praise to God. Her wholehearted singing helps me praise the Lord too.

When the singing ends, Pastor Declan prays, thanking God for friends.

"Amen," we all say.

"Tonight," he says, "we're talking about friendship and loving others."

During the discussion time, I pay attention when Titus speaks. His thoughtful, heartfelt words make me think. More than once, Maya and Timothy get us laughing about their epic friendship fails. They seem so comfortable talking about their mess-ups. Should I be more open?

As we pray together at the end, my heart aches. Silently, I pray. "Help me to see people who go unnoticed and be a friend to them. And help me to help Natalie. Amen."

I turn to Natalie. "Have you thought of using the method Pastor Declan taught us?"

"I did. But I didn't know where to start. The Bible is such a big book."

"When I started getting more serious about reading the Bible, my mom told me to start with the book of John. It's a great book because it has lots of stories." I open my Bible to a multicolored page. "This is what my Bible looks like after doing the color thing for a while."

Her eyes light up. "Great, Cassie. Thanks."

As I crawl into bed that night, I pull out Mom's challenge again and think about the past few weeks. My small group is beginning to trust me. Tonight, Natalie came to me with an important question. Is she the one I'll end up mentoring?

On Monday evening, after I finish my homework, I pick up my journal, plop down on my bed, and write. I haven't written in several days. I don't have time to write down all the details like I could have if I'd written daily, but I'll summarize the important things.

We placed third last weekend, which was amazing. But Coach talked to me today. He still thinks I didn't give everything I had. He still thinks I'm holding something back. I ran hard, especially right at the end, but maybe he's right.

Maybe I was holding back because I don't want everyone to focus on me. I wish I could do this with an invisibility cloak and still help the team. Please help me, God, to give it my very best until the State championships.

Coach usually talks about three things. (1) Eat right; (2) Exercise; (3) Get enough sleep. When I do those things, I do feel better. I need at least eight hours of sleep at night, and I run better if I get more. If I don't, it's hard to pay attention in class and still have energy for cross-country.

Does mentoring mean I share what I'm learning in my own life, not just Bible stuff? Should I ask Natalie about her exercise and eating habits? Should I share what I'm learning about exercise and sleep with my small group? Maybe I should ask Pastor Declan.

Thanks, God, for your help. Help me to use what I'm learning to bless others, especially Natalie. Amen.

I put my journal on my side table and grab my computer from my backpack. If mentoring is not just about praying for others and helping them when they have questions, I need to figure out what else I could share with my small group. Jesus said we're supposed to love Him with our hearts, minds, strength, and souls. So in mentoring, it's not just about Bible reading and prayer. It includes all of life. What are some big categories where I have something to share? Personally, it would be physical, emotional, spiritual, and mental. Maybe I'll change it, but that's where I'll start.

CHAPTER 15

Saturday mornings sometimes leave me with too much time to think. Last night, I dreamed about Mom again. She was running through a field of flowers, her red hair streaming behind her. When she stopped, little children came to her with fistfuls of flowers in their hands. Longing woke me. I wanted to be one of those children taking flowers to Mom. Now, the tears won't stop.

A post-it note on the kitchen counter reads. "Gone to the cemetery." I'm glad he's gone, and I have the quiet house to myself. I don't think either of us can comfort each other today. Even my Bible reading seemed empty this morning. All I want is for Mom to be here with me. Her birthday is tomorrow.

Wrapping both hands around my warm mug, I inhale the steam, letting its chocolaty sweetness soothe my senses before setting it down on the bedside table. Then, when I think I can talk without crying, I grab my phone. My fingers scroll to Alex's number. If Alex were home this weekend, it would be easy. We could support each other. But she's not, so now I have to decide what to do.

My cell phone buzzes in my hand. Natalie. I juggle the desire to ignore her and cry or pretend like I'm OK and answer. I take a deep breath and say cheerfully, "Hey, Natalie."

Her exuberant voice encourages my aching heart. "I'm so glad I caught you. Do you have time to meet today?"

I'd rather wallow in my grief, but I'm not going to tell her that. "Sure," I say, "if you give me an hour or so. I need to finish my cleaning and laundry." We agree to meet at Grindstone Café in two hours.

I pull my knees up, wrap my arms around them, rest my head, and pray. "Lord, please help me. It breaks my heart that probably no one except us will remember that tomorrow is Mom's birthday. Please help me, and let me bless Natalie today."

I bike the short distance to the café, lock it on the rack, and walk in. The smell of coffee greets me first, and then Natalie locks me in a bear hug. A few minutes later, with a mocha for me and a Mexican hot chocolate for her, we find an outside table in the sunshine. We sip our drinks and watch people coming and going. I wait for her to talk.

"So," she begins, "I'm doing better with my Bible reading, as you know, but I'm really struggling." Her mouth quivers. "My parents are not getting along, and it's really affecting me. It's hard to study. My brothers spend a lot of time out of the house because the atmosphere is so glacial, but because I'm younger, I can't go out like they do."

Oh, no. How do I respond to this? All I can do is help her with her fears and responses. "You can't fix your parents. You know that, right?"

She nods.

"All you can do is respond correctly to the situation." I dig out my phone. "I'm going to look up some verses that might help you, but I need to know first what bothers you most about what's happening."

"I'm afraid they're going to split up."

We talk for a few more minutes, and I realize she needs help with fear and not dwelling on negative thoughts. I open my Bible program and type in "fear." Then, as I find the verses I need, I write down the references on a napkin. At the top, I write the verse I've memorized that helps me often: Isaiah 41:10. Then I add two others: 1 Peter 5:7 and Philippians 4:6. I shield my phone from the sun so we can read the verses together.

"It's tempting to take what we're feeling today and think those feelings or circumstances will get worse," I tell her. "But we don't know that. We make it worse for our-selves when we heap tomorrow's problems on today." My mind goes back to my struggles anticipating Mom's death. I share that with her. When I finish, my mind goes back to my struggle this morning of not wanting to go to church tomorrow. I was assuming what tomorrow would hold. But I don't. None of us do. I need to take my own advice.

She gives me a slight smile then, but the worry still radiates from her eyes. I remember one of the things Dad talked to me about when Mom was dying—making our thoughts obey God. I tell her of my struggle to fight neg-ative thoughts. "You need to fight this, too." I send up a quick prayer for help and then look up one more verse posted on our home refrigerator. "Philippians 4:8 tells us what's supposed to be uppermost in our minds. Pay at-tention to this little word. I point to it. The things that are lovely. Is there anything lovely about the way you are feeling and thinking?"

She shakes her head.

"How can you change your thoughts when you're afraid? When scary thoughts like these come into your mind, what can you think about instead?"

She doesn't answer, and I'm tempted to fill the silence with suggestions. Instead, I wait. When the silence continues, she lifts her eyes to mine and shakes her head.

"It could be anything," I say. "That verse we read gave us a list of ideas. Whatever is lovely or pure or excellent or worthy of praise or good. What about praising God for something good? Thinking about a project or an assignment that's coming up? You could make a list of things to do. Singing a song. The important thing is to find something that works for you to take your mind off the negative and focus on the positive." I check my phone and notice the time. "Look, I need to go, but I'll see you tomorrow in church, okay?"

She drains the last of her hot chocolate. "Sure, but can you pray with me before you leave?"

I nod. In my mind, I walk into God's throne room and ask Him to still her fears and help her fight them. Aloud, I ask God to resolve her parents' issues, help her fight against negativity, and give her peace.

When I open my eyes, she's wiping tears from hers. "Can we do this regularly? I really need a big sister right now."

"Of course. Let's chat tomorrow and figure out when we'll meet next."

We both stand, toss our cups, and hug each other. The gloom on her face has retreated. As she walks from our table's umbrella into the sunshine with the list of verses in her hand, I marvel at how God met my need by sending me someone who needed me. She doesn't even know how I was struggling this morning. Maybe I'll tell her tomorrow.

When I get home, the car is in the garage. I find Dad in his study and tell him about my meeting with Natalie.

"Well, it sounds like you're making great progress on mentoring. Do you want the next letter?" His red-rimmed eyes let me know he's struggling too.

"Soon. I want to be sure she's okay with my having an intentional mentoring relationship with her." I check my phone to see the latest text from Gemma. "Dad, do you think I could invite Gemma for lunch tomorrow? Her parents are away this weekend."

"Of course, so long as you agree to do the blessing activity with me tomorrow. I think I need it, especially on Mom's birthday."

I get up and give him a brief hug before going to my room. A song of praise runs through my mind as I thank God for the blessing of a godly dad.

As we pull into the parking lot at church the next morning, I turn my attention to the sky. September will soon be over, bringing cool, crisp air. Blue skies with wispy white clouds form a perfect backdrop for the gold and red leaves on the trees. It's one of those fall days that Mom always loved. I can still hear her lilting voice. 'Even though God didn't paint the leaves just for me, I'm glad He brought me into the world at a time when the trees celebrate His creativity." The memory makes me want to smile and cry at the same time.

The parking lot is buzzing with life as car doors open and slam shut. Hope pulls me in for a hug as I walk through the door. 'I know it's your mom's birthday today. I've been praying for you."

I dig in my purse for a tissue and wipe the tears that threaten to mess up my mascara. 'Thanks for remembering."

Gemma walks in behind me and whispers in my ear. 'God knew you needed that hug this morning." Smiling through my tears, we find our seats.

After we sing a few songs, Pastor Declan puts down his guitar, grabs his Bible and moves to the podium. 'Look in your Bibles for John 14." Bible pages rustle. Two seats down from me, Ben pulls out his cell phone to look up the Scripture passage. After we've found our places, Pastor Declan begins to teach about heaven. As He describes God's care in preparing a home for us, I can almost feel God wrapping His arms around me, letting me know Mom is happy. I breathe deeply as I imagine what today is like for her in that beautiful place.

When Sunday school ends, I share with Natalie my ideas about mentoring her—praying for her every day, texting, and meeting regularly to touch base and pray together. A smile comes over her face. 'I love it! This is exactly what I need."

At lunchtime, Gemma grabs a pitcher and pours water into glasses while I find a candle and put it in the tall wrought iron candlestick in the middle of the table. 'Mom," I whisper. 'Even though you're not here, we remember it's your birthday. I know you're having a better day in heaven, but I'm lighting this candle for you."

I realize my whisper reached Gemma's ear when she puts her arm around me. 'Do you want to sing 'Happy Birthday' for your mom? I'll sing with you."

'Without a cake?" I shake my head. 'She's happy with God. I still miss her terribly, but the candle is enough."

'Okay, girls," Dad interrupts. 'Time to eat!"

We sit down at the table and join hands. Dad's clear, strong voice thanks God for his children, friends, good food, and the many happy memories of his wife. His voice cracks, and I squeeze his hand. When the silence continues, I steal a look at him. Tears are pouring down his face, so I finish. 'We love you, Father God. Amen."

Dad clears his throat and wipes his face with the back of his hand. I pass the roast to Gemma, and we load up our plates. We dig into the pot roast, vegetables, and mashed potatoes. Only the quiet ticking of the clock breaks the silence while we savor the food.

"So, what were your blessings this morning?" Dad asks me.

"I could list several, but Hope pulling me in for a hug was the most obvious blessing I received. The blessing I heard was Pastor Declan's teaching on heaven because I needed that today. The blessing I gave God was my sincere praise during the singing, and I'm still trying to think about a blessing I gave someone else."

"I'll give you the answer for that one," Gemma says. "Your invitation to me for lunch was definitely the blessing you gave to someone else."

Dad goes next. "My blessing received was your willingness to look for four blessings today. I needed something to get me outside of my sorrow. The blessing I gave, I hope, was asking you to do that with me." I nod as he continues. "My blessing to God happened even before church when I determined that I would focus on Him today instead of my loss. And the blessing I heard was the song we sang, 'He Will Hold Me Fast.'"

Gemma taps her fingers on the table one at a time. "So a blessing received, a blessing given, a blessing heard, and a blessing to heaven. Four blessings. I'm going to talk to my parents and see if we can do that. Maybe it would help us too."

I lean back in my chair and smile as I look at the flickering candle in the middle of the table. Mom's life here may be over, but she is still very much with me. I send up a silent prayer. "Thank you, God, for Mom's life."

CHAPTER 17

The next morning, I find Dad putting a bowl of mixed fruit on the kitchen table and warming muffins in the microwave. An empty mug sits near the coffee maker, and I fill it with dark liquid. Two minutes later, the muffins emerge piping hot from the microwave, and we sit down to enjoy breakfast together.

I watch the butter melt on the hot muffin. "Dad?" I wait for him to look up. "So Natalie is the person I've started mentoring. She's been looking to me for advice more than the other two in my group. Do you think I'm ready for the next challenge?"

"I thought you might be asking for the next one soon." He reaches into the backpack by his chair and pulls out a pink envelope.

"You had it in your backpack?"

"I knew you were ready. I wanted to have it with me in case you asked for it while we were out somewhere." He drains his coffee cup, grabs his backpack, kisses me on the cheek, and heads for the door. "See you tonight."

As soon as he leaves, I tear open the envelope.

My darling daughter Cassie,
I wish to talk to you about your progress through these
challenges, but as I write this third one, I am confident

you will complete all of them. The first two were ongoing, but this one is something you can get done easily. Hopefully, it will help you as much as I hope the other two are already doing.

You already know a lot about loving others. One of the things I've emphasized to you through the years is that loving others is not about feelings but about actions. The Good Samaritan was Jesus' example because of what he did. We have no idea what he felt, but he loved the Jew who was hurt by the roadside by helping him.

Follow his example and find at least three people who need love. Then, do something tangible to meet a real need in their lives. If you're not sure what I mean, ask Dad. I don't have the energy to list all the verses and thoughts in my head, but he can help you. However, since we have had these discussions in the past, I think you know what I'm saying.

Loving others is about actions. If you are having difficulty in a relationship, finding a person's real need and meeting it will help. It applies to marriage, parenting, job and church relationships, and every other human relationship. It also benefits you with the joy of giving.

So have fun with this one! Invite a friend or two to help you if you need to. They might enjoy hearing about our family's perspective on love.

I love you to heaven and back. And even though I can't do anything tangible for you right now, God has left His Holy Spirit for you. He is doing more than I ever could.
Mom

I need to think about this one, but not too long. Now that I've made progress with the first two, I want to complete all nine. And I have no idea what the others will be or how long they will take.

CHAPTER 18

Cross-country, touching base with Natalie, and homework fill my weeknight hours. Occasionally, Aunt Sandi comes over for supper if she's off early from work and Dad's working late. But usually, I don't have much time. On weekends, though, I try to finish my homework and chores early so I can do other things.

I'm admiring my clean room when my cell phone rings late Saturday morning. Gemma's face appears on the screen. Plopping down on my bed, I put the phone to my ear. "Hey friend, what's up?"

"Just finished my chores, and now I'm scheming to get my best friend to do something crazy with me!" When I hear the smile in her voice, I imagine her eyes narrowing into a squint and a grin crossing her oval face.

"Crazy?" I quickly respond. "Crazy like usual or more than that? You know me. Born to be mild.." She's the bold one. Not me.

"More than usual, but not so much that you'll refuse outright. But don't say 'no' right away. Think about it for a minute, okay?"

"Now you're scaring me. Out with it." I stare at my foot tapping the hardwood floor, soundless in its gray woolen sock.

"Remember how you said it would be nice to do something for people without them thinking they needed to do something nice back?"

I mumble a yes.

"And you know how Pastor Fuller was saying on Sunday that loving others means we meet a need in their lives?"

"I do remember that." I was surprised to hear him preach on that just after I got Mom's love challenge. It almost made me think they were in cahoots.

Gemma's on a roll. "Well, I was thinking about some kids that hardly get noticed. To do this right, we're gonna have to listen to what the kids around us are saying. We'll make a list of those who need some extra love in their lives." Crunching follows her words. What's she eating? Probably a carrot or celery stick. I'd be popping candy or munching on tortilla chips. "Then we'll get together to discuss our lists to see what we can do to meet that need."

"Okay. I guess I can do that. Maybe Maya can help. She knows a lot more people than I do."

Gemma murmurs her agreement and continues. "We'll keep it a secret. That way, they can't try to pay us back!" Her munching continues.

"What are you eating, anyway? An apple?"

"Yup. I know I'm not a basketball player like you are, but I'm aiming for the trash can."

Clattering comes across the line. "Nothing but net!" she yells. "Maya would have loved that one."

After we hang up, I pull out Mom's letter again and think about the Good Samaritan. True, the injured man knew who helped him, but Mom's letter doesn't say that I have to disclose my identity. Gemma doesn't even know she's helping me with Mom's love challenge. Keeping the project a secret will make it easier for me.

Maya, Gemma, and I gather at Gemma's house on a balmy October Sunday afternoon. Gemma's mom brings in a plate of pumpkin cookies and apple cider, and we sit cross-legged on the living room floor with our notebooks in front of us.

Gemma grabs a cookie from the plate. "I found one person at church and one in my home school group who need encouragement. How many did you two find?"

"I found two." I take another bite of my cookie.

Maya rustles around in her backpack and pulls out a notebook and pen. "I found three. I'm sure I could find more if we need more, but we probably need to keep it small."

Gemma puts up her hand. "I'm glad you stopped at three, Maya, because you're right. We don't have unlimited time or resources. Now let's see who we have and why we thought they needed to be encouraged."

As the minutes roll by, we share what we learned. Lacey is battling depression. Zach's dad left them. Tanya's dad went to jail. Madison. Chloe. Reggie. Skye. We talk about the ones we didn't include, like Melanie. She has friends and a loving family who will help her with her anxiety issues.

Gemma turns her dark eyes to me. "What about the gray girl?"

"No. Absolutely not." The vehemence of my reply startles her.

Maya tilts her head. "Who's the gray girl?"

Gemma looks at me again, waiting to see if I'll say anything. "Someone she knows at school. I don't know the whole story."

Dread fills my stomach like a stone. "You're right. You don't." The vehemence in my voice surprises me. "Look.

That's something I need to deal with. For you to help her, I'd have to tell you about her, and I'm not ready to do that. Okay?"

Gemma reaches out and puts a gentle hand on my arm. Concern fills her eyes, and I look away. "I'm just not ready, okay?" A single tear rolls down my cheek.

Maya stretches her legs out in front of her. "I have one more. Yesterday, a girl at school asked if she could talk. She was crying, and it was hard for her to tell me what was going on, but I'm glad she did. She had an abortion."

Gemma gasps. Her eyes flash as she shakes her head. "But Maya, if we help her, aren't we sending a message that we think abortion is okay?"

Maya's braids bounce as she shakes her head. "I don't think so. Besides, doesn't she need to see a real example of God's love from us? God still loves her. He still wants her to turn to Him. Maybe our love will help."

I've heard some of the girls talk about abortion, but never to me. I guess I'm not friendly or trustworthy enough for them to confide in me. "Maya," I ask. "Do I know her? Is she a Christian?"

Maya studies our faces. "Sorry, I can't tell you who she is. She doesn't want anyone to know. Even though most kids at school accept abortion, she knows she ended her baby's life. Her parents were going to kick her out if she didn't do it, so she felt like she didn't have a choice. But now she realizes she did have a choice, and her guilt is putting her in a dark place. I told her God's love is un-conditional and encouraged her to seek His forgiveness. I'm going to check in on her every day for a while. She knows I'm telling you, but I told her I wouldn't say who she was. I need to go alone when we figure out what we will do for her. You two can sign a card with comments instead of your names so she knows it's not only from me. But she told me in confidence, so I have to do this one myself."

I ache for the baby. I ache for this girl whose parents pressured her to make this choice. I'm ready to include her. But Gemma has always been outspoken against abortion. Will she agree? Would Jesus ask us to withhold our love for those who are hurting based on the type of sin they've committed?

Gemma leans forward, her black hair swinging around her, anger etched into her features. "Last week, the Williamsons talked about wanting to adopt a child." Pain echoes through the room as she talks. "I would not be sitting here now if the government had discovered my birth mom's pregnancy. Why are some people so quick to have an abortion instead of looking for adoptive parents? Why don't people see this as a taking of a life? It makes me so sad."

Pushing her hair aside with trembling hands, she looks at us with a tight smile. "I know. We can't change the past. And God forgives everyone who asks." She turns to Maya. "Don't ever tell me who she is." Fury and sadness mingle on her face. "I don't think I could handle it. But if this will help her understand the love of God, then let's do it."

Together, we prioritize our list in case we can't help all of them. At the top? The unnamed girl. But deep inside me, I know the gray girl should be on that list, too.

Now that we've agreed on our list, Gemma returns to strategizing. "I know Lacey and what she likes. I'll make a list for her." Maya and I make lists of ideas for the ones from school that we know. What should we do? I need to listen more to see if I can find out how to meet their needs.

Gemma rips the page of ideas from her notebook and puts it on the coffee table. 'Here are some ideas for my two, but how will we make this anonymous?"

'I know." My idea came out of nowhere, but it might work. After all, Halloween is around the corner.

On Halloween night, my watch confirms our on-time arrival when Gemma's mom drops us off. Before we can even grab our backpacks and get out of the car, Maya's dad emerges from the house. "We'll take the girls home when they're done," I hear him say.

"Bye, Mom!" Gemma yells as we rush to the front door.

Stepping over the threshold, I sniff the air. "Smells like chicken and something else?"

"Dumplings, of course." Mrs. Johnson's face gleams with satisfaction as she walks over to give us each a hug. "Maya, your guests are here," she calls and turns to look at us. "Have you eaten yet?"

"Oh yes, Mrs. Johnson. We ate before we left, though I think your food smells better than the leftovers I had."

Maya bounces down the stairs. "Come on up, and we'll change."

We haul our backpacks up to her room. In Maya's room, we turn our backs to each other and begin to dress. When the rustling stops, Maya asks, "Everyone finished?"

"Yup," we say together.

"Okay, then. Turn around on three. One, two, three."

We all turn around and stare. Gemma is wearing all black, but the sequined, blue-and-black butterfly wings make her look even smaller than she is. With an upward swoop, she twirls, showing off their full size. A matching sequined mask covers her face. You would never know who she was unless you knew how she walked and talked.

Maya's bulldog pajamas with padding underneath give a nice roly-poly look to her graceful figure. Gemma doubles over in laughter when Maya wags her short tail. Somehow, she can move it even when she's standing still. With her braids tucked under the hood, the plastic bulldog mask, her rounded figure, and her waddle when she walks, no one will recognize her.

I had a hard time with my costume. I could have bought one ready-made, but they were expensive. Instead, I found some old black jeans, bought a hoodie at the thrift store, and painted orange tiger stripes on them. Layers under the hoodie round out my figure and will keep me warm while we're out. My plastic tiger mask muffles my voice, but I twirl around and growl at Maya, who barks back a warning while Gemma flits around the room.

"Are we ready?" Maya grabs her cell phone and holds it in the air. "Selfie time." We try several poses and agree to text our photos to each other.

Maya's parents look up as we come down the stairs.

"I only know who's who because I know which three girls are in this house." Maya's mom reaches for her cell phone, and the camera clicks and flashes. "Now, go and be a blessing."

In Maya's driveway, I type the address to the first house into my phone's map program, and the computer voice gives directions. Gemma hums a youth group medley in the back seat.

As Maya slides her family's black sedan into a parking place across the street and several houses down from our first address, Gemma finds the box wrapped in pumpkin paper and a big orange bow with Zach's name on it. The card reads, "Zach, we want you to know we care about you, and God cares even more than we do. With care and prayer, Three Friends." On the other side of the page, we wrote out the words to John 15:12-14 and included an information sheet about our Bible club at school.

She passes the orange gift box to Maya. Inside are a pair of new Nike sneakers. At the last soccer game, two guys behind me snickered about his ratty shoes. When I heard it, I knew we had our answer for him. Maya can talk to anyone about anything, so she struck up a conversation with the guys' team about shoe sizes to find out what size he wears. I hope he loves them.

The porch is dark, but lights glow through the drawn curtains. I ring the bell and step back from the door.

The light comes on, and Zach's older brother opens the door, a scowl on his face.

"Treat for Zach," Maya says and hands him the box. We take off running. Gemma lifts her wings as we go, and they sparkle in the lamplight.

We jump into the car and burst out giggling. "That was fun!" Gemma says. "Where do we go next?"

It's after 9:00 when we get back to Maya's house.

"How did it go?" Maya's mom asked us as we plop down on the couch.

"That was so much fun." Gemma can hardly talk fast enough to keep up with her thoughts. "I don't think anyone knew who we were. You should have seen their faces. At Zach's house—"

Maya interrupts. "Zach's brother looked angry when he came to the door, but when we handed him the gift for his brother, he didn't know what to do."

I laugh, remembering his look. "And Tanya's brother was ready to yell at us, thinking we were ignoring their lights-off signal. When I handed him the package and said, 'Treat for Tanya,' he stood there with his mouth open."

"At the next house, Chloe came to the door with a candy bowl." Gemma mimes the two-handed candy bowl presentation. "Maya and Cassie were afraid she might recognize them, so I handed her the package and said, 'A treat for you,' and we took off running. I wish we could do it again tomorrow night." She sighs and leans back in her chair.

"Were you able to find them all?" Mrs. Johnson asks.

Maya shakes her head. "At Madison's house, no one was home, but we were able to do the others. Since I need to do one by myself anyway, I'll take care of that one too."

Mrs. Johnson jingles her car keys, and I check my watch. It's getting late. Looking at me, she asks, "If I borrow your costume, I could accompany Maya, and then it would look like you were involved."

"That's a great idea, Mom. And Gemma, would you be willing to loan yours to my little sister?"

Gemma nods.

I'm a little offended that her little sister will meet her unnamed friend. I thought nobody could know her identity? "That would be great for Madison, but what about the other one?"

"No, not that one. I won't be costumed when I take our gift to her." Maya yawns and stands to her feet. Stretching her arms to full height and wagging her little tail, she laughs. "That was fun."

CHAPTER 20

The light is on in Dad's study when Mrs. Johnson drops me off. I run up the stairs. "What do you think, Dad?" I twirl around in my tiger costume.

"It looks great. Why don't you come and tell me about it?" He motions me into the room, and I take the corner chair. My face hurts from smiling when I'm done telling him about all the stops we made.

"So I guess that means you're ready for the next letter from Mom."

"Sure am. I've been thinking about it all day since I knew I would get it after we finished tonight."

His deep dimples emphasize his huge smile. He ducks into his bedroom and returns with another pink envelope, a tiny #4 handwritten in the top right corner. He stops me as I try to push out of the chair to go to my room to read it. "Why don't you read it here? I know what it is, and it involves me."

Curious, I grab his letter opener off of his desk and carefully slit the top.

Dear Cassie,

Three challenges down. Six to go. So that you won't get discouraged, I made this one an easy one. Take Dad with you to visit a couple of colleges. If I had not been

> *sick, the three of us would have gone together. You already know Dad's school, and you've visited the U of M in Saint Paul and Mankato State, but choose two other schools you'd like to visit with him.*
>
> *Choosing a college is a choice between good options. For some people, choosing not to go to college is the best option. Sometimes, the choice we have to make between several good ideas is the hardest - when there is no right and wrong, and every choice has good points. Ask Dad about that. How do you make a decision when many of the choices seem valid? I'm praying now that God will prepare the paths ahead of you.*
>
> *I love you to heaven and back.*
>
> *Mom*

Dad looks up as I finish reading. "So, what do you think?" He turns the computer screen to face me. "We need to find a time we can both go."

The screen shows both of our calendars. I look at the spot where his finger is pointing to a school break. We'd have three days. Two schools immediately come to mind: Word University and Northern Bible College. We can get to both in that amount of time.

"Dad, what happens if I don't finish all nine of them?"

"You don't get the prize she asked me to give you." The smile on his face matches the twinkle in his eye. "But don't worry. None of her requests are as hard as raising children, and you want to do that one day."

"Yes, but I don't have to do that within a year." I lean back into the chair to study him. "And you're not going to tell me what it is."

"Nope." He turns to the computer again and punches in the dates we'll be gone. "If you don't complete them all, you still get the blessing of doing the challenges. They may be worth more than the prize, even though you will hate losing out on the grand finale."

"Will you tell me what it is if I miss it?"

He swivels his chair toward me. My heart pounds in my chest while I wait for his answer. Will I want to know what I missed? I think so.

"Yes, I'll tell you then."

"Good." I start to get up. "Hey, Dad. Can Gemma come with us on this trip? If she doesn't end up at Juilliard, she's interested in going where I go."

"Sure. If it's OK with her parents."

I pull out my phone to text Gemma and mark the dates on my phone's calendar. I ask if she'll get permission to spend the night at my house the day before we leave so we can get on the road early in the morning.

The next day, Timothy stops me in the hallway between classes. "Hey, thanks for helping Natalie. She really needed someone. Titus and I deal with things differently than she does. She's so emotional."

"Glad to help. Your sister is precious to me."

"Yeah. We've seen Mom and Dad go through things like this before, and they'll get through it. But she was too young to notice the last time. I tried to let her know they'll be okay, but it didn't help. She needed someone else. So, thanks."

As I duck into my class, I'm delighted by how Mom's challenge is blessing me and others.

Later, when the school bus drops me at the corner, I zip my jacket closed for the short walk home. The streetlights come on as I walk, but no lights shine from our windows. I let myself in and check the garage. No car. Strange. Dad didn't tell me he was working late tonight.

I lug my backpack up to my room and send him a text. *Working late tonight? Should I start dinner?*

He texts back. *That would be great. I'm stopping at a student's house to drop off some homework for him. See you soon.*

I find his menu for tonight on the refrigerator door. Chicken Wraps. Good. That's something I've made before. I wash the lettuce and tear it into bite-sized pieces. Then I cut up the chicken, tomatoes, and avocado and grate a carrot. I gather the Parmesan cheese, croutons, black olive slices, and dressing. I set the table and arrange the ingredients on a platter. I'll warm the tortillas when he walks in.

Then I grab my physics textbook from the table and wander into the living room to study while I wait. An hour later, I check my watch. Why isn't he home yet? I dial his number, and it goes straight to voicemail. Strange. He doesn't usually ignore my calls. Fifteen minutes later, I'm pacing. He should be here by now. What should I do? Call Alex? No, there's nothing she can do.

My fingers find Aunt Sandi's number. She picks up immediately. "I was just going to call you. Your dad just arrived at the ER at Abbott Northwestern. I don't have any details other than that. Shall I call someone to come and get you?"

My heart hits the floor. I sink down onto the sofa and try to think. "No. I'll take a Lyft. I do it all the time. By the time you send someone, I could be there." My heart is pounding in my chest as I open the app to order a Lyft driver. The app says the driver's six minutes away. I return my textbook to my backpack, run upstairs to grab my journal and a jacket and run down again. Pulling on my jacket and turning off the inside lights, I see the Lyft driver outside. I run down the steps to meet him and jump in the car. "Hurry," I say. The dark-haired driver smiles in the mirror at me but doesn't say anything. I wish he could speed to get me there, but at least he won't dawdle.

On the way, I can't focus my thoughts. What happened? He was fine when we texted. A car accident? A heart attack? I find myself praying silently. "God, you can't take him. Mom just left, and he's all I've got." Tears slide down my cheeks, and I brush them away, not wanting the driver to see me in tears. Twelve minutes later, he pulls up to the emergency room. I dash out of the car, not even stopping to say "Thanks" or "Bye."

The woman at the front desk looks up his information. "We'll get someone to show you the way," she says to me with compassion in her eyes.

Minutes later, I follow a volunteer through the maze of halls, past the surgical section, and into the ICU. A nurse shows me to his cubicle, where tubes snake across his chest to an IV stand and the machine recording his vitals. An ugly bruise is forming on his cheek, and a bandage is on his head. The heart monitor breaks the silence with its steady beep, and I let out a breath I didn't know I was holding. A straight-backed chair sits in the corner, and I pull it up next to the bed and hold his limp hand.

"Dad," I whisper. "It's Cassie. Wake up. Talk to me."

He opens his eyes, turns to me, and smiles. Then his eyes shut again, and deep breathing returns.

Just then, the green curtain moves, revealing a woman in blue scrubs and a white lab coat with a mask hanging from her neck. "I'm Dr. Levinson. Are you Cassie?" When she sees me nod, she continues. "He was unconscious when they brought him in because he'd lost a lot of blood. Now he's sedated to manage his pain, but when he woke up from surgery, he was asking for you. I'm the surgeon who worked on him." She puts out her hand, and I shake it.

"What happened? Do you know?" The quiver in my voice surprises me.

"No, but I'm sure he'll tell us the whole story later. I extracted one bullet that went into his abdomen. Another on his side went all the way through and out the other side."

"He was shot?"

She nods. "Fortunately, it was a small caliber weapon. The bullets missed his vital organs, and I expect him to make a full recovery. The police will want a full report tomorrow." She moves to the bed. "We think he fell when he was shot, and that's how he bumped his head. He'll have to stay here for a few days." She looks up at me. "Any questions?"

I shake my head. I don't know what questions to ask, but Aunt Sandi will.

She walks over to the sanitizer on the wall, rubs her hands together, and turns back to me. "I'm available for questions if you need me." She smiles at me and leaves, and I wonder if she has a kid my age.

A moment later, Aunt Sandi walks in, and I stand. "Oh, Auntie, I'm so scared."

She hugs me, her cheek resting on my shoulder, and then steps back to take my face in her hands. "I just talked to Dr. Levinson. Your dad is going to be fine. The danger has passed. But it will be a while before he can return to work."

Aunt Sandi pulls the curtain back from around his bed, allowing more light from the hallway to stream into his room. Then, she checks his chart, and Dad stirs, groaning. She sanitizes her hands, walks over to the bed, and holds his hand. "Adam, can you hear me?"

He slowly opens his eyes and looks at her. Then he turns and sees me. "I guess I caused some excitement." He smiles, and his eyes close again. I'm so glad to hear him talking. Aunt Sandi's right. He's going to be okay.

"By tomorrow, he'll seem more like himself." She motions to the chair. "I'll bring you a blanket if you like, and you can rest there, but I have to get back to work. I rushed down here on my break." As she moves toward the door, a knock interrupts us. The door slowly opens, and Alex walks in. She rushes to the bed, grabs his hand, and kisses his cheek, but he keeps sleeping. She looks up at us, and Aunt Sandi fills her in with as much as she knows. In the hall, a voice announces that visiting hours are over, but we'll stay a while longer.

It's almost midnight when we finally get home. Alex lugs her weekender case up the stairs, and I fall across the bed, exhausted. When I awaken in the morning, I'm still fully clothed.

After breakfast, Alex calls my school to explain, and we go to the hospital to stay with Dad. When we walk in, he's sleeping, so Alex walks to the nurse's station to ask how he's doing. Her smile tells me it's good news when she walks back into the room. "He ate breakfast, but the pain was bothering him, so they gave him some more medication. They say he'll probably sleep a lot today."

Alex and I talk softly together. Even though both the surgeon and Aunt Sandi said he'd make a full recovery, I'm still on edge. When will he be up and around again?

How long will he be out of work? Will the shooting change him? I've heard of other people going through PTSD after something like this. How will we get around without a car? I'm such a mess.

Alex's phone buzzes, and she leaves the small room to answer it. I sink into the chair and pull out a novel to read. Deep into my mystery, I startle when Alex walks back in.

"That was Jon." The smile in her eyes had already told me that. "He's going to come down and get me on Sunday afternoon." She settles on the other chair and sends messages on her phone. Seeing the room clock, I notice that almost two hours have passed. When Dad stirs, Alex jumps up from her chair and sits on the corner of his bed. When his eyes open, she says, "Hi, Dad."

He reaches out a hand to touch her face. "Hi, sweetheart." His voice is gravelly, and the stubble on his face makes him look older. He smiles, looks around the room, and sees me.

I stand on the other side of the bed. "So, Dad, what happened?"

He grimaces as he pushes the button to raise the bed. "One of my students was sick, so I agreed to drop off some homework." He stops to drink water, and when he resumes, his voice is clearer. "As I was leaving his house, I saw a man with a slim jim breaking into my car, so I ran up the street, yelling. He turned. A gun was in his hand, and he started shooting." He stops, winces, and puts a hand on his abdomen. "I remember falling, but that's all."

A soft knock at the door interrupts us. A man I've never seen before walks in with another man behind him. He introduces himself as Detective Mitchell. The nurse steps in as well and motions for us to leave. This tiny room is now way too crowded, and our presence is restricting her ability to check on him.

As we leave, Alex introduces herself to the detectives and turns back. "Dad, you can fill us in later." He nods.

We wander through the hallways, browse the gift shop, and go to the cafeteria. The food in the buffet line looks good, and it is almost lunchtime, but I don't want much. I ask for a small bowl of chili, grab an apple and a bottle of water, and then find a table. When Alex joins me, we sit for a minute, just looking at each other.

"I can't believe we almost lost him," she says, tears brimming in her eyes. I nod, and a tear rolls down my cheek. She grabs my hand, closes her eyes, and thanks God for our food and for keeping Dad from dying, too. Her voice quivers as she asks for a quick recovery. When she says "Amen," I study her. I think this has rattled her even more than Mom's death.

We eat in silence, noticing the other quiet conversations in the room. How many other wounded hearts are trying to force down food to keep their strength up when they'd rather cave to the pressure? When we clear our trays and return to the room, I wonder if the detectives will still be there, but when we walk in, Dad is alone and eating lunch. When he finishes eating, he holds on to the cup of coffee and pushes the tray away. We join him, standing on either side of the bed.

"So, Dad," Alex begins. "What did they say?"

"Well." He grimaces again when he moves. "I guess it was a good thing I fell. If I hadn't, I might be dead. The police found eight casings nearby. I don't remember anything after falling until I woke up here in the hospital. One of the neighbors heard the shots and came out to check things out and saw me lying on the sidewalk. He called 911."

I offer up a quick thanks to God for the alert neighbor who made sure he got to the hospital quickly. While Dad chats more with Alex, I pull out my laptop to study, but I have a question. Is it okay if I ask it even though it's more important that he heal? Turning back to my laptop, I finish one short assignment for English class and then let my mind wander to the future. Will I finish Mom's letters now that Dad's laid up? I hope so.

"I'm taking a quick walk," I say as I stand and move to the door. As soon as I reach the hall, the tears start to flow. Should I even be thinking about Mom's challenges when I almost lost Dad? But what if I get stuck on this one? Then I remember my words to Natalie, telling her to think about things that are lovely when she's scared, sad, or anxious. This negative thinking isn't helping me. As I turn the corner of the hallway, I see the sign for the chapel. I walk into the hushed room, move to the front to kneel at the altar, and start to pray. The tears flow—grateful ones, disappointed ones, happy ones, and lonely ones.

"I need You, God, to be everything I need right now. Mom's letters and Dad's advice were helping me get me through this year, and I almost lost both. Help me to depend on You and to be grateful for what I have. Even if I don't finish them all by the time the year is up and don't get the surprise, I'll still get to read Mom's words and cherish her advice."

When I finish praying, my heart is at peace.

CHAPTER 21

The days fly by. Dad comes home from the hospital and starts physical therapy. Going up the stairs to his room zaps him of his energy at first, but before long, he manages without having to stop and rest. Many days, on my way home from school, I wonder if the college trip will ever happen. We don't have a car, and he's not driving yet. What will happen if I get stuck on this challenge? I'm still doing most of the cooking and cleaning at home, though last night I came home to the smell of chili slow cooking in the crock pot. The air feels crisp and cold as I walk home, wondering again how long I'll have to wait to visit colleges. Walking up the driveway, I see a red Hyundai sitting in the open garage. After I check out the car, I find Dad in the living room drinking coffee.

"I thought we'd take our new car for a spin and treat ourselves to supper out," he says. "The physical therapist approved me for driving and for a trip. I just got off the phone with your school, and you get to skip school for this. Since I don't start teaching until after Thanksgiving, we'll go tomorrow. Gemma will be here later."

My mouth drops open, and I run to his chair and lean over to give him a hug. "Really?" I don't know what to say. Maybe I'll be able to finish all the challenges after all!

The morning we leave to visit colleges, I wake up before my alarm. Picking up my phone and Bible, I grab my robe and creep out of the room, careful not to wake Gemma. I usually have my quiet time at night before bed, but who knows if that will work tonight.

The smell of fresh coffee from our programmed coffee maker lures me into the kitchen. I pour myself a cup, add a little hazelnut cream, and move into the living room. It wasn't that cold last night, but I turn on the gas for the fireplace and sit in the adjacent chair, relishing the warmth radiating toward me. The glow from the fireplace is almost enough to see my Bible, but not quite, so I reach up and pull the string on the lamp.

The ribbon in my Bible marks my next reading—Psalm 66. As I read, I notice the phrases "come and see" and "come and hear." I read through the things the psalmist urges his listeners to notice and underline them in green. During the past year, there have been times when God clearly showed Himself to me. While I have never seen Him part a sea to create a path for a million people to walk over to the other side, I have seen Him do amazing things in my own life. He gave grace to our family. He kept us going through all the grief. He has comforted me.

Through the window, the pale dawn spreads its light. Why do I doubt and fear when He has already done more for me than I can count? "Forgive me, Lord," I pray, "for all the times I think I'm the one who is supposed to conquer my fear when all I have to do is trust You. I need to see and hear You. Help me focus on You more and not worry about the future. After all, You are already in my future. Even though I can't see it yet, you can."

Soft footsteps pass my chair, and I open my eyes to see Dad heading for the kitchen. Soon, we'll have breakfast and be on our way. I finish praying and climb the stairs to see if Gemma is up yet.

Blue skies form a backdrop for the changing leaves as we leave the city. I tell Gemma about my morning devotions. "When I see all this beauty around us, I wonder why everyone doesn't believe in God as the creator of the universe? Most of the students at my school don't. They think it just happened that way by chance. I'd love to be at a college where people don't think I'm strange if I talk about God."

Gemma's eyes turn from the GPS to me. "When I went for my interview at Juilliard, the admissions counselor gave me a tight smile when I said anything about God. Like she thought, I would grow up and stop believing once I got there. It hurt. I went out afterward and cried." She stops talking long enough to take a picture of the sky.

"You never told me that." I try not to sound hurt.

"I know, Cassie. That's because I went to a college group at Joyful Church that evening and told them about it. They prayed with me, and I felt peace. I decided that if I go to Juilliard, I'll talk about God every chance I get. I don't want to be afraid to shine. The best way for me to do that is to keep sharing what matters most in my heart."

Paper rustles in the back seat, and I know Dad is listening while he works on lesson plans.

"Dad, what was it like when you were in college? Were you mocked because of your belief in God?"

The rustling stops. My eyes stay on the road, but my ears perk up, hoping for insight into this decision. For the next hour, Dad tells one story after another. Most are encouraging stories of guys coming to ask him questions about what he believed. A few are stories of being mocked or put down. "But times have changed," he says. "Tolerance is widely taught. For some of your co-students, that will help, but others will think it doesn't apply to you because you are not tolerant when you say that Jesus is the only way to God and that we should obey what the Bible teaches."

It's quiet in the car until we arrive at the Northern campus. Students, workers, and teachers come and go from the various buildings. It reminds me of the school where Dad teaches. The male teachers are easy to distinguish from the students with their sports jackets and ties, but it's harder to tell with the women. The parking lot in front of the administration building is almost full, but I find a location at the far end. We get out and go in.

Looking up from her computer, the receptionist grins. "Hello, Cassie and Gemma. I'm Lucy." She hands us a schedule for the day and a map. "Come back here after the last class, and one of the students will take you on a campus tour. I don't have you down to stay in the dorm tonight, but if you change your mind, let me know, and I'll find a spot for you both." She looks up at my dad. "You can attend classes with them if you want, but I suggest the library if you have to work. It has a good internet connection, and it's usually quiet."

Lucy shows us the next class on our campus map and directs Dad across the street to the library. As we leave the warm building into a brisk fall breeze, we agree to find him when we finish.

The next few hours blur together: English class, chapel, Bible class, lunch in the cafeteria, history class, choir rehearsal, and a campus tour, including the dorms, gymnasium, and sports fields. We end up at the library, where we say goodbye to our student guide, find Dad, and drag ourselves to the car.

"I'll drive," Dad says as we return to the car. "You must be exhausted after all that. Besides, I've had enough lesson plans for one day." As he turns onto the highway, he asks, "So? What did you think?"

I don't wait to see if Gemma wants to answer. "Dad, did you know they start every class with prayer? And during discussion times, even in English, the teachers bring the discussion back to something in our lives. It was amazing. I asked one of the students during lunch if that was normal, and she said it was. I think I could grow in my relationship with God here."

"What did you think, Gemma?" he asks.

"This is the experience I always thought I'd have in college. I wanted to be surrounded by people who genuinely love God. But I think God may be leading me to Juilliard. It would be so much easier to be here. During lunch, I heard another table discussing theology. Where will I find something like that if I go to Juilliard?" Gemma's eyes brim with tears.

"On the other hand, God asks us to let our light shine so that He will be known to those who don't know Him yet. Being in a school with people who believe all different things means I'll be able to share what I believe all the time. That part really appeals to me. Honestly, I feel torn. I'm asking God to make it clear. If the doors to Juilliard open wide, I will walk through and trust Him for the strength to do what He wants me to do. If not, I want to go to a Christian school with Cassie."

Almost as soon as we merge onto the highway, my eyes feel heavy. When the car slows to pull into a gas station, I sit up with a jerk, realizing I've been asleep. Yawning and stretching, I look around. "Where are we?"

Turning off the ignition, Dad turns to me. "About half an hour from our hotel for the night. You missed a beautiful sunset."

"Awww. I love pretty sunsets." Away from the city lights, the stars above sparkle with brilliance, and the crescent moon begins its march across the night sky.

The next morning, after an early breakfast, we leave Dad at the hotel and drive the short distance to Word University. Near the front entrance, we find the administration building. At the information desk, a tall, thin guy smiles at us. When we introduce ourselves, he turns to the woman behind him. "Lisa, these are the students you are showing around today."

Lifting a hand from her crutches, Lisa gives me a firm handshake and a broad smile. "Welcome to Word. Today, you get to go to all my classes with me. I'll give you a campus tour during my free period. If you have questions, ask away. We'll have extra time during lunch and after the last class."

"Follow me." Her crutches click on the tile floor as we cross the lobby to the door. "You get to ride in style today," she says as she climbs into a golf cart parked outside, slipping her crutches behind her. "Since this campus is large, and it's hard to find parking, the school lets students with disabilities use golf carts. I still do plenty of walking with my crutches to keep me in shape." Students wave to us as we drive by, calling out greetings to Lisa.

"You know lots of people here," Gemma notes as we ride.

'I am the golf cart queen of the campus. Everybody wants a lift sometimes. I thought my handicap would make things hard for me in college, but it has made it easier here. People know who I am. The cart gives me a way to help them when they always want to help me, even though I keep telling them I can handle things myself. It has connected me to a ton of people I wouldn't otherwise meet."

The rest of the day blends together as one. In class after class, though, the teachers impress me. They work at drawing the students out of simple study to the application of what they are learning.

After supper, Lisa rides the elevator with us to the fifth floor of the closest dorm, opens the door and hands us the key. I wander to the window to look out over the sprawling campus. Below me, students are wandering. One boy on a bicycle almost runs into a boy who steps into his path without looking.

Lisa turns to us and points through the window. 'Breakfast is in that building from 6:30 until 8:30. I'm in room 310 if you need anything. I'd stay longer, but I have a ton of homework for tomorrow. Are you set here?"

Gemma looks at me, and we nod.

I reach into my backpack and pull out a bag of chocolate truffles. 'You said you like chocolate, so I hope you enjoy these. Thanks so much for all you did for us. If we end up here, you'll be the first person we'll look for."

'Thanks! And oh, I almost forgot." She reaches into her pocket and hands us a business card. 'Here's all my contact information. If you decide to enroll, please let me know. I'd love to introduce you to my friends."

On the way home the next day, I turn around to see Gemma in the back seat, engrossed in a novel. I dig out my journal and begin writing. What a whirlwind. But I'm no closer to knowing what to do than before we started. Lord, what should I do? I pause and sigh.

Dad maneuvers around a slow truck and pulls back into our lane. "So, what did you think?"

Just then, he slams on the brake. My pen flies out of my hand, and I brace myself against the dashboard as I see the tail end of a yellow car cross the traffic in front of us. We miss it by inches.

"Everyone alright?" Dad asks. "That car came out of nowhere."

"Dad, I'm so glad you were driving. I might not have braked fast enough." I look down at my journal and see a long black pen mark across the blank page. Now, every time I see this page, I'll remember what happened.

When my heart settles, I return to Dad's question. "The school visit was great. But I'm still no closer to knowing what to do than before we started. If anything, this trip just made it more confusing for me. Now I have more options."

"Options are good, but too many can be overwhelming. Let's break it down. List your options for next year for me." He already knows this, but I can tell he wants me to say them out loud.

"Well," I start counting on my fingers. "I could go to the community college where you teach."

He nods. "What are the advantages to that?

"It's inexpensive, and I'd get to live at home."

"But?" he probes.

"It's a two-year school, and with the college credits I already have, I wouldn't be there very long. It feels like putting off my decision."

For the next hour, he asks questions and I answer. I dig out some peanuts and pass them around. "Mom said in her letter that I should ask you about making good choices when there are many options."

"That's what we're doing. But there is one thing I haven't mentioned yet that should be foremost in your thinking." He tosses some peanuts in his mouth. "What will make the most difference for eternity?"

An exasperated sigh escapes. "I have no idea!"

"Think, Cassie."

"Well, you're always reminding Alex and me to focus on the things that matter for eternity, like people. Not possessions or how much money we can make. But I don't see how that helps me decide on a college."

"Let me put it to you this way." He puts out his hand, and I pour more peanuts into it. "When you drove to visit the college yesterday, there were multiple routes you could have chosen. If you had stopped for gas at one station or another, it wouldn't matter because the college was your destination. What is your ultimate destination in life?"

I know this answer. "To please God. To be His girl."

"Then, choosing a college is like stopping for gas somewhere. What matters is whether you are looking to God. He can lead you into your future from any college because He's that big."

Wow. He's right. I've been stressing over "getting it right" when God is big enough to lead me anywhere from anywhere, as long as my heart is following His. I turn back to my journal.

So many choices. I don't have a clear idea about majors or careers. Many people I know went to college for one thing and worked in an entirely different field. God, You know all the choices before me. Right now, I declare that I will trust YOU. I don't need to know the end, but I do need wisdom.

John 10 says You are my shepherd. I will listen for Your voice and follow where You lead.

I close the journal and breathe deeply. It's so good to know I can trust God with my future.

After we take Gemma home, we pull into our garage. I pull out my duffle bag, pillow, and purse, and Dad grabs the rest. I open the door with my key and take my things upstairs to my room while Dad stops in the kitchen to drop off the bag of snacks.

A few minutes later, Dad appears in my doorway. "I'll give you your next envelope tomorrow, but tonight, I want you to think, evaluate, and pray about what you learned in the past few days."

Disappointment fills me. I long to read another of Mom's sweet letters. But he's right. Once I have the new one in hand, I won't want to process the last two days.

"Dad, if God can guide and keep me so long as I'm trying to follow Him, that makes this big college decision less scary. Thanks for helping me see that."

He smiles, walks in, and sits on the edge of Alex's bed. "Cassie, God has given you a good mind and a desire to follow Him. In the choice between good options, He usually lets you decide and will guide you from there. Keep trusting Him, and you'll be just fine." He stands. "Who you are matters more to God than where you go to college. Keep focusing on Him, and He will always be your guide." He smiles as he exits, closing the door behind him.

Grabbing my journal from my backpack, I ask myself what I want to remember about today. I pick up my pen, divide the page into four blocks, and write Northern Pros in one block and Northern Cons in the next. In the bottom two blocks, I write Word Pros and Word Cons. I'll start there. When decision time comes, I may need a bigger chart that includes Dad's community college, U of M, Mankato State, these two schools, a gap year, and not going to college at all. Unless I get a sense in the next few days that one of these is the answer, the bigger chart will be part of my process.

As I fill in the blocks, I think about what Dad said. Even though this is the biggest decision I've had to make, God will guide me. After the blocks are filled with my thoughts, I add my prayer to the bottom of the page.

God, whatever happens, I choose to follow You. I will watch for Your leading and listen for Your voice, but most of all, I will trust You to keep me through the years ahead.

The Bible on my bedside table reminds me that I haven't read God's letter for my personal relationship with God today. The bookmark opens to John 10. There, I see my thoughts reflected. I am one of the Shepherd's sheep. I will listen to His voice and follow where He leads.

Leaning back against the headboard, I clasp my Bible to my chest and close my eyes, thanking Him for letting me finish this challenge. I wonder what's next.

When my alarm rings in the morning, I don't remember turning off the light and going to bed. At the breakfast table, a pink envelope lies beside my cereal bowl with a post-it note in Dad's scribbled handwriting. *Have a great day. I'll see you tonight.*

Before I pour myself a bowl of cereal, I slit the envelope with a table knife.

My dear daughter,

So you've been to visit colleges. I wonder which one you'll choose. I know you'll be a blessing to others wherever you go.

It must be November now, and the stores are putting up their Christmas decorations. Last year, December was hard. But this year, I want Christmas to be special for you.

For the past few years, I've wondered if our way of celebrating Christmas is the best. Does it honor Jesus on His birthday, or is it more about us? We did what we knew-what your dad and I did growing up, without much thought of what Jesus might like from us. So this is your task: Find ways to make Jesus the focus of Christmas this year.

When you have some ideas, share them with Dad. If he agrees, he'll talk to Alex for you. Then go all in and enjoy Jesus. Make this year all about HIM!

Whatever you decide, I hope it will help you worship Jesus more—not just this year, but for the rest of your life.

Love you to heaven and back,

Mom

Hmmm. A different Christmas. Did she suggest this because she knew this Christmas would be extra hard? I'd hoped this envelope would hold another quick and easy assignment like the last one, but this will take some time. When I see Aunt Sandi at Thanksgiving dinner, I'll ask her to help me.

CHAPTER 23

On Thanksgiving afternoon, Alex emerges from the kitchen carrying the golden turkey on a platter and places it in the middle of the table. My stomach rumbles when I see the steaming vegetables and a basket of rolls. My growling tummy was so loud that Dad laughs. It's so good to see him enjoying this day after all the days of pain and rehab.

Jon and Alex sit on the far side of the table, and Aunt Sandi and I on the other. Dad takes his place at the head. Alex hums a note, and together we sing, "Now thank we all our God with hearts and hands and voices."[1] Alex's clear soprano voice, with the rest of us filling in with harmony, makes us sound like a quintet practicing for a concert. When the last note dies down, Dad leads us in prayer, thanking God for the many blessings in our lives, especially the gift of family. He chokes at the end, and when we open our eyes, all of us are wiping tears from our eyes.

Aunt Sandi passes the turkey to Dad, who carves it into pieces. While he works on it, the rest of us pass around the other food. Aunt Sandi turns to Alex. "What's this I hear about Jon applying for a job nearby?"

Alex hasn't stopped smiling since she got here. "Yes. His internship will be here in the city, and if they like him, they'll keep him on full-time."

Dad pauses briefly in his carving. "And where are you going to live, Jon?"

"I'll look for a place during Christmas break. I hope I find one that puts me between here and work." Jon's doting smile rests on Alex, and she reaches out to squeeze his hand.

A pounding on the front door makes me jump. Who could that be? Don't they see we have a doorbell?

Dad gets up. At the door, a soft, low voice asks, "I'm sorry to bother you, but could you spare a sandwich or something? My wife and I are down on our luck."

My dad can be a sucker for a sob story, so I get up to see what's happening. I don't have to get close to the man in the green jacket for my nose to tell me he hasn't bathed in a while, though his hair is neatly combed. His five-o-clock shadow has morphed into the beginnings of a beard on his light face. His pants look clean.

"Tell you what," Dad says. "We're just sitting down to our Thanksgiving dinner. Would you like to join us?"

I duck out of view. Did he see my face? How can Dad do this? He'll wreck our family dinner by bringing strangers in.

"Oh, no. We weren't asking for that. We were hoping for some leftovers."

I glance back through the doorway as the man looks down at his boots. Did he choose our house, or is he just going from house to house? I stare past him to the driveway, where a woman sits in the car.

"I insist," Dad says. "Let's go invite her in." He motions down the driveway. "Nobody should be alone on Thanksgiving. We're grateful to be able to share."

Dad and the man walk down the driveway together. I see the woman shake her head as she says something.

Maybe she won't agree. But soon, the car door opens, and she gets out, holding on to her husband's arm and limping.

"Cassie," Dad calls as he turns and sees me standing in the doorway. "Put on a couple of plates. We have guests."

I turn to obey. What is wrong with him? Doesn't he know they could be con artists or thieves looking for an easy mark? Put on smelly clothes and find a house with cars parked in front? Yeah, I could do that too.

"Do it for Me." The words come unbidden into my mind.

"But Lord," I argue back. "They're probably con artists." A quiet coldness pokes my heart, and I remember that it's not wise to argue with God. While I gather plates and silverware, and we all shift our plates to make room for two more, I try to imagine that Jesus sent these two strangers to us. I still don't like it.

Dad seats our guests at the table. We soon find out that Mike lost his job three months ago. That is, if he is telling the truth. They couldn't pay their rent, so they moved in with relatives for a while. But then the relatives moved, so they had to leave. Now, they are living out of their car.

I wanted to hear more about Jon's apprenticeship, but that will have to wait. Instead, I begin to listen to the couple talk about their lives.

"I was a waitress," Michelle explains. "About two years ago, I was in a car accident and almost died. I was in a coma for four weeks. When I came out of it, I had to relearn everything—how to talk, do math, feed myself, and walk. My leg was broken in several places and hasn't healed correctly, so I can't do anything that requires me to stand on my feet all day, so I haven't found a job yet. I'm thankful, though. We had insurance when it happened, though the remaining medical bills are draining us dry. I'm grateful, though. It could be so much worse."

"Worse?" It sounds awful. "How could it be worse?" I ask.

Michelle looks around the table at us. "We don't owe anyone money, so we don't have debt collectors calling. We're trying to keep it that way until Mike can find a job again." She changes the subject by complimenting the food and asking questions about us.

When we finish eating and are all royally stuffed, we move toward the living room. Mike and Michelle start to say goodbye.

"Wait," I say, as the memories of our Love Project fill my mind. I approach Michelle and whisper, "Would you like to use our shower before you go? I'm sorry, but I couldn't help but notice."

Her face turns a fiery red, and she gives me a tentative smile. "Let me go to the car and get some clean clothes."

She walks over to her husband and whispers in his ear. He agrees, and they go out to the car together.

"Dad," Alex says. "We can't let them sleep in their car again. It's supposed to drop to zero degrees tonight."

"I was thinking the same thing. If they agree, I will call the Shepherd's Home to see if they have room. Maybe they can stay there until he finds a job."

Mike and Michelle return with clean clothes, and I lead Michelle up the stairs. Wincing with every step, she breathes a sigh of relief when she gets to the top. In the bathroom, I show her the towels and hairdryer. I can hear Dad downstairs talking with Mike. When I return, Dad's on the phone.

The conversation is short, and Dad's smile turns to a frown. He turns to Mike. "I'm sorry. They don't have room.

But it's too cold to sleep in your car tonight. Maybe you can stay with us."

Where, Dad? On the couch? Your room? Mine? For how long? And didn't you see how hard those stairs are for her? I'm tempted to voice my thoughts, but Dad's talking to Mike, not me.

Mike looks around like he's considering. "Um, I don't know. I'll have to ask Michelle."

Aunt Sandi returns from the kitchen and looks at me, then Dad. "Adam, you don't have room here, and you're still recovering." She turns to Mike. "Stay with me. I have a guest room with its own bathroom. You can stay as long as you need. And it's all on one level."

He swallows, chokes back tears, closes his eyes, and nods. "I think that might work. But not for long. If possible, we need our own place by Christmas."

When Michelle returns, he tells her what he's decided. She sags into her husband's arms. "Thank you. We've been okay so far, but I dreaded another night in the car. We won't stay long, I promise."

"Don't promise." Aunt Sandi reaches out to touch Michelle's shoulder. "We'll pray that God will give your husband a job, but stay as long as you need a warm, comfortable place. I'll enjoy the company."

I knew Aunt Sandi was generous, but this goes beyond anything I've seen. Maybe that's why everyone at the hospital likes her so much. But I'm going to pray that Mike finds a job so they don't stay too long.

"In fact," Aunt Sandi continues. "Why don't we go now? Michelle needs to rest, and you can shower at my house."

As I watch them leave, my mind is churning. Dad settles into a chair by the fire, and Alex and I finish clearing the table.

"You're quiet," Alex murmurs as we walk into the kitchen. "Something wrong?"

"Yeah. I'm just thinking about Mike and Michelle. All of you were so quick to think about helping them. Except for me. Why am I always so suspicious? Why can't I be more like Mom and Aunt Sandi?"

If Mom had been here, I would have seen her excitement in helping others, and I would have gotten on board. But, instead, I thought the worst of them. I was only thinking about what I wanted instead of others' needs. The sobs rise from somewhere deep within me. Guilt wants to swallow me whole.

Alex puts down the dishes and wraps her arms around me. She rubs her hand over my hair and shoulders and lets me cry. When the tears settle, I hear her humming. The lyrics to the song flow through my mind.

"Children of the heavenly Father
Safely in His bosom gather
Nestling bird nor star in heaven
Such a refuge e'er was given."[1]

It was one of Mom's favorite hymns. When I was little and had nightmares, she'd sit by my bed and sing it to me until I fell asleep. Now the memory of that safety net quiets my heart, and I brush the tears away.

Alex pulls back to look at me. "You are God's child, Cassie. God's Spirit dwells in you. Yes, we are both learning and growing, but God is molding you into the woman He wants you to be. Don't compare yourself to Mom or Aunt Sandi. Just be yourself."

---

[1] *Children of the Heavenly Father, hymn by Carolina Sandell, translated into English by Ernst Olsen, public domain.*

"But I fail so miserably. How will I ever be the woman God wants me to be?" I bury my face in my hands.

"If you feel like you failed today, ask for forgiveness. Then get back up and move on. He'll help you learn and grow." I stand back, and Alex hands me a paper napkin. "Your mascara is smeared," she says with a smile.

I wipe under my eyes and throw away the napkin. I'm glad Jon wasn't here to witness my meltdown. Or Dad, for that matter.

As we load the dishwasher, Alex starts humming again. Before long, the song bubbles up in my heart. I am God's child. He will keep me through the years ahead. He will accomplish His work in me. Without even thinking, I start to hum along.

Iturn up my collar and wrap the orange woolen scarf tighter around my head as I walk against the biting wind. Turning the corner, I wait for the traffic light and begin to hum, "Silver bells. Silver bells." On the light poles, decorations sparkle—red and white candy canes, white snowmen, yellow stars, and green Christmas trees. I love this time of year.

From the other side of my mind, like a freight train bearing down on me in my moment of Christmas joy, the beast of sorrow forces me into darkness, a black hole that can still suck all the cheer and energy out of me. "Mom," I whisper into my scarf, "Why did God take you from us?" I choke back the sobs that rise from deep inside. Tears freeze on my cheeks. Will being with Aunt Sandi help? I walk a little faster.

The light changes, and I start across the street, thinking about Aunt Sandi's steadiness through all the ups and downs. Maybe her nursing helps her stay calm when life falls apart. As I walk, the Christmas trees shining in the windows of some homes shout with joy to my aching heart: "It's time to celebrate that Jesus came." Last night's snow left four inches on the ground, and the white powder reflects the colored lights. It's only the Monday after Thanksgiving, but many houses glow with lights, candles, and trees. Not ours. Our house doesn't have a single decoration.

I turn up the walk to Aunt Sandi's house. Her Christmas tree shines in the early darkness, showing off its ornaments and tiny white lights. If Aunt Sandi is ready to celebrate Christmas, I want to, too. I rap on the door, open it, and step over the threshold.

"I'm here, Aunt Sandi," I call. Breathing in the sweet smell of chocolate drifting from the kitchen, I remove my green parka and hang it on the hall tree. As I bend to take off my snowy boots, Aunt Sandi walks into the front hall. She wraps her arms around me and gives me a squeeze.

"I'm so glad you could come." Taking a step back, she reaches up to take my face in her hands and stares at me. "You look so much like your mom. It's like she left a piece of herself with us when she left. I know you're you, but seeing you is a gift to me. It helps me deal with the fact that my sister's gone."

I smile. Sometimes, my resemblance to Mom bothers me, especially when Dad looks at me like he's remembering Mom instead of seeing me. But Aunt Sandi makes it seem okay again. "Are those chocolate chip cookies I smell? And are we going to have hot chocolate with them?"

"Of course." She smiles, and we walk arm-in-arm to the kitchen. Fresh from the oven, cookies are on the cooling racks, and two snowman mugs are on the counter, ready to be filled with hot chocolate. She hands me one, and I fill it with her secret recipe from the saucepan on the stove. The cookie tray beckons me. I choose two.

The house is quiet, welcoming me into its presence like an old friend.

"Are Mike and Michelle still here?" This will be a quick visit if they are.

"Yes, though they're out tonight looking for an apartment. Mike found a job the day after Thanksgiving, so they won't be here much longer."

"I'm glad." I sip some hot chocolate. "So they're going to be okay?"

"They are. Michelle is excited about getting their furniture out of storage and setting up a house again."

I savor the cookie, enjoying the chewy dough, the crunchy nuts, and the chocolate chips. A little warm chocolate dribbles out, and I lick it with my tongue before it drips on my clothes. "I almost didn't come. I wanted to see you, but I had a horrible day, missing Mom so much."

Aunt Sandi leans back in her chair and looks around at her decorated home. Instead of the picture of a family saying grace around the table, a sign reads, "Jesus is the reason for the season." Looking at me again, she says, "Do you have any thoughts about this Christmas?"

I draw in a deep breath, let it out slowly, and tell her about Mom's latest challenge. "Until I received Mom's letter, I thought I wouldn't want to celebrate Christmas. But now that she's given me an assignment and I realize that Christmas can be more about Jesus, I'm ready." I pause to look at her Christmas tree. "Christmas will be awful if we don't do something different. It will just remind us what we've lost."

"So, what are you thinking?" Aunt Sandi asks.

"I don't want to use our ornaments. They'll remind me too much of Mom. I'm not ready for a tree. She always got so excited about choosing the right one." How do I phrase what I'm thinking? "What if we made our nativity set the centerpiece of our decorations and made evergreen garlands? I could make some Christian symbols to add to some garlands or buy a few. If our ornaments focus on Jesus, maybe that will help."

Aunt Sandi grabs her laptop and opens it on the kitchen counter. For the next few minutes, we look at several sites online. I grab a pen and a notebook to take notes of the symbols we like and make a list of materials we need.

"Well, I don't think we'll need many, and I can buy some." In my mind's eye, a garland wraps around the staircase with paper crosses, stars, and lambs. Candles adorn the garland in the bay window with words like Emmanuel, Jesus, and Prince of Peace. Another garland over the fireplace. And greens and candles around the nativity set.

"Hey, look at this." Aunt Sandi stops her scrolling through Pinterest and enlarges a picture. It's an evergreen cross someone hung on their front door.

"What a cool idea. I could make that. I only need two sticks of wood, floral tape and wire, and evergreen branches. I could even put some lights and symbols on it. Auntie, would you help me with the symbols?"

Aunt Sandi looks up from the computer screen. "I will if your dad and sister don't want to, but ask them first. Even though you think he's not ready to celebrate, he may be hurt if you leave him out. If neither of them can help you, ask if it's okay if I do."

Walking together toward the door, it swings inward. Mike and Michelle walk in.

Michelle is beaming at me. "We found a place! It's small, but it's close to Mike's work. I can already imagine a Christmas tree in the corner of the living room. We move in this weekend."

Aunt Sandi hugs her. "Will you need help moving in? I could round up some friends from church. Unfortunately, I have to work this weekend, or I would definitely help you!"

"You have been so kind," Mike says, "but my new job is paying for a moving company." He turns to me then. "You have an amazing family. Your aunt has gone above and beyond helping us, and what you and your family did for us on Thanksgiving Day was such a blessing."

Michelle looks at her husband and nods, so he continues. "We were far from God when we met you, but you have made us rethink our priorities. We're going to start looking for a church."

"Come to ours," I urge. "We love it there, and I think you would too."

On my way home, I look up at the crescent moon and around at the fresh snow, wrapping the world in a soft, white blanket. As I near the house, porch lights illuminate the cleared sidewalk. One light shines upstairs in Dad's study. Stepping into the entryway, I place my boots on the tray inside the door and hang my coat.

"I'm home." My voice dispels the quiet.

Footsteps walk across the upper floor and descend. "How was your time with Aunt Sandi?"

"Good."

Dad rubs his eyes and yawns. "Would you like a hot drink after your cold walk? I need something after all that studying."

"Sure." I follow him into the kitchen.

He removes two mugs from the cupboard, fills them with water, and puts them in the microwave. I dig for the box of tea and choose Candy Cane for myself. I hand the box to Dad.

Well, here goes. "Dad, I have some ideas about Christmas."

"Okay." He pulls out a chamomile tea bag and looks at me, tension etching his face. "What are you thinking?"

"I'm not ready for everything we used to do," I say slowly.

He nods. "Neither am I."

"So, I was wondering. Can we get a bigger nativity set and make it our centerpiece instead of a tree? Then we can hang garlands and string lights, but the nativity set would be the focus."

The microwave dings and we grab our mugs. He stares at his cup as he dips his teabag.

"I love that idea," he says. "We can put it on the coffee table in the center of the room. That would give it the focus you want. I'll call Alex in the morning and talk to her about it. In the meantime, let's get some sleep."

"Dad?" I look into his dark eyes. "Will we be okay?"

He puts down his mug and draws me in for a hug. "Christmas will not be the same without your mom, but putting our focus on Jesus will help. I'm glad she made it one of your challenges."

I nod, hug him back, and climb the stairs to my room as I sniff my minty tea.

CHAPTER 25

A week later, I'm back at Aunt Sandi's. We draw patterns on paper and use the patterns to cut the poster board into crosses, angels, and stars. With glitter, sequins, paint, and pipe cleaners, the shapes transform into decorations fit for any home. At 8:00, her grandfather clock chimes. A couple dozen symbols lie on the end of her table. We have quite a few, but we need some more.

After stacking the supplies in a pile, she grabs a sponge to clean the table of glue and glitter. "Did you talk to your Dad?" she asks.

"I did. He called Alex, and she'll help us gather evergreen tips for garlands when she comes home."

The ache in my heart is still so massive. "Aunt Sandi, do you ever really heal from something like this?"

"In a way, you do." She looks up from wiping the table. "In another way, you learn how to go on. When my mom died, I felt like I'd lost a limb. I still miss her, but you learn how to live your life without her. Only when we get to heaven will we be truly healed." Reaching out to pat my arm, she adds, "But there can be great happiness, even though a part of you is missing."

"I hope so."

Auntie throws her long brown hair over her shoulder. "What are you going to do about gifts? Maybe you should talk that over with your dad."

"I suppose." I stop to look into her blue eyes. "It's weird how we say Christmas is about Jesus, but we give each other gifts instead of Him. If people threw me a birthday party and then came and gave gifts to everyone else, I think I'd be offended. Jesus said that giving to the least of these is like giving to Him, but we're not doing that. Usually, we're giving to people who already have so much. So, if we're celebrating Jesus' birthday, I need to give Him something. But how do you give a gift to someone who owns the universe? What would He want from me?"

"That's a great question, Cassie. Do you have a little more time to talk?"

"Sure. I finished my homework this afternoon."

I text Dad quickly to let him know I'll be home later than I planned. Then Auntie puts down her mug and walks out to the living room. A few minutes later, she reappears with two Bibles in one hand and paper in the other. Moving the drying ornaments off to the side, she hands me a Bible and some paper. She looks up "gift" on a Bible program on her computer while I do the same in the concordance in the Bible she's given me. The clock ticks. Delicate Bible pages rustle. Ballpoint pens click and scratch. My list of verses grows. I look over at Aunt Sandi's paper and see that she has a fairly long list, too.

"I think this will get us started and give us an idea of how to give gifts to Jesus. If you still want more verses, you can use your computer at home to cross-reference these verses, and you'll have even more." She puts her list next to mine so we can compare them. Some verses are the same. "From what we see here, what are some of the things God wants as gifts from us?"

"Well, He wants our praise, and He wants us to give to the needy and those in ministry. It surprised me when

I read that He would rather we forgive others than bring Him a gift." A weight settles on my heart. Have I forgiven the gray girl? Not really. But I don't want to think about that now.

Aunt Sandi is waiting for me to go on. "Auntie, I want to give something tangible like we would give to others at Christmas. I know ministries need money, but I want to give something more personal than that."

"Well, my dear Cassandra, I think the first order of business is prayer. God knows your heart and will direct you to something He wants you to give."

I smile. "And, since He has everything, I don't have to worry about offending Him if my gift is small. I give because I love Him and not because He needs it."

She prays with me and gives me a long hug. "Be careful out there. Always be on the alert. Text me when you get home, okay?"

"I will," I promise.

The wind is behind me on the way home, making it seem warmer even though the temperature has dropped another couple of degrees. Light snowflakes drift slowly down. I stick out my tongue to catch one. Times with Auntie ease the hurt a little. I'm happy with the ornaments we made for decorating. Now, I can focus on the gifts.

The gray girl pops up in my mind. I try to push the thought away, but it won't leave. What do I do about her? God's gentle voice whispers to my soul, "If you do not forgive others their sins, I will not forgive yours either."[2]

But how? How do I forgive her?

---

[2] *Paraphrase of Matthew 6:15*

CHAPTER 26

At school on Monday, I find Yasmin. She's become the first person I look for, a friend I never thought I'd have. I was happy alone, or at least I tried to convince myself I was. But then God gave me Maya and now Yasmin. He knows me better than I know myself.

After homeroom, Yasmin starts talking about her interest in Malcolm. I listen intently, trying to ignore the gray girl walking toward us on the other side of the hall. "Hi, Cassie!" she calls.

I pretend I don't hear her.

Yasmin stares at me. "What's that about?"

"What?" I ask.

"That girl," Yasmin says. "That's not the first time I've seen you ignore her."

"Long story." I pick up my pace, anxious to get to choir and not think about her.

Yasmin stares at me. When we sit down in the choir room, Yasmin is still staring.

I fidget with the edge of my sweater. "What?"

"It's not like you, Cassie. I know you're shy, but that was different. That was unfriendly."

Shame fills me. I've been trying to convince myself that just because I avoid her doesn't mean anything. But it's not true. Bitterness has taken root. And if I don't forgive her, Jesus doesn't want a present from me for His birthday. It's not like I haven't tried. I've tried, but the hurt keeps coming back. How God? How do I let this go for good?

Mr. Clark leads us in vocal exercises, and my shame-filled thoughts take a back seat to the notes on the page before me.

That night, tucked under my down comforter, I reach for my journal.

Lord,

I want to give YOU a gift this Christmas, but what? I have no idea what to give.

Almost immediately, the verses I read with Aunt Sandi from Matthew 5 remind me that Jesus doesn't want a gift from me when unforgiveness still lurks in my heart. Yasmin's questions today make it clear. If I can't forgive the gray girl, have I even begun to understand how much God forgave me? He forgave me so much more. Help me, God, to forgive her.

Last year, I saw her in the cafeteria praying before she ate her lunch, so I asked if she was a Christian. Though we didn't have classes together, we became lunch buddies. I was surprised because she was prettier and more athletic than me, though she was a loner like me. But after I got to know her a little, she began making little comments that hurt. I tried to hide it, but her ideas wore away at me. Day after day, she pointed out how she was godlier than I was with little jabs, like 'How can you read that when you need to be reading the Bible more?" or "Why do you play those silly video games when you could spend your time memorizing Scripture?" One day it was, 'I guess my dad loves me more than yours," because my dad let me do things her dad didn't. I felt like such a failure around her. When she chided me that I didn't have enough faith and that's why Mom was dying, I talked to Mom about it. Mom encouraged me to see things from the big picture. That she was going to heaven a little ahead of me, that was all, and that God knew best.

After that, I sometimes found a place to eat alone, but sometimes I still sat with her. But then, after school was out for the summer, she wrote on Facebook that some so-called "Christians" were not Christians at all. The example she used was me, though at least she was kind enough to not use my name. But anyone who knew about our friendship may have guessed who it was. That was it. I was done. I gave up and decided that I wouldn't be her lunch buddy, even if we happened to have lunch at the same time. Then, in August, I found out that her "super-spiritual" dad was taken in by the police for drunk driving and is still in jail. Secretly, I felt like she deserved the misfortune. But now my bitterness toward her has shown itself to Yasmin in all its ugliness. I bury my face in my pillow and smash my fists against the mattress. I want to scream out my frustration, but Dad might hear me.

She thought she was so perfect, and everything I did was less perfect. My version of following Jesus was never as good as hers. I didn't read my Bible as much. My church was not as good as hers. My clothes weren't right. What began as feeling sorry for myself has transformed into savage resentment, and now I realize my own judgment of her is just as much of a sin as her judgment of me. Even deciding to call her the "gray girl" instead of "Stormy" was because I was being hateful.

I know I face a crossroads. One way leads to forgiveness, both asking for it and giving it. If I go the other way,

I get to keep my pride and justify my actions. But if I hold on to that, I'm turning away from God. I can't do that. He has been with me every step of the way, especially during this horrible last year.

Yet Jesus is clear. He doesn't want my gift until I forgive. In this morning's Bible reading, after Jesus taught the disciples to pray, He told them that if they didn't forgive others, their Heavenly Father wouldn't forgive them either. Ouch. That hurts.

I get out from under my warm covers, slip on my heavy robe, and kneel beside my bed. "Okay, God, I can't hold onto my bitterness any longer. You've forgiven me so much more than what she's done to me." All the hurts replay in my mind, but then I see Jesus suffering for me. I never suffered what He did, and yet He forgave me. "Okay, God, I forgive Stormy."

A huge sense of relief slides through me. Why didn't I do this sooner? I continue. "Every time the bitterness starts to creep back in, I'll forgive her again. I'll keep doing it until I don't have to do it anymore. And please forgive me, too, for being judgmental against her. I thought I was just protecting myself, but now I realize that I was doing the same things to her as she did to me."

For the first time in a long time, warmth slides into my heart, replacing the coldness I've held against her for so long.

I shed my robe and crawl back into my toasty warm cocoon. As I drift off to sleep, a smile creeps across my face. Is God smiling too? I hope so.

CHAPTER 27

The car's thermometer reads 28 degrees as we drive down snowy roads to Dad's sister's farm. When we jump out of the car, memories of finding Christmas trees here flood my soul with a wave of grief. I bolster myself and follow Dad down the driveway to the barn behind the big farmhouse. He slides open the barn door, and we duck inside the dim room. A big tractor dominates the space, and as my eyes adjust, I see the tools and implements lining the wooden walls.

"Over here," Uncle David calls out to us. He walks over and hugs each of us. "Here are some pruning shears and a saw. The saw is in case you need it, but you probably won't. A path into the woods to the left of the newly planted trees will lead you to full-grown cedars, firs, and pine trees, all of which we've used in making garlands. Help yourselves."

Our bootprints join others on the well-trodden snowy path through the woods. Ahead of me, Alex scoops up a ball of snow and turns to face me. Splat. The snowball disintegrates on the front of my parka. I return fire. Soon, Dad joins in our fun, and we're laughing and squealing as we dodge snowballs and throw them at each other.

"Truce," Dad calls with a chuckle, and we drop the balls we're holding. "Time to get to work, or we'll be here all day."

With pruning shears in hand, we gather soft tips off nearby tree branches and lay them on the tarp beside us. I breathe in the smell of fresh pine and fir. Our house is going to smell great.

"Look. Bayberries." Alex plucks some silver-blue berries off a branch. "These will help our house smell great, too."

"And we can use them for decoration." I join her, and we find a couple of bayberry-laden branches.

"Girls, I think we have enough." Dad joins us, breaks open a berry, and puts it to his nose. "I've always loved this smell."

We take turns pulling the evergreen-loaded tarp out of the woods. When we emerge, Dad hands me his pruning shears. "You girls take the tools to the barn and meet me at the house. I'd like to see Aunt Rachel before we leave."

We hang the tools in the barn and walk back to the house. Uncle David opens the door wide for us, and we join Dad in the kitchen. "Did you get everything you needed?"

"Yes, and we found some bayberries. Okay if we have them?"

"Sure. We've got more than we need. But why aren't you getting a tree this year?" Uncle David asks.

Dad looks at me and nods, encouraging me to explain.

"Well," I begin. "Mom asked me to find ways to make this Christmas more about Jesus, so we decided to make a nativity set the centerpiece of our decorations. The tree can be such an attention grabber that people don't even notice a manger scene."

"Interesting idea, but I hope too many people don't follow suit. I'd have to shut down the tree farm," he says with a wink. "Anyway, I'd ask you to stay for lunch, but Rachel is out, and I'm not great in the kitchen."

"Too bad." Dad's face deflates with disappointment. "Tell her I'm sorry we missed her, but we need to get back home. Thanks for everything."

We load the tarp full of branches into the trunk. The scent glides into the passenger cabin, and I relish the smell of balsam fir. One more thing done to make things special for Jesus' birthday, but I still haven't figured out what gift I will give Him.

My internal body clock wakes me up at 6:00 a.m. Starlight moves when I lift my head off the pillow to see if Alex is up, but she's still snuggled under her comforter. It's so nice to have her here.

"Happy birthday, Jesus," I murmur under my breath. Reaching out to the bedside table, I pick up Mom's photo. How I miss her. "Mom," I whisper, "I don't know if you see what happens here on earth, but I hope you will be pleased with how we're celebrating Christmas today." Will we like it? Or will we go back to the way we've always done it?

Today will be different. I'm glad, but I'm also a little sad. I don't think I realized how selfish I was when it came to Christmas—how it was about what I got and the gifts I gave to my friends and family. Never once did I think about giving Jesus something. It's just the way we did things, and I loved it. I will miss that, but I hope I'll like this new way too. We'll see what I end up teaching my children someday.

I roll out of bed, slip on my slippers, and grab my robe. The smell of coffee draws me downstairs. The warmth of the blazing fireplace contrasts with the cool upstairs.

Dad pours me a cup of coffee. "Good morning, pumpkin."

"Dad, you haven't called me that since I was a kid," I add cream and a tiny bit of sugar.

"Well, today, with your unruly red hair, that's what came into my mind. How are you feeling about our changes?"

"Mixed emotions," I explain.

"I know what you mean," he agrees. "I'm glad Mom asked you to do something different. Otherwise, I don't think I would have done anything at all. But you're right. We'll always associate the way we did things before with Mom, and that may mean that one of these years, we'll want to try adding some of those elements back when it doesn't hurt as much." Tears glisten in his eyes. "As soon as Alex is up, we can eat breakfast. In the meantime, I need to do one more thing." Coffee cup in hand, he trudges back upstairs.

I settle into the big chair beside the fireplace in the living room. Pulling up the settee, I lay a blanket over my feet and stare at the lighted garlands with their handmade ornaments. More greenery adorns the bookshelves. Electric candles and words for the names of Jesus hide among the branches on the bay window. I love it, though it took hours for us to gather the greens and then weave them together into garlands. This is a Jesus-focused Christmas to remember. "Thanks, Mom."

"Happy birthday, Jesus," I whisper, and a spring of deep joy rises in me.

Music plays, soft at first, then gets louder. Deep, resonant strings play "Silent Night." Alex must be up. She can't live without music. The music from Alex's phone connects with the speakers to fill the whole house with Christmas praise.

"Morning, sis." She grins as she bounces into the room. Her tousled blond hair makes her look gorgeous, even though she would call it "bedhead." She plops on the couch and wraps her fluffy lavender robe around her.

"Morning," I say. "Sleep well?"

"Like a rock. But I had a dream about Mom. She was here. This morning. Celebrating with us. And it made her happy that we were celebrating Jesus. I think she'd like your ideas. My dream is right. She'd be happy." Alex's million-dollar smile says it all.

"Everyone ready for breakfast?" Dad reaches to put an envelope under the garland on the mantle. "The breakfast casserole is ready, and the cinnamon rolls you girls made are warming in the oven."

We gather at the kitchen table, Alex. Late last night, Alex tied festive, red ribbons around our napkins and stemmed glasses. Dad pours orange juice into the glasses and motions for us to sit.

"Wait." Alex reaches for a lighter and ignites the single white candle in the center of the table. "Happy birthday, Jesus," she says with a smile. "We should sing." She leads out in "O Come, All Ye Faithful." It's just us, but the harmony of our three voices stirs contentment in me. When the last note fades, Dad prays, thanking God for sending His precious Son into the world to open a personal door between us and God.

We linger over breakfast. What a different Christmas from last year when we barely wanted to acknowledge that it was a special day. Aunt Sandi came and fixed dinner, and we exchanged a few gifts. But with Mom coughing and barely able to get out of bed, it was hard to muster any excitement over Christmas. Yet today, less than a year since I lost her, I'm celebrating Jesus.

A couple of hours later, in the living room, Alex and I take selfies in our red sweaters and laugh about the goofy looks on our faces. We quickly delete half of them. More pictures. Us by the nativity set. Us on the stairs with the decorated handrails framing us. In front of the fireplace with the evergreen-draped mantle and lit candles behind us.

Dad settles into the big leather chair by the fire while we plop on the couch. He grabs his Bible from the table beside him and says, "I think we should read the Christmas story, sing together, and then talk about our gifts."

I glance at the front door. "Aren't we going to wait for Aunt Sandi? She said she'd be here soon."

"And what about Jon? He'll be here after his family finishes their gift opening. I'd like him to experience this firsthand instead of hearing it from me."

"If you girls want to wait, I'm all for it. We never could have waited when you were little, but things have changed." We laugh together at the memory of trying to hurry our parents out of bed so that we could open our gifts. Now, waiting is part of the fun.

An hour later, the doorbell rings, and Alex jumps up to answer it. Jon pulls Alex into a warm embrace. "Merry Christmas." He removes his coat while Alex waits by the door for Aunt Sandi, who's pulling into the driveway. Soon, we're settled in the living room. Not to be left out, Starlight jumps up in my lap.

Dad opens his Bible. "I want each of us to pick a character in the story and place ourselves in their situation. What would it have been like to be there that day? When I finish reading, let's share our thoughts." We agree, and he reads from Luke 2, a story I know so well.

I choose the angels. I listen, trying to visualize that night on the Judean hills when the angels showed up. Maybe I should have picked someone else. After all, I have no idea what it would be like to be an angel. But l stick with it.

When Dad finishes, we share our thoughts on our character. Jon chooses Joseph. Aunt Sandi shares her reflections on Mary. Alex talks about the shepherds. Dad asks about the innkeeper, even though he's not mentioned in the story. Was he there or not? Why does Luke mention there was no room? He raises lots of good questions, none of which we can find any answers to in the Bible. It's fun to imagine, but it's good to know it's our imagination, not Scripture.

When he stops talking, he looks at me. So does everyone else. "I chose the angels," I say.

"But you don't know what being an angel is like," Alex says, the double meaning loud and clear in her tone as she grins.

I nudge her with my elbow. "I wanted to think about it, though. What would it have been like to be sent from heaven to announce the birth of the King? What would you think about making that announcement in a field of sheep to a few shepherds instead of a palace or even a stadium with lots of people?" I talk about seeing the startled looks on the faces of the shepherds and what it would be like to be joined by a multitude of angels in praise to God and in giving blessing to us humans.

I love this discussion. It makes the story come even more alive, even though I've heard it a million times. Okay, that's exaggerating, but I have listened to it a lot. After a while, the discussion dwindles.

Dad clears his throat. "As you know, we decided to do things differently this Christmas. It's hard without Mom here, and she knew it would be. So, as I think you all know, she gave Cassie an assignment to focus on Jesus more. Sandi helped Cassie make all the symbol ornaments you see around the room."

Aunt Sandi and I exchange a look of satisfaction.

"We've done what we could to put our attention on Jesus." Dad sighs and looks around at the decorations. "It's beautiful, and it has done my heart good to see this place decorated for Christmas. And that brings us to the gifts. Our presents this year are just for Jesus. There will be other times for us to give each other gifts. Since He's not physically present, the person giving that gift will open it."

Alex gets up first. She opens her envelope and pulls out a photo of a beautiful six-year-old girl from Thailand. Her gift will continue to provide meals and school supplies until this little girl grows up. I guess she figures that she can afford it since she'll have a real job soon.

Next, Dad opens his. He has a receipt for the money he sent to a Bible college in Ghana that is building a new classroom to train pastors.

I hesitate. Thoughts race through my mind. Should I even share mine? Should this be private? Between me and Jesus? I don't want to impress anybody with this. I want Him to be pleased. Am I just afraid to share because it's not much compared to what Dad and Alex have done? I'm uncomfortable with all eyes on me.

"I couldn't do much," I stammer. My heart is beating so fast that I'm sure the others can hear it. "I don't have much money. I tried to think of what is really valuable to me. Right now, I'm trying to save money for college. The money from almost every babysitting job or the hours I work at the Burger Joint ends up in my college account. So, I think my time is my most valuable asset. So then I thought about what I could do with my time that would please Jesus. So, I called Olivia's parents and asked them if I could give them a free night of babysitting once a month so they can go out together. Olivia told me they don't like leaving her alone with all eight of her younger siblings, but they can't afford a regular sitter. It's not much, but I couldn't think of anything else."

"That's a wonderful idea, Cassie." Dad beams, and I bask in the warmth of that smile.

Aunt Sandi reaches into her purse. "Well, I guess it's my turn to share mine. I sent money to a Christian hospital in Greece for medical supplies. They are near a refugee center and have been inundated with patients this year. So I had to help."

Jon reaches out and grabs Alex's hand. "I love this idea," he says. "Let's talk about incorporating this into our future Christmases."

She smiles. "I was hoping you would say that. I feel bad that I've focused more on me, my family, and my close friends than on Jesus. I like this."

I lean back into the couch. Where will I be in ten years? Will I be sitting by a tree with a husband and maybe a child or two? Will he want our focus on Jesus or on gifts? Do you talk about things like that when you date a guy? I want to ask Dad but now isn't the time.

That afternoon, Gemma video calls me. "What did you get for Christmas?" she asks, a twinkle in her eye.

"Nothing." Relating Mom's fifth challenge puts a smile on my face.

"So you didn't get anything?" Surprise raises her eyebrows.

"Nope. And it was wonderful. After all, it was Jesus' birthday, not mine."

"Hmmm." The red polished nails of her hands wrap around a strand of her long hair. "I guess I figured the Christmas Eve service was my gift to Jesus, and the rest, well, was just Christmas. I hadn't thought much about giving Jesus a gift since He already has everything He needs."

I don't know how to respond, but I don't feel like I need to either. Gemma continues. "So you finished the fifth challenge. What's the next one?"

"I don't know yet. Dad said he'd give it to me on New Year's Day."

"It must be so hard to wait," Gemma says.

"It is," I agree. "But it's giving me more time to think about Mom's Christmas challenge rather than jumping right into the next one."

When I hang up, I smile. The hole Mom left is enormous, especially today. But shifting my focus to Jesus instead of myself really helped.

CHAPTER 29

It's almost 11:00 p.m. on New Year's Eve when Dad, Alex, and I slip into the auditorium. Music from the string ensemble soothes my aching heart; it reminds me how much Mom loved this service and bringing in the New Year with God.

Christmas lights run through the garlands, around the windows, and highlight the platform. I spot Gemma by the piano and wave briefly to her as we find our seats.

Pastor Ian Fuller steps to the podium and welcomes us. "A big ball will drop in Times Square tonight, but we won't see it. Instead, we have chosen to join our brothers and sisters in saying goodbye to this year and welcoming the new one. Some of you have come to love this service as much as I do."

As the clock nears midnight, the lights in the auditorium dim. Only the Christmas and platform lights give the auditorium a soft glow. Then, someone turns off the Christmas lights, section by section, until only the ones on the platform provide any light. As Pastor Fuller's voice fills the room, even the stage lights darken until only the red exit lights give any light to the room. It's almost as though I am alone in the room until someone coughs.

In the darkness, Pastor Fuller's voice reminds us. 'Let the darkness be a reminder that we are starting over. This year is gone. Use the remaining minutes in the darkness to confess, give thanks, and say goodbye to the past year. Then expect God to do great things in and through you in the coming year."

A hush falls over the room. I hear the rustle of people moving, and I know they are turning around in their seats to kneel. I bow my head and begin my confession. "Lord, forgive me for not trusting You more with my life. Forgive me for paying more attention to what others think than You." As I continue to pray, tears stream down my face. I reach for my purse to find a tissue. "Lord, let me live this coming year in the confidence of Your strength, power, and love for me. Show me how to be confident in You and all You provide. Let me truly shine for You."

When the lights come back on, we rise to our feet. I'm not the only one wiping my eyes.

Pastor Fuller's voice booms over the microphone. "Happy New Year, everyone!"

"Happy New Year!" we shout back. I look at my watch. Two minutes past midnight. All over the auditorium, people hug those next to them. Gemma makes her way down the aisle to me. "Happy New Year!" She reaches out to hug me.

When the chatter dies, the string quartet plays the introduction for this year's theme song. Some people know it and sing along. I hum the first verse and join in on the second. It's true. Christ will hold me. Not only this year but for the rest of my life. This song will help me keep going when my confidence evaporates, which happens almost daily. I realize as I sing that I usually don't feel insecure when I'm concentrating on something positive, but otherwise, I do.

That's it! I need to figure out how to train my mind when insecurity comes, just like I told Natalie she needed to do. That's the answer.

The first day of the new year dawns with new snow glistening on the ground outside. I snuggle under my down comforter for a while and think back over last year. It was the hardest year of my life so far. But today begins a new one.

Alex is still asleep, so I pick up my Bible and new journal, slip out of the room, creep down the stairs, and settle into the chair by the fireplace. The crisp, blank page of my journal begs for words to appear, so I pick up my boring black pen to write.

Happy New Year, Lord. I'm excited to start this new year with You.

I'm glad we went last night. I want to leave last year behind me, press on to know You better, and walk in confidence. Too often, I let my mind sabotage my efforts. I compare myself to others rather than Your Word. I listen to the lies that our culture tells me. I don't believe the things the Bible says because I'm paying attention to what others say. I listen to the lies in my head.

Dad says he uses lies as a springboard to re-focus on the truth. So when I hear a lie in my head like, "Nobody really loves me," I will sing "Jesus loves me," and repeat Romans 8:32. Maybe the biggest lie I hear is, "You can't do this," or "You'll never be good enough." I will counter those lies with the truth from Isaiah 41:10 and remind myself that You will always help me.

My pen stops as I think about this year stretching out before me. I still don't know where I'll go to college this fall, though I'm leaning toward staying home and going to the U of M. Or maybe I'll go to Word or Northern.

Lord, I'm willing to follow You anywhere. It would be so much easier if You would give me a map. But Dad says that's what faith is - following when you're unsure. I know my final destination is heaven, and the path I should follow is pleasing you, but many stops and decisions face me along the way. Help me, Lord, to walk each day in Your path so that when the right doors open, I can walk through them.

Dad passes by and kisses me on the head, holding out the anticipated pink envelope. I grab it, and he wanders into the kitchen.

Carefully, I slit it open. Instead of the matching pink paper, blue snowflakes border a white page.

> *My darling daughter,*
> *Happy New Year.*
> *I asked Dad to wait until today to give this to you because I wanted to be with you today. Since I can't be there in person, at least you know that my thoughts jumped ahead to what this new year would be like for you.*
> *I am curious about this Christmas. You can tell me all about it when you join me in heaven. I hope it was a very special day as you focused on Jesus.*
> *If today is like the start of many other years, snow covers the ground.*

She's right. The snow outside my window swirls lazily down to the ground, beginning a new layer to cover the crusty gray beneath it.

The long, dark winter always reminded me of two things. First, the long nights remind me that we need God's grace during the darkest times of our lives to shine His love and warmth into our hearts. Second, the snow covering the hard ground and sparkling in the trees reminds me of His grace that covers our imperfections and sins to make us beautiful in God's eyes.

Since God's presence and grace are two of His precious gifts to us, this is my sixth challenge for you. Share your story of how you met God with someone who doesn't know Him yet.

Oh no, Mom, I can't do that! It's hard enough to share something so personal with my close friends, let alone someone who doesn't even understand what I'm talking about. Yasmin's sweet face pops into my mind. Okay. Maybe she would listen to me. But how do I bring up something like this? They'll think I'm weird.

I've seen you get so excited about games you've won that you can't wait to share the victory with others. Isn't God's presence and grace far more impressive? I admit God's work is different from an adrenaline rush. It's more than that. It's life-changing. May God give you the courage and joy you need to share His goodness with someone else.

If you need help, talk to someone like Alex, Aunt Sandi, or Dad. Or Gemma or your mentee. They can also give you some encouragement. But to move on to the next challenge, you need to share your God story.

Love you to heaven and back,
Mom

> *P.S. I am praying for you as I write this that God will give you someone in your life who needs to hear the good news of Jesus. I believe He'll answer my prayer so that by the time you read this, you will know exactly who needs to hear your story.*

She's right. I've known Yasmin since the beginning of the school year. I've told her I'm a Christian, but I doubt she knows what that means to me. It's time to tell her. But how? When? There isn't enough time during the school day. I need to figure this out, or I'll be stuck here for a long time. I slip the paper back into the pretty pink envelope and resume writing in my journal, recording my confused thoughts about how to complete this challenge. Then, with a desperate heart cry to the Lord, I simply ask, 'Help me, Lord!"

CHAPTER 30

On the first day back to school after Christmas break, I scan the halls for the gray girl. I mean, Stormy. When I see her, I need to make things right between us. I check during lunch and after physics class. Last semester, I often saw her heading for the bus, but I don't see her today.

A familiar voice calls, "Cassie!"

I stop to look behind me. Gemma saunters up, her backpack hanging off one shoulder and a violin case in her opposing hand.

"I have something for you." She holds out an envelope. "It's my invitation to my 'Gotcha Day' party. Mom and Dad said I could invite friends this year. I hope you can come."

I tear open the envelope to check the dates. "Ooh, fun. I hope I can come, too. I'll check with Dad."

"Of course. Let me know on Sunday, okay? I want to invite Yasmin and Maya, too. Do you know where they are?" Gemma's eyes scan the hall.

"At basketball practice. I'm going there now. Come on. You can watch us practice for a while if you want."

The sounds of bouncing balls echoing down the hallway grow louder with each step. When we walk through the gym door, Gemma moves to the bleachers while I enter the locker room to change. When I return to the court, Maya stands at the free-throw line. Whoosh! Nothing but net. Gemma applauds. Maya hears it, turns, and waves.

Gemma calls out words of encouragement for the next hour as we work up a sweat, dribbling, passing, and shooting. Finally, Coach Hardy calls us into a huddle. "Keep up the good work, girls. I'll see you tomorrow afternoon."

Maya, Yasmin, and I cross over to the bleachers to see Gemma.

"That was great," Gemma says. "Maya, you sink a ball with such finesse. It's almost like dancing!"

"Too bad you're not here for every practice," Maya returns. "I think I play better when you're around."

"Well, I'll be at your next game. I want to see how many baskets you make. What's your record so far?"

"I don't like to think about that," Maya bounces the ball around her and between her legs as she talks. "Basketball is a team sport. I don't play as well if I focus too much on how I'm doing. Coach said scouts are still looking for players for next year. I really hope I'll get a scholarship. Even if it's not a full scholarship like yours, I'll need the help. Otherwise, I don't know how I'll manage college."

"Are they really offering you a complete scholarship?" Yasmin asks.

"They only guarantee the first year. After that, it depends on how I do. But even if they pay for one year and then I have to switch schools, that's okay."

"I wish I knew what I was doing about college." I sigh. "My guidance counselor says my grades are good enough for a scholarship, but she doubts it will be much. Only geniuses like Nora receive big academic scholarships. So I guess I'll be working my way through college."

Maya spins the ball on her forefinger. "But maybe you'll at least attend a Christian school. I doubt I will, especially if I get a scholarship. Dad says Christian schools don't usually offer big scholarships."

"Why does it matter to you if you go to a Christian school?" Yasmin asks. "I suppose if a Muslim school were around, I'd be interested. Isn't the degree what matters?"

"Yes and no," I say. "You see, the most important thing for me is that my faith in Jesus Christ keeps growing. It seems like a Christian college will help me do that better than a state school. If I keep my heart on God, I can do that in either place. But I also know myself and attending a Christian college may help me keep Jesus first in my heart."

"You girls are different from some of my other friends." Yasmin catches the ball Maya tosses her way. "Most of them say they are Christians too, but you talk about it like it's really important to you."

"It is important to us." Gemma stands and walks down the bleachers. "Oh, I almost forgot. The whole reason I came to watch you practice was so that I could give you these." She hands the red envelopes to Yasmin and Maya.

Maya and Yasmin open their envelopes and read.

Yasmin's forehead wrinkles as she reads. "What's a 'Gotcha Party?'"

"I'm adopted. Every year, my parents celebrate the day my adoption was complete. They call it my 'Gotcha Party' because it's the day they 'got' me for good. Even though I love my birthday, this party is probably even more important than my birthday. If it weren't for my parents adopting me, I'd probably still be in an orphanage in China. So, can you come?"

"I'll need to check with my parents," Yasmin says. "My dad will probably want to talk with your dad before he lets me go. Do you have his number?"

Gemma digs around in her bag for a pen, hands it to Yasmin, and rattles off her father's number. "That's his cell phone. Call me if he doesn't answer it, and we can both put our fathers on the phone."

"Deal. I'll get back to you as soon as I know."

After we change back into our street clothes, we return to find Gemma waiting. It occurs to me that maybe her party will give me the opportunity I need to tell Yasmin my God story.

CHAPTER 31

On Saturday, January 18, an hour before her party, I stop to stare outside with a balloon in hand. "Look, Gemma. Sun snow!" Snowflakes drift lazily from the sky, but the sun peeks through the dark clouds, spotlighting Gemma's front yard.

Gemma jumps down from the stepladder to stand at the picture window with me. "Wow! My favorite. It's like God is smiling on us today. Come on. Let's get these balloons and streamers up before the girls arrive."

She grabs the red crêpe paper roll, tosses one end to me, and climbs the stepladder, taping one end to the corner while I twist and tie the other to the chandelier over the dining room table.

"I love the red and white, Gemma."

"We've always used those colors. Red is the color of celebration and joy in China. White is for innocence because I was a baby when my parents adopted me. They chose the two colors for my first Gotcha Party, and we've kept them ever since."

"Tada!" Gemma's mom walks in carrying a triple-layer red velvet cake with white buttercream frosting. Red roses surrounded the words, "Happy Gotcha Day, Gemma."

"Mom, it's beautiful. You do such a great job." Gemma sticks her finger in the frosting at the bottom edge and lifts it to her lips.

"Gemma!" Her mom purses her lips.

"What? My hands are clean. I just washed them. Besides, I need to check to be sure it's as good as it looks," she explains with mock innocence." She licks the frosting off her finger and sighs. "Just the way I like it. Plenty of butter and cream cheese."

The doorbell chimes, and Gemma runs to open it. "May I take your jackets?" she asks as Maya and Yasmin step over the threshold.

Maya hands hers to Gemma. "My parka is long enough to cover almost all of you."

Gemma puts it on and struts around the room. "Do you like my full-length coat?" We laugh together as we move into the dining room.

An hour later, after a supper of sloppy joes and french fries, Yasmin leans back in her chair and pats her stomach. "I am stuffed. I don't think I can eat another bite!"

Gemma grins. "Oh, come on. You can't be done. We haven't eaten any cake yet, and that's the best part." She points at the cake sitting on the side table. "I must say, though, if I ate this much every day, I'd turn into one of these red balloons." She grabs one as it floats down from the ceiling and pops it with her fork.

I jump, startled.

She giggles. "It was too tempting, drifting my way like that."

"Are we going to play your adoption game?" I ask. Gemma told me about it years ago.

"We are." Gemma looks around the table at all of us. "You see, growing up, I was always full of questions. It was constant. So my parents decided to do something about it. They told me to keep a list of my questions, and they would turn it into a game for my party. The week before the party, they divided my questions among the family. It was their responsibility to answer the question. After a while, I didn't have those questions anymore, and we stopped doing it. But tonight, I'm turning it around and asking you to ask me questions. Come on."

We get up, and Gemma takes a box out of the hall closet. She opens it, pulls out a brightly colored, homemade board game, and puts it on the coffee table. Mrs. Lindberg sets red-striped butter mints, red and white M&Ms, and peppermint pretzels on a side table.

"Choose a token." Gemma holds out her hand. "When you land on a question mark, you get to ask me a question. The first person to reach the finish line wins the first spot at the dessert table. Since this is my 'Gotcha Day,' the questions should be related to my family and me."

Maya stares at the family photo on the wall. "So I can ask about your tall, single brother?" She turns to Gemma with a smirk.

Gemma glares at her in mock anger. "You know what I mean."

Maya's laughter starts all of us laughing, but we settle down as we scoot closer to the coffee table. Maya's token is the first one to land on a question. "Gemma, does it bother you that your birth mom gave you up?"

"When I was in junior high, it did. Not anymore. Now, I'm so grateful for this family. It doesn't mean I don't want to meet my birth mom someday. If I ever get the chance, I want to thank her for giving me life."

Yasmin is next. "Gemma, do you ever wish you still lived in China?"

"No. But I would love to visit one day. I've learned a lot about what a beautiful country it is and its amazing people, but I wouldn't be part of my family if I lived there.

And I wouldn't live in Minneapolis or have met all of you!" Her bright smile removes any doubt anyone might have. "I love my life here."

When my token lands on a question mark, I'm ready with my question. I already know the answer, but the other girls don't. "Gemma, how did your parents decide on your name?"

"My birth mother pinned a note to my blanket that said my name was Meiling, and my birthday was May 21. My parents considered changing it to something like Mae Lynn, but then they decided to keep it as my middle name and give me a new first name. Meiling means 'beautiful and delicate.' I was a tiny baby, so they felt it fit me. They decided on Gemma as my first name because they said I was their gem from China. I love my name and how loved it makes me feel."

"They were right. Those names fit you." Yasmin's bright smile tells me she's feeling comfortable here.

Maya asks the next question. "Gemma, why is your 'Gotcha Day' even more important to you than your birthday?"

Gemma sits quietly for a minute. "This is the question I was hoping you would ask. I've been trying to figure out how to answer it in a way that makes sense. My birthday celebrates *who* I am. My 'Gotcha Day' celebrates *whose* I am. They are both important to me, so that question has two answers."

"I already told you about my name and how my parents got me. But a few years ago, I asked Jesus to forgive my sins and be my Savior. When I did that, He adopted me into His family. Now I know being adopted is a privilege. I have no idea where I would be today if my parents did not adopt me. If Jesus hadn't adopted me into His family, I don't know where I would be today either."

"What do you mean that you asked Jesus to be your, um, what did you call it? Your?" Yasmin's voice fades away.

"Savior,"

Gemma replies, her face serious but kind. "I asked Him to save me from my sin."

"Sin? Like doing things you know you shouldn't?" Yasmin's face looks puzzled. "I don't get it. How can you be saved from sin? I get that we do things we shouldn't. Everyone does. But all we have to do is try harder. Try to do right, and Allah, who is merciful, will forgive us."

This is it. The chance I've been praying about for weeks. "Yasmin, it's like this," I begin. "We all have a war going on inside us. One part of us wants to do right. Another wants to do what we want even if it's wrong." She nods tentatively. "Like my two-year-old self, we want to be in charge and do things our way."

Yasmin adjusts her hijab, but she doesn't say anything, so I push on, silently praying for the words to say and that God will make it make sense. "My parents tell me that my first word after 'Mama' and 'Dada' was 'No.'" She giggles. So does Maya. "Nobody taught me that. It was in me already. I didn't want to obey them. I just wanted my way, even if it was the wrong way. Even when I didn't know the right way. That helps me see that sin was in me from the day I was born."

"So what?" Yasmin's fingers fiddle with the button on her sleeve. "If everyone is like that, why does it matter?"

"Everyone likes to believe that we can be good on our own. We keep trying to fix ourselves, but no matter how hard we try, we can't be perfect like God." I pause to let that sink in. "Is this making sense so far?"

Yasmin grabs some M&M's to toss into her mouth. "I think so."

She passes the bowl to me. I grab a few and put the bowl back on the table. "Describing our amazing God is like putting the ocean in a bottle. Let me start with my own story. Maybe it will help."

Out of the corner of my eye, Gemma's clenched hands in her lap tell me she's praying.

"I was only eight when I asked Jesus to save me from my sin and be my Savior," I tell her. "The day is etched in my mind like it was yesterday. I'd been disciplined that day for lying. Even though I asked my parents to forgive me, and even though I prayed for God to forgive me, my lying was bothering me. No matter how hard I tried, I kept lying to get out of hot water, which only got me into deeper trouble."

"That night at bedtime, I asked Mom a bunch of questions about God, and she patiently answered. I don't remember everything, but she told me I kept wanting to do wrong because we were all born with a desire to sin. But Jesus could set me free if I asked Him to forgive me, come into my life, and set me free. I was tired of trying to do right by myself and failing every time. So that night, I did that. Even though I was only a child, I felt new and clean inside. I was so happy."

Yasmin's eyebrows pull together in confusion. "I don't think I understand. How could God make you feel new and clean inside?"

"Jesus came to earth to fix our broken relationship with God. He came as a human with flesh and blood like us, but He was also still God while He was here. He lived a perfect life. Unlike me, He never said 'No!' to His mom. He never even had a bad attitude. Throughout His years of ministry, He taught people about God. He healed people's diseases. He made blind people see. Everywhere He went, crowds came to Him, wanting to hear Him teach and watch Him do miracles. But some people didn't believe God sent Him. They decided to put Him to death on a cross. Jesus died for wrongs He didn't commit. He died for our sins. But He didn't stay dead! Three days later, He came out of that grave to tell the world He was alive."

"What? How did He do that?" Yasmin's eyes widen.

I smile. "Hard to believe, isn't it? That's how I know He wasn't just a good man or a prophet. He was God. Through His death, He forgave us. By returning to life, He showed His power over sin and death." I continue to explain as best I can.

Finally, Yasmin turns to Maya. "So, have you also asked Jesus to forgive you too?"

"I have. And it's the best decision I ever made." Maya's big smile dispels some of the tension from the room. "I was pretty stubborn. My dad is a pastor, and he was anxious for me to seek God as my Savior. My parents knew God needed to be the One to show me I needed a Savior. I thought I was pretty good and didn't need God's help. Then, when I was 14, I felt like God was knocking on my heart. Letting me know He was real. I resisted for so long. Finally, I didn't want to resist anymore. I asked Him to take over my life. It has made such a difference in my life. I feel freer than I ever have before. I have a sense of belonging because now I belong to the King of Kings."

My heart yearns for Yasmin to understand. I know it's strange to her. Our conversation continues for at least another half hour, with the three of us answering Yasmin's questions.

Finally, Yasmin stops. "So, if I wanted this relationship with God that you have, what would I need to do?" Her eyes search mine.

Inside, I'm praying, begging God for words she'll understand. "All you do is ask. His love is a gift. It's something you can't earn. Talk to Him, and ask Him to save you."

Gemma reaches for her Bible. "Do you have a Bible at home?"

"Are you kidding? We're Muslim, remember?"

I pull out my cell phone. "Let me show you an app I use to read the Bible sometimes." I scoot in closer to her and show her my screen. "You could use an app like this to read."

"This is a lot to think about." A furrow lines Yasmin's forehead, and unease creeps into her eyes. "I don't think I could do what you did."

"But Yasmin, you can," I insist. "God's offer of forgiveness and grace is for everyone."

Yasmin shakes her head. "You don't get it. It's different for me. I'm Muslim. That's all I've known since I was little. I live in a mostly Muslim neighborhood. We celebrate the Muslim traditions. All my relatives are Muslim. Can you imagine what it would be like for me to change that?"

I lower my head to hide the tears in my eyes. No, I can't.

Gemma's face loses some of its intensity, and she smiles. "Let's have some cake."

"And presents," I add.

"Presents?" Gemma frowns. "I thought the invitation specifically said 'No presents.'"

"But we wanted to. Besides, we went together and bought one present. I think you'll like it. It has to do with being adopted." I hand her the small package wrapped in red paper with a white bow.

Gemma smiles as she tears off the paper and opens the small black box. Inside, nestled on black velvet, is a gold cross necklace with a heart-shaped garnet. "Wow. That's beautiful. But it's not my birthstone."

Maya nods. "No, it's January's birthstone to celebrate your 'Gotcha Day.' My dad knows a jeweler. He designed it and gave us a deal on it. Now look on the back."

Gemma takes it out of the box and turns it over. On the back is her full name—Gemma Meiling Lindberg. She traces her name with her finger.

"And," I add, "since your name is an important part of your adoption, and you told us that you want your 'Gotcha Day' to be a reminder of the day God accepted you into His family, your name on the back of the cross celebrates both ideas."

"This is stunning! And it's something I'll be able to wear at Juilliard. Thank you." She reaches out her arms to the three of us. "Group hug."

We stand and wrap our arms around each other.

"Now, would someone put this on for me?"

Maya takes it from Gemma's hand and fastens the tiny clasp behind her neck.

Gemma steps to the side to look into the mirror hanging on the wall. Her eyes sparkle. Then she turns around to announce, "Now, let's have that cake!"

CHAPTER 32

Buzz. Buzz.

I reach into my bag to answer my phone. It's Alex. A video call. "Hey. You got time to talk?"

"Sure. What's up?"

"I wanted you to be the first to know. Don't say anything to anyone else, not even Dad." Even though she sounds serious, there's a twinkle in her eyes. "Okay?"

I nod.

"Jon asked me to marry him!"

I shriek and almost drop the phone. "When? How? What exactly did he do? I assume you said yes!" I'm so full of questions that I don't know where to begin. I like Jon. He's like a brother to me. He's been part of the family since they started getting serious two years ago.

"Last night, he took me to dinner. I could tell something was on his mind, but when I asked, he said, 'Later. I'll tell you later.' It was bugging me. Why wouldn't he tell me?"

"He distracted me by getting me to talk about Dad. Then he asked how you were doing. He was hardly eating. I asked him again what was wrong. 'Nothing,' was all he would say. I knew I needed to let it go. When the desserts came, he'd ordered chocolate crème brûlée for me and chocolate cake for himself. Again, not like him. We usually share."

"Come on, Alexandra. Get to the good part." I know she loves the whole story, but come on.

"So the desserts arrived. He hardly touched his. I was oohing and aahing over how good mine was, and he was watching me with a smile on his face. Then, I put in my spoon to give him a big bite to taste, and it nicks something hard. I scoop it up, and a piece of plastic sticks out from the edge. 'Oh no,' I said. 'They managed to let some plastic fall in.'"

"'Pull it out,' he said. 'If we show it to them, maybe they won't charge us.'"

"So I pulled it out. A tiny plastic bag held a diamond ring!" She shifts her camera from her face to her hand. A sparkling solitaire diamond in a gold band sits on her ring finger. She shifts back to her glowing face. 'I held it up, all covered in chocolate. He took it from me, wiped off the bag with a napkin, removed the ring, got down on one knee, and said in a husky voice, 'Will you marry me?' Of course, I said 'Yes!'. The whole restaurant burst into applause when it was over. Afterward, we did a little re-enactment so we'd have pictures on our phones."

I let out an excited squeal. "So when is the wedding?"

"May. Right after our graduation. But we don't have many other details. When I come home next time, you can help me plan. And, of course, I want you to be my maid of honor."

When we hang up, I dance a little jig around my room. "My sister's getting married! My sister's getting married!" I figured it would happen eventually because she and Jon have been talking about it for a while. But now that it's here? It's so exciting.

That night, I pull out my journal.

My sister's getting married! I'm so happy for her. And Dad will give her away. Thank You, God, that he's still a part of our lives. But I wish Mom could be here.

I haven't asked for the next challenge yet. I don't know if sharing my story at Gemma's party was enough. Do I need to say more? I showed Yasmin a bunch of verses, but I could tell she felt pretty lost. And she hasn't brought it up again when we've been together at school. When I try, she changes the subject. I'll talk to Dad about it tomorrow.

Before I fall asleep, I pull out my phone and text my friends in our group chat.

I'm praying for you. If you see me in school tomorrow, give me a high five!

Olivia, Emily, and Natalie send back thumbs up and hearts. Having heard from all "my girls," I plug in my phone, turn off the light, and climb under the covers. In the darkness, I ask God to protect them. And I dream of Alex's wedding.

CHAPTER 33

Dad is packing his backpack for school the next morning when I find him. "Dad, I'm wondering about the next challenge. I told Yasmin about Jesus, but was I clear enough?"

"Have you tried talking with her about it some more?" His gentle eyes soothe the ache in my heart for my friend.

"I have, but she changed the subject."

"Well, from what you've said, I think you did what Mom asked. Jesus tells us to spread the good news. How we live our lives affects whether people want to listen, but God does the work in each heart. It's not our job to make anything happen. The Holy Spirit is the One who brings people to understand in a way that they can believe. We are instruments He can use, but that's all." He lifts the heavy backpack onto the couch and adds his computer from the side table. "Do you want the next one?"

"Yes. But I hope I'm not done telling Yasmin about Jesus."

"That's the way to look at it. Many people need to hear the good news of God's salvation several times before they understand it. So keep praying for her and telling her how great Jesus is to you." He zips up his backpack and sets it by the door. "Stay here. I'll get the next letter."

A few moments later, he returns, the corners of his eyes crinkling in the smile. "If I remember correctly, you'll like this one." He passes me the envelope and hugs me quickly. "See you tonight."

"Bye, Dad." I bounce into the kitchen and find a clean knife to slit open the letter. The ache of missing Mom grows momentarily stronger when I see her familiar handwriting and smell the lotion she often used wafting up from the paper.

My sweet daughter,

I wish I could have been present when you told a friend about Jesus. Speaking up has never been easy for you, but I hope it freed you from some of the fear that you would say the wrong thing. The Holy Spirit helps us in our weakness, but He doesn't let us off the hook from sharing our faith. I'm sure you know that by now, so I'm glad you've gotten to this point in our challenges because it means you stretched your faith by telling someone about Jesus.

This one will be easier for you, and I think you'll have fun doing it, too.

Through the years, I've watched you struggle to know who you are-your gifts, abilities, purpose in life, and where you fit in God's grand scheme of things. So, it's time to work on that.

Every person has three identities-how God sees them, how they see themselves, and how others see them. I'm asking you to work on the first two. Books can help if you investigate this further, but the task is simple for now.

I stop reading. "I Can" will be a short list. That's my problem. I don't feel like I have any particular gifts or talents. But if I write down everything, maybe I'll think of something that works.

I ponder the things I enjoy. I like to run, and I can run fast enough to help my team win, so that one would be in both columns.

Yup. I thought I couldn't lead a group, but here I am doing it.

I want to write so much more, but my body is aching for rest, so I have to stop. But never doubt this: I love you so much, but God loves you even more. He will take care of you on the journey ahead.

Love you to heaven and back,

       Mom

Dad's right. This is going to be fun! And since this is already my seventh challenge, I can take some time with it and not feel rushed.

I tuck the envelope into my backpack, grab my jacket from the closet, and walk out into the bracing wind.

CHAPTER 34

It's Saturday morning, and bridal magazines, open to various dresses and decorations, clutter the floor in our bedroom.

"Remember." Alex looks up from her laptop, where she's researching wedding sites. "These are only for ideas. I'm throwing them all out if I start getting covetous over what I can't do."

I agree, but I'm still oohing and aahing over the dresses and the lavish settings.

"What are you going to do about a dress? These are so expensive." I can't believe someone would spend that much money on a dress they wear only once.

"I'll check out thrift stores and consignment stores first. Then sales. We are not going into debt for this. After all, this is one day, but our marriage is for a lifetime."

The faces of smiling couples stare back at me from the glossy pages of my magazine. I know they are models, not real couples. But it makes me wonder. How would I know if a guy was a good match for me?

"Alex," I say, lifting my eyes from the page to look into hers. "I liked Jon from the first time you brought him home. He's a great guy. But what made you say he's the right one for you?"

'First of all, sis, various guys could be right for me, so long as we get along well."

"You mean, like Elijah?" I ask in mock seriousness. Elijah was a guy who liked her in high school.

"No!" She throws the pamphlet she's holding. "Not Elijah, you goof." I fall back and clutch my chest as though stabbed while she retrieves the pamphlet. "We didn't have enough in common, nor were we headed in the same direction. He was all about getting rich. Not my goal in life."

"So what made you think Jon was right?"

"First, I asked God to let me see any red flags."

"And were there any?"

"None that made me say I should end the relationship. We come from different backgrounds, so we'll have to adjust to each other. But that's just two people coming together."

"But you were ready when he asked you, right?"

"I was because of three things." Holding up her left hand, she grabs her pinky. "First,"

"Three points and a poem? Is this a speech?" I jump to my feet, turn slowly around, and say in my deepest voice. "Single ladies from the four corners of the earth, may I present to you the very esteemed Alexandra Joy Nelson, whose deep knowledge and thought prepare her to speak to us today on the significant subject of finding a husband." I bend from the waist in a deep bow. "Thank you. Thank you," I say to my imaginary audience. Laughing, I sit back down on the floor.

Alex's musical laughter rings out, and she stands. "Well, if you want a speech, I can give you one." She grabs a hairbrush off the table to use as a microphone and wanders around the room, grinning at her pretend audience. "First, all of you should find someone not too different from you, whose personality is not completely opposed to yours. Yes, opposites can attract, but those marriages often have more friction. Marriage has a lot of adjustments just because two different people are forming a close union."

I'm giggling, but I'm listening. Because even though we're both being silly, I know this is important.

"Second." The diamond-ring finger disappears into her hand. "Women, don't settle for less if you want a godly guy. My fiancé showed me this through his actions. I saw he was trying to honor God. He'd tell me about turning to God and the Bible for counsel. He even does things contrary to the world's values because he believes in the Bible."

I raise my hand. "Teacher!"

"Shhh. This is a speech, not a class." She works hard to keep a straight face, but the grin creeps out.

I lean back against the bed, listening.

"Third." Her left hand pulls away from the right, holding up three fingers as she walks back and forth in our tiny room, speaking into her hairbrush. "Ladies, listen closely. Try to imagine yourselves down the road and ask, 'Are we headed in the same direction?' Do we have the same goals in life? If you want your life to serve God, you need a life partner who also wants that. Otherwise, you will be in constant conflict. Your goals in life need to line up." She bows to me and sits down. "Now, what was your question?"

"Were there other guys who might have worked? I mean, you're pretty and have lots of talent. Many guys must have wanted to get to know and date you." I sigh. That will never be the case for me.

"In my first two years of college, quite a few guys were asking me out. But, you know how Dad always says we shouldn't date until we are ready for marriage?"

I nod.

"So my first year was easy. I gave that as my excuse for not dating. Most of them didn't interest me anyway. Then, in my sophomore year, I realized that I could get married, and I wanted to start looking, so I said 'yes' occasionally. I still didn't date much. Either I wasn't interested, or he didn't strike me as a godly guy. I noticed Jon during my sophomore year. We did a few things together in groups, and the more I saw, the more I wanted to get to know him. It wasn't a sudden 'love at first sight,' and I didn't want that. I wanted a partner for life. The best way for me to know if he'd be a good partner was to get to know him before we started dating. So if I heard of an outing and found out he was going, I'd go too. It made it much easier when he finally asked me out."

I hold up a picture of a gorgeous wedding dress for her to see. "But most people don't do it that way."

"You're right. Some people get to know each other during their dating or courtship period, but I'm glad I knew him before he asked me out. Later, I found out he was checking me out too. By our third date, I knew I wanted-ed to get to know him even better. And, once people knew we were 'in a relationship,' most guys backed off. One or two kept asking, but I think it was more or less to see how serious I was about Jon. I was glad they stopped asking."

"Why? Wasn't it fun to date?"

"In a way, yes. But it was hard work knowing when to say 'yes' and when to say 'no.' I would normally give a guy two chances to make me think the relationship was worth pursuing. After that, I said 'no.'"

As I mull over what she said, I keep flipping through the pages of the magazine. Every once in a while, something catches my eye, and I show it to her. Then, we discuss whether we could do anything similar on her limited budget.

"Do you have a color theme? Or do you care?" I stop at a gorgeous layout of a buffet table draped in apricot and cream and show it to her.

"That's pretty," she agrees. "I'll avoid black, but I haven't decided on colors yet. I thought you and I could go shopping. I'll look for wedding dresses, and you can look for a bridesmaid dress. Whatever color you find, that will be our theme color."

I grab my cell phone. "I'm going to look up budget weddings and see what comes up." I almost choke when I see the price of renting a room for the reception. "They call this budget?" I show it to her."

"You think that's bad. You should see what people are willing to pay. I'd rather put that kind of money as a down payment on a house than on a wedding."

"Hey, you forgot the poem for your speech. Here's one you can use. Thinking quickly, I say, 'Lilies are white, and roses are pink. Weddings are wonderful. Don't you think?"

She groans, and I laugh, rolling over onto my stomach. Our voices mix together in happy companionship.

CHAPTER 35

The earth sheds her fluffy, white winter cloak in the spring, and the brown earth appears. Trees bear tiny buds, and the jonquils push through the cold ground. If I could have chosen when to have my birthday, it would have been the first day of spring. But since the spring equinox moves around, I'm happy my birthday is just a day or two before, on March 18.

Dad bought a chocolate cake with raspberry filling and chocolate frosting. It's decorated with frosting sunflowers and big, bold letters that say, 'Happy 18th!" I love it. Last night, Alex hung a 'Happy Birthday" banner. A few yellow and orange helium balloons give a festive feel to the room. Outside, five balloons dance in the wind around the mailbox to let the girls know this is my house. Jar candles on the mantle, coffee table, and windowsill will let me turn down the lights later. Stunning orange roses sprinkled with baby's breath and greens adorn the table, Dad's gift to me this morning. Leaning into the bouquet, I sniff their perfume and dream of orange roses sprinkled among white ones on my wedding day. That's all my decorating. Just enough to look festive and not so much that I spent too much time or money on it.

Alex puts her arm around my waist. 'Ready?" she asks.

I sigh. Part of me is excited to have my friends celebrate with me, but another part would like to hide. I force a smile on my face. "Ready as I'll ever be. Do you think I'll ever get over this feeling of wanting to hide?"

"Maybe. Maybe not. You have the right idea of being honest with these girls about who you are. Maybe it will help them to open up, too."

"I hope so. What if it falls flat?" I ask.

"I don't think it will. I think it will resonate with them. At least, it did with me when you talked to me about it." Alex smiles as she squeezes me one more time.

Footsteps on the stairs announce Dad's descent. He looks around, taking in the decorations. "It looks lovely. You two did a great job."

Alex catches his eye. "Dad, Cassie's feeling nervous about this party."

"Well, I think we should pray about that before your friends come." He joins us to form a small circle, one arm on Alex's shoulder and one on mine. Then, shutting his eyes, he bows his head and prays.

"Thank you, God, for my baby girl celebrating eighteen years of life today with her friends. She is unique, wonderful, and smart." His voice catches, but he continues. By the time he says "Amen," tears are pooling in my eyes.

I stand on tiptoe to hug him, and he bends down to kiss me on the cheek. "Thanks, Dad. I needed that." Being surrounded by my family and hearing Dad pray for me settles my nerves. Movement outside catches my eye as Gemma comes up the walk. I run to the door, swinging it open to catch her with her hand in midair, about to knock. Her surprise turns into a big smile as she leans in to hug me. "Happy birthday!"

"You're the first one here. I'm glad because I want to show you something."

After Gemma kicks off her shoes by the door, we scamper up the stairs to my room, passing Dad on the landing. I close the door. On the back of the door, a long teal blue dress with lace covering the bodice and arms draws her eye. "What's that for?"

"That's what I wanted to show you. Jon's brother, Xavier, called Dad and asked if he could take me to some fancy concert. Do you think it's okay? Or is it too much? Should I wear something more casual?"

She takes the dress down. Still on its hanger, she holds it up to me. "It will look gorgeous on you."

"But is it too much?" I ask nervously.

"I have no clue." Gemma runs her fingers down the folds of the dress. "Can you look up pictures online from last year's concert to see what they were wearing?"

"I did. There's a mix of short and long dresses. But that's not my concern. I'm not trying to impress Xavier. I want to look nice. But I'm afraid he'll think I'm trying to catch his attention if I wear this."

"Where did you get it?" she asks.

"It was Mom's. Dad brought it to me when I told him I had nothing to wear."

"Wow. That makes it special. I say, wear it.' And tell Xavier about your mom and how you wanted to wear this to honor her. I think he'll understand, even if he's impressed." Gemma smiles as she hangs the dress back up on the back of my door.

The chime from the doorbell interrupts us. As we speed downstairs, she asks, "So, your dad changed his mind about you dating?"

"Not really. Xavier called him, and Dad asked me if I wanted to go. Xavier's friends told him if he didn't find a date, they would. He told Jon and Alex, and Alex suggested that he ask me. It'll be a chance to spend time with Alex and Jon too. I haven't met him, but I've seen pictures of him. And he called once to say 'hi.' He sounds nice. Being with Alex and Jon makes it feel like less of a date. I guess that's why Dad's letting me go."

I pull on the heavy door. Maya and Yasmin enter, shrug out of their coats, and hand them to me.

As I hang their coats in the closet, the doorbell chimes again, and I turn to open the door. Julia, Lily, and Sophia huddle together on the steps. Gemma takes their coats from them and hangs them in the closet, and they plop down on the leather sofa. Julia picks up the candle on the coffee table to smell it and passes it to Sophia. "Mmm, pumpkin spice. My favorite."

Sophia looks around the room, and her fingers go up one at a time. "Are we going to light all the candles?"

"When it gets dark."

The sun is already low in the sky, casting orange light into the room. It won't be long now.

CHAPTER 36

Once they're seated in the living room, I clear my throat. "Thank you all for coming. I have a couple of activities planned, but after that, it's just ice cream and cake." I look behind me to see Alex standing by the dining room table. "Alex, please join us."

She lifts a dining room chair and adds it to our circle.

"The things I decided to do today result from something my mom asked me to do," I tell them about Mom's latest challenge and how I've always questioned my value. "I know this is different from most parties, but that's why."

"I don't think all of you know each other, so the first activity is to introduce ourselves. But instead of just giving us your name and what year you are in school, I would like you to tell us something you like about your name and something that most of us might not know about you."

Julia stares off into space, but the expectant look on Lily's face makes me assume she's ready with her answer.

"To give you a minute to think, I'll start." I look down at my still, calm hands and then up into their faces. "My full name is Cassandra Faith Nelson. My parents chose my first name by starting with the letter "C" after my mom, and my mom wanted something that used my aunt's name, too. Her name is Sandra. So it's a combination of my mom's and my aunt's names. My name means 'to shine upon mankind.' I want my life to be a shining light to others."

"My second name is Faith. Mom wondered if she would have another child because it took so long for her to get pregnant. When I was born, she wanted Faith in my name as a reminder to keep believing in God even when He doesn't answer our prayers quickly. And Nelson. That's my family name, so that's a given, but it tells you that my dad comes from Scandinavian heritage." I look around the room. "Who wants to go next?"

"I will." Maya sits up straighter. "My full name is Maya Journey Johnson. I was named Maya because my mom was a big fan of Maya Angelou and liked it, especially when she discovered that one of its many meanings is 'great.' She wants me to be great and often prays that I would be great for God and do great things for Him. Maybe that's one reason I want to be a doctor. She has been steadily encouraging me to be the best I can be for God. Before games, she prays that I will be great for God on the court. Anyway, that's my first name."

"My parents chose Journey because they wanted me to remember that life is a journey and that our final destination is heaven. When I was little, I liked Journey better than Maya. And my last name is Johnson. We have traced our heritage back to the days when my great-great-great-great...you get the picture...grandfather was a slave in Missouri. For me, the Johnson name means that we've persevered through good and bad. My parents. Oh, you should meet them. They are so strong, and so is my grandmother. I'm glad to be part of the Johnson clan."

The remaining girls share their full names and the stories behind them. By the time they finish, darkness shrouds the view outside. Alex reaches behind her chair to close the curtains, and I turn on the table lamp beside me.

Yasmin adjusts her green hijab with practiced fingers. "That was fun. I learned things about all of you, and it was much more interesting than simply sharing our names. When I see Maya at school, I'll think of her being on a journey."

Maya beams. "And when jasmine blooms this summer, I'll remember you when I smell it. I should have guessed that's what your name meant, but it didn't occur to me."

Six sets of eyes turn toward me, and I pull my wandering thoughts toward the next activity I'd planned. "I asked you to bring something that says 'you' tonight. So please pull those out, and we'll get started."

Chairs creak, and backpacks rustle as the girls dig for their objects. When they finish, Alex and Yasmin sit empty-handed, so I lift an eyebrow at Alex.

"Don't worry," she assures me. "I remembered. You'll see."

"Me too," Yasmin agrees.

I nod. "Then, let's get started. This time, I'll go last. Who wants to go first?"

"I will." Maya holds up a set of keys. "This keychain tells you something about me because it holds the keys to my family's house, and my family is my home. It has a basketball attached to it because I love to play basketball. Then there's the key to my bicycle lock. When the weather's warm, I love riding my bicycle." She smiles and turns to Sophia.

Sophia opens her hands to show a book. "My parents named me Sophia because they want me to be wise. This book is the best book I know to keep teaching me wisdom." As she fans it open, I see the small print and realize it's a

Bible. "I don't go anywhere without a Bible, though sometimes it's just the one on my phone."

Gemma jumps in next, fanning herself with a red oriental fan. "My parents bought me this fan when they went to China to adopt me. I don't take it out of its box very often. Red is the color of happiness in China, reminding me to be happy for my heritage. But it's also a fan that stirs the air and cools, and I want to be like that. I want my music to stir people and be like a refreshing, cool breeze." She closes her fan and points it at Julia. "You go next."

Julia holds up a library card. "For those of you who know me, I love to read. I could live in a library and keep reading for the rest of my life. If you ever see me looking at my phone, I'm probably not on social media. I'm reading a book." She turns to Yasmin.

"When I thought of something that symbolizes something special about me, my hijab came to mind first. It tells everyone I'm Muslim, and I like how it frames my face and makes people pay attention to my face instead of my hair or neck." Her big smile emphasizes her point.

Alex leans forward in her chair. "When Cassie asked us all to bring something that represented something about us, I decided the best thing I could bring would be my engagement ring." She holds out her hand for everyone to see.

"You're engaged?" Julia jumps up to get a closer look at the ring and turns an accusatory eye toward me. "Why didn't I hear about this?"

Defensiveness rises in me, but I calm myself. "It's Alex's news to share, not mine." I glance at Sophia and Lily. Are they mad too? "At least you got to hear it before most people at church."

Julia glares at me but then bubbles with laughter. "Gotcha! Bet you thought I was mad." She plops down in her chair and grins, combing her fingers through her short brown hair.

When the girls finish admiring her ring, Alex continues. "This ring tells you that I'm committed to marrying Jon, and Jon is committed to me. The simple diamond will last until after we are both gone, just like God's love never ends but will be there even after our deaths. Right now, nothing matters more to me than God's, Jon's, and my family's love."

Lily sighs dreamily. "You should have gone last, Alex. Nothing can top yours." She looks down at the colorful book in her hands. "I brought this children's ABC book because I want to be an elementary teacher. I love doing things with children—working in the church nursery, babysitting, and helping in Vacation Bible School. I also love that I have younger brothers and sisters that I can help teach. So that's me."

I'm last. "I didn't have to bring anything because I wanted you girls to symbolize who I am. All of you have been important to me. Alex has been part of my life since I was born. I've known Gemma since I was little, and the rest of you entered my life at important points. I believe God made us to be a blessing to each other, and I wanted you all to know that you have been a huge blessing to me." I stop because I can feel the tears stinging my eyes. I brush one away and continue. "Now for cake and ice cream, and then we'll finish with the last activity."

Alex links her phone to the speaker, and soft string music filters through the room. Steaming hot apple cider wafts up from the paper cups, and we each take one. Alex lights the candles on the cake, and the "Happy Birthday" opening streams from the speaker. Everyone sings, shouting "Happy Birthday!" at the end.

"Speech! Speech!" Maya calls out as she holds up her paper cup.

"I already gave my speech," I stammer. "I can't say much more except 'thank you'. Thank you so much for coming. I'm glad you came to share turning 18 with me."

I grab my plate of cake and ice cream and return to the living room. Our conversation stops as we focus on our dessert. Gemma passes around a bowl of nuts, and I grab a few. When we finish eating, Alex gathers the paper plates and takes them into the kitchen while I light the center-piece candle on the coffee table. "Would each of you choose one of the jar candles?"

Julia has already smelled all of them and knows exactly which one she wants, but the others take time to choose theirs. The last two are for Alex and me.

Alex reaches up to shut off the overhead light. Now, the three-wick candle glows brightly as the only light in the room.

Pointing with my chin at the candle, I begin. "That candle represents God to me. He is the brightest light in my world. Through the last few years, His light gave me comfort and peace when everything around me felt as black as midnight. Some days, I felt like I was in a hole so deep I would never get out. But God and His light were always there. So, I asked you to come and celebrate with me to-night because you also brought light into my darkness. You helped me on those dark days.

I keep going even though my voice is wobbly. "I usually feel like a nobody. But God gives me a reason to exist. He is my center. From Him, I get my light. I want each of you to light your candle from the center light. As you do, ask yourself these questions. One. Who are you? Two. Why did

God give you life? You don't have to say the things out loud, but I will share mine so you see what I mean."

Six sets of eyes watch me as I reach over with a long matchstick to the candle in the middle. It catches, burning brightly, and I light my candle and blow out the match. "I'm Cassie, and I'm God's girl. Two. I think God gave me life to be a blessing to others."

Lily scratches her head. "Wow, Cassie. God's girl, huh? I like the sound of that, but I've never thought about it before. But I can say this. I'm Lily. I want to be like a lily and be a sweet scent in this smelly world." To make her point, she holds her nose, and we laugh.

When Yasmin picks up a match, her dark eyes look around the room. "I know I'm the only Muslim here. I believe in God, but not in Jesus like Cassie does. So I'll say, 'I'm Yasmin, and I want to help others."

Silently, I ask God to show Jesus to Yasmin and that He would allow us to be part of the process. Gemma, Maya, Sophia, and Alex also share their thoughts about their candles. The candle-lit room has shifted from gloomy to glowing, each girl's face lit by the candle she holds.

This glowing space is filling a dark void in my heart. "Can you imagine how dark this room would be if none of you were holding a lit candle? You were like little lights in my life, and your kindness and encouragement gave me hope on my darkest days. That's why I didn't want presents tonight. I wanted you to know that I consider you my gifts." I nod at the big candle. "God was my best and biggest light. Without Him, it would have been awful. And I want you to have these candles as reminders to be lights and encouragement to others."

"Thanks, Cassie." Lily holds hers up closer to her face. "I love candles."

"Dad said he'd come in at the end, so Alex will get him now. He wants to pray a blessing over me. But before he comes, I want to show you something." I pull out the rolled poster beside my chair and open it. Telling them about Mom's challenge, I show them everything I found that God says about me. "I'm using this every morning to remind myself that I'm not nothing. Not only am I God's girl, but I'm all these things the Bible says about me."

Gemma holds out her hand. "Can you pass that around so we get a closer look?"

I pass it to her, and Maya leans over to look at the poster. When it gets around to Yasmin, she studies it and reads each statement. "Wow. The Bible says this about you? You're chosen? You have a huge inheritance?"

I nod. "Yes! Well, those things aren't just about me, but about everyone who asks Jesus to save them from their sins."

Yasmin continues to study it, and Maya and Julia look at it over her shoulder. When Alex returns with Dad, I smile into his searching eyes.

"Did you leave me any cake and ice cream?" he asks.

"We did," the girls respond.

"Mr. Nelson, you don't have a candle," Julia observes.

"I have one upstairs. Cassie brought me one earlier when she explained what she was doing tonight. Did you girls have a good time?"

"We did!" everyone exclaims.

Dad stands behind my chair and puts his hands on my shoulders. "I'm going to pray a blessing over Cassie. If any of you want this blessing in your life, you can use my words to ask God to do these things for you, too.

Dad begins to pray. "Father, I'm asking You today to bless Cassie. Bless her with wisdom to know the difference between good and best. Bless her with strength, knowing that You can always supply what she lacks. Bless her with character that stands strong in the face of temptation. Bless her with joy even on her darkest days. Bless her with a sense of purpose that will propel her through the rest of her high school days and keep her going through college. Bless her with peace that calms every storm. Bless her with grace so that she never thinks she can earn Your love but instead relies on You every step of the way. I could request many more blessings, but mostly, I ask for the blessing of Your presence in her life—every day, every hour, every minute. I ask these things in Jesus' name and for His glory. Amen."

I stand and walk around the chair to hug him. "Thanks, Dad."

"Mr. Nelson?" Gemma moves her candle to the side table and stands. "Do you think you could put me on your prayer list? I would love to have someone praying like that for me."

"I imagine your parents do that for you," Dad says with a smile.

"I doubt it. They love me, but my parents don't get me. Sometimes, I think they only care about my success as a violinist."

Dad doesn't respond. We don't know the Lindbergs well, and I've never heard Gemma's dad pray. Maybe she's right.

Lily looks like she's about to ask for the same thing. Maybe none of them have dads who pray for them. Well, not Maya. I've heard her dad pray like Jesus was standing right in front of him. But what about the rest?

Dad looks around the room. "Tell you what. I already pray for Cassie's friends. I'll add your names so I can pray specifically for you if you want. Let me know if you have particular requests, and I'll jot those down."

Lily beams. "Thanks, Mr. Nelson. I sure appreciate that."

Dad cuts himself a piece of cake at the dining room table and pours himself a glass of soda.

"Well, we have to go." Julia stands to her feet. "Cassie, I've been to lots of parties, but I don't think I have ever walked away feeling like I knew everyone in the room better than before I got there. Thank you. This was special."

Out of the corner of my eye, I see Yasmin talking softly with my dad. I wonder what that's about. One by one, the girls grab their coats and leave with their candles in their hands. I watch out the window as they get into their cars and drive off.

"So, how do you think that went?" Dad pulls me in for a brief hug.

"Much better than I thought it would. Thanks for your encouragement and your prayer of blessing. It meant a lot, not just to me, but also to my friends."

"Did you see Yasmin talking with me?" When I nod, he smiles wistfully. "She asked me if all Christian fathers love their daughters as much as I love mine."

"Wow. What did you say?"

"I had to be honest. Not all do, and I often fail to love you girls like I should. I told her that Jesus set a high bar for how Christians should love one another. I also said that since God calls himself a Father to His children, dads are responsible for loving their children, demonstrating God to them, and teaching them the right way. She said her dad likes teaching them how a Muslim should live, but she always felt it came more from duty than from love. I encouraged her to read the story of Jesus from the Gospel of John. Maybe it would help her understand."

My heart swells with appreciation. "Thanks, Dad. I'm glad she saw the difference God makes in your life. Hearing you pray for me tonight may help her come to understand Jesus better."

By the time we stop talking, Alex has almost finished cleaning up. "Nope. No help from you tonight. You're the birthday girl." She smiles and pushes me away, so I take the stairs two at a time. Changing into my pajamas, I pull out my journal to write.

Lord,

Tonight is just a night to say "Thank you." I could list so many things, but I'll need to go to sleep before I can, so I'll only list a few.

Thank you for:
- *the six girls who came to my party tonight.*
- *the blessing each of them has been to me.*
- *the realization that, more than anything, I belong to You. I'm Your girl.*
- *Alex's strong, loving presence in my life.*
- *Dad's prayers for me. Thank You that You left him here and haven't taken him to heaven yet.*
- *Yasmin's noticing that Dad is different from some of the dads she knows.*
- *Dad and his stability through this, even though it's been harder on him than anyone.*
- *The orange roses and gold hoop earrings from Dad.*
- *The cross necklace from Alex.*
- *Alex's cleaning up after the party. She's done that for me*

every year, but this is the first time I've noticed it as a gift.

- The ideas You gave me for the party tonight.

But most of all, I want to thank You for saving me, keeping me, helping me, and being my Rock that I can run to whenever things are tough. Thank You for being my Light, especially when things seem dark. Thank You that You are my God.

Amen.

CHAPTER 37

"Cassie, you're going to wear a hole in the carpet with all your pacing." Dad looks up from his book and then at the clock. "Don't worry. They'll be here."

I have never been so nervous in all my life. And it's not like a real date because we're going with Alex and Jon. Through the living room window, I see Jon's car pull in. Alex opens her door and then closes it. Behind her, Xavier gets out, and my stomach flip-flops. He looks just like his picture. Sandy-brown hair, easy on the eyes, and tall, but not as tall as Jon. His languid walk toward the front door keeps me rooted to my spot at the window. Then, he sees me and smiles before tapping on the door.

Dad swings the door open wide. "Come in. It's good to meet you finally. I've heard a lot about you from Jon."

Xavier steps through the door carrying a small white box. "Good evening, Mr. Nelson." He extends his hand, and Dad shakes it, and I extend mine for a handshake, too. After removing his black gloves, he opens the box, revealing the white rose corsage inside. "Cassie, I hope you like it."

"I do, but won't it be crushed under my coat?"

"We'll wait until we get there, and Alex can pin it on for you. Is that okay?"

I nod.

Dad hands my coat to Xavier, who holds it while I slip into it. Then he opens the door for me, and I lead the way with him close behind.

"Don't be too late," Dad calls from the door.

Xavier opens the car door, and I slide in. "Hi, sis. Oh, and you too, Jon." He laughs.

Alex turns in her seat to look at me. "You are going to love tonight. The orchestra is amazing. At least, it was when I heard it last time."

Xavier closes his door. I listen to the banter between them as Jon drives. Every once in a while, Xavier turns to look at me, but I pretend I don't notice. Instead, I watch the city lights.

"We're not far now." Jon stops for a red light. "You're awfully quiet back there, Cassie. We don't bite, you know."

"Jon, you know she's quiet." Alex pulls down the visor to check her makeup. "Cassie, we warned Xavier that you would rather listen than talk, and he said he's fine with that. Right, Xavier?"

"Right. I want you to enjoy the evening. If that means you don't talk much, that's fine with me."

I nod, my racing heart slowing. Maybe I'll be fine tonight after all.

The car slows in a line in front of the orchestra hall, and we jump out, and Jon leaves to park the vehicle. Xavier offers his arm again. I'm thankful for his security while I walk up the steps in my high heels, holding the long folds of Mom's teal dress to keep from tripping. The lobby boasts sparkling chandeliers and shining black and white marble floors.

"Ladies, may I take your coats?" Xavier helps me out of mine while Alex slips out of hers. Then he hands her the little white box. "Would you help her with this?"

"Happy to." She takes the corsage from the box and pins the white roses to my dress.

I feel so elegant in Mom's dress. Around me, men in tuxes and women in sweeping gowns let me know that I would have felt out of place in a simple dress.

When Jon arrives, the ushers, dressed all in black, show us to our seats, about two-thirds of the way back on the main floor. Heads turn as we walk in, but I see the eyes on Alex as she glides forward in her purple gown, her blond hair twisted into a simple French braid and curled into a bun at the base of her head.

"The website says that the sound is best in this area." Alex sits next to me with the two men on either side. "You can't see as well as you can in other seats, but I shut my eyes to listen half of the time anyway."

For the next hour and a half, the music draws pictures of majestic mountains, wind blowing through grassy fields, children laughing, the ocean surging, and angels singing. Some people hear notes, but I see beauty as they play. Sometimes, even stories form in my mind as I listen. What must Mom be hearing now if music can be so wonderful in our world?

I hear the climax of Mendelssohn's "Fingal's Cave," and it turns my attention to all the changes this past year has brought to my life. I may never enjoy being the center of attention, but Mom's challenges and God's grace are teaching me that God has a purpose for me. I can't just sit on the sidelines. I need to actively participate in whatever God has for me. I'm not the same person that I was at this time last year.

When it ends, I long for more. I could listen to something like this every night. I stifle a yawn, and Xavier smiles. "Tired?"

"A little. But I could listen to more. Tonight was perfect. Such beautiful music. Thank you."

"You're welcome." Once again, he offers me his arm as we leave the auditorium.

He goes for our coats while Jon fetches the car. Then, alone again with Alex, she asks, "Did you enjoy yourself?"

"It was wonderful. Thank you for suggesting to Xavier that he invite me."

I look down at my rose corsage, surrounded by baby's breath. "Do I need to take this off before I put my coat on?"

"If you want to keep it, you probably do." Xavier's voice behind me answers my question.

As he hands Alex her coat, I unpin the corsage and gently place it back in its box. "Thank you for this, too. I've never had a corsage before."

He helps me into my coat, and we walk down the front stairs of the orchestra hall. The music still reverberating in my heart, I begin humming the last song.

"Happy?" Xavier asks.

"Yes." Smiling up into his brown eyes, I wonder if we'll ever see each other again. Well, he is Jon's brother, so it's likely.

As we get into the car, Xavier asks Jon to drop him at Caribou Coffee before taking us home. When he gets out, he says to me, "I really enjoyed tonight. Jon wants to stay a while and talk, and I have studying to do. I hope I'll see you again soon."

That night, when I crawl into bed, the soft murmur of Jon's and Alex's voices downstairs drifts up to me. She'll be up soon, but before she gets here, I need to record some of my thoughts in my journal.

Garbage in. Garbage out.

That's what Dad often told us when we wanted to see or listen to something that wasn't uplifting. Tonight, the music is still reverberating through my thoughts. If hateful lyrics instead of beautiful music were cycling through my head right now, I'd have a double battle to fight. Not only would I be dealing with things out of my control, like Mom's death, but I'd have to fight the negative thoughts from the lyrics. No wonder Dad always wanted us to be careful of what we watch, hear, and read.

So, Lord, help me fill my thoughts with pure and beautiful things so that I will be helped and not hindered on this journey of life.

Thank You for a wonderful evening. I didn't really get to know Xavier, but it was nice to meet him and to spend time with Alex and Jon.

I lift the phone off the bedside table to text my group: *In bed, but I want you to know I'm praying for you. I hope I'll see you all at church on Sunday.*

CHAPTER 38

Dad's voice calls me from the living room. "Cassie, would you come here for a minute?"

"Sure, Dad," I call back. "Let me finish cleaning up the kitchen, and I'll be right there."

I grab the last plate and put it in the dishwasher. A final look assures me the kitchen is clean, and I wander into the living room.

Dad's head is down with his eyes closed, and a Bible is open on his knees. I watch for a minute, wondering when he'll notice I'm here.

He looks up. "Oh, sorry. I didn't hear you come in. I was praying."

"I thought so. You wanted to talk?"

"I do." He settles back into the blue wingback chair and looks at me. Tears form in his deep blue eyes. "You look so much like your mother did when I met her. It takes me back to that time." He pulls a red bandana out of his pocket and wipes the tears. He shakes his head. "But that's not what I wanted to talk to you about."

He looks down again at the Bible in his hands and shifts his weight in the chair. That's strange. He's not usually nervous with me. He clears his throat. "I saw you bring some dresses in this afternoon. Are those for the junior-senior banquet at church?" He rolls his head from side to side, stretching the muscles in his neck, and then looks at me, waiting for my answer.

I smile. No wonder he's nervous. He's never up on women's fashion. If that's what he wants to talk to me about, he's clueless. Well, at least that's something I can help him understand. Here, we go into awkward territory.

"Yeah. I wanted a new dress for the banquet, and later, Maya, Gemma, and I will dress up and go out for dinner together."

"And, like your mom, you brought some home because you couldn't decide at the store?"

I nod. "I was having a hard time. But the lady who helped me was so nice. She told me to try them on with my friends and return the ones I don't want next week. Maya and Gemma will help me, and maybe I'll ask Aunt Sandi's opinion, too."

"Would you mind trying them on for me?" he asks sheepishly.

A knot rolls into my stomach, and I bite my lip.

Dad sees me hesitate. "Mom used to help you with your clothes shopping, and I'm not a great replacement. But maybe I can give you a man's opinion? Your friends will tell you what they think, but would it help if you heard my opinion too?"

I don't get it. He's never asked me to do anything like this before. Of course, Mom and Alex used to help me choose my clothes. But Mom's gone, and Alex isn't home. Is that why? I shift my weight from one foot to another, not sure what to say. Finally, I stammer, "Why?"

"Cassie, this stage of life is hard for me as a dad. Letting my little girl go off on her own more and more. I've noticed that some girls have more trouble with modesty when they dress up. I'll be more relaxed letting you go if I know what you're wearing ahead of time. It probably seems silly, and I know you can take care of yourself, but I want to send you out the door without worry. So would you do this for me?"

I study the pattern in the rug at my feet, afraid to meet his eyes. I twist Mom's Grace ring around on my right ring finger. I start to say something but stop, afraid I'll say the wrong thing. I can do this for him, but he needs to understand me, too.

"Okay, but Dad, I need to tell you this first. I always look for modest dresses. Sometimes, when Mom and I went shopping, she'd say, 'No, that won't work. Your dad wouldn't approve.' Or she'd say, 'Remember, it needs to be long enough, high enough, loose enough, and thick enough.' So I looked for dresses that she would like. I'm pretty sure all of them are okay."

Dad looks up at me. Sometimes, I think his love will jump out of his eyes and wrap itself around me in a tight squeeze. Even though I'm uneasy about his "help," I never need to wonder if he loves me. I shoot up a silent prayer of thanks to God for my dad, and I feel the knot in my stomach relax.

"I know you were careful, Sweetie." The crease in his forehead deepens as he talks. "But maybe it will help you to know why she thought that way. I'd like you to hear my perspective. So let's do this. You try on the dresses one at a time. How many are there?"

"Four. One that I could wear on Sundays and three formal gowns. I'm also considering the one I wore to the concert, but you've already seen that one."

"Okay. We'll set up the living room like a runway." He shows me what to do. "When you finish, I'll tell you what I noticed. You get to pick the one you like, but I would like you to know my impressions. Does that sound fair?"

"Sure, Dad." My voice wavers. "But I'm afraid then that it won't be my decision. I'll just do what I think you want."

"I won't tell you which one I like best. I'll only give you the facts."

"Okay." I sigh. "Let's get this over with." I trudge up the stairs, wanting to hide in my room until school tomorrow rather than do this. I know he means well, but why can't he leave this alone?

In my room, I remove the dresses from the garment bag and lay them across the bed. Four beautiful dresses. Which first? The black formal with sequins on the shoulder? I love the feel of the green velvet gown. I bite my lip as I remember my mom in a similar dress. No, not that one first. Dad might not be able to handle it. The champagne lace formal? Maybe the red sheath with the scalloped hem? Which one first?

I grab the black formal with the sequined shoulder and slip it over my head. Rummaging around in my closet, I find my black high-heeled shoes and put them on. I check the mirror. Hair up or down? I pull it up behind my head and then let it hang again. For this one, definitely up. Otherwise, the sparkle on the shoulder won't show. Grabbing a hair tie, I pull my red curly mess into a ponytail.

I descend the stairs and stop at the landing, listening. It sounds like Dad is thumbing through the CDs.

"Are you ready?" I call.

"Just a minute," he replies. "Let me put on some runway music."

Before long, a Mozart symphony drifts through the room. I stifle a laugh. Not exactly the kind of music an actual runway would use, but it'll do.

I peek around the corner to see Dad gazing up the stairs.

"Okay. Here I come!" I do my best to look like I'm floating down the stairs instead of walking. What's wrong with Dad? Doesn't he approve? I stop. His mouth is tense, and a single tear makes its journey down his cheek.

"Are you okay, Dad?"

"Sorry. Just wishing your mom could be here for this."

"Me too." I exhale and continue my descent. "Okay, here goes."

At the foot of the stairs, I get my bearings. He's moved the furniture around. The coffee table is off to one side, and now the book is on the floor in the middle of the room. I walk across the room, sit on the blue wingback chair across from him, and stand again. I crouch down and pick up the book. Am I being ladylike? I hope so. I rise again and finish walking to the end of the room where I reach up to put it on the top shelf of the bookshelf. Slowly, I turn and smile into Dad's watching eyes, walking back across the room to head upstairs. When I reach the stairs, I turn.

"Was that what you wanted?"

"It was perfect. And I said I wouldn't say anything, but I have to say this now because I won't last for three more dresses. You look beautiful."

I giggle and run up the stairs, holding the front of the gown in my hand. Only Dad would think that about me, but I'm glad he does.

Back in my room, I peel off the silky black and slip into the champagne lace formal with the scalloped neckline. I love how the bodice is form-fitting, but the skirt flares from the hips. I twirl in front of the mirror, watching the dress spread like an opening flower. Kicking off my black heels, I replace them with my gold sandals.

Once again, I go through the paces, walking, turning, sitting, squatting down to get the book, and reaching up to put it away. Dad's eyes follow me through the room. When I pass him on my way to the stairs, I see a smile tugging at the corners of his mouth. He scribbles something on his pad. Too bad my shoes won't allow me to take the stairs two at a time like I usually do, but my heels slow me to a more graceful run.

With each dress, Dad's smile gets bigger.

"Are you bored yet?" I ask. "I know women's fashion shows aren't your thing."

"But it changes everything when my daughter is the model. Go change, and then I'll tell you what I thought."

I turn with a final flourish, my hair swinging outward. Then, slipping off my shoes, I dash up the stairs, two at a time. After hanging up the dresses, I return in my t-shirt and jeans.

Dad looks up as I sit down. "Thank you for doing that for me. Let me explain why I wanted you to do it. First, anything you wear should draw attention to your face. Your face tells people about you more than any other part of you. Your eyes, smile, and expression are the most important part of your looks. Those are your features that point people to God."

"So does that mean I shouldn't wear t-shirts with sayings on them?" she asked. "After all, the first thing people try to do is read what the shirt says."

"You've made my point. If you want people to read the saying, that's fine, but they won't look at your face first. But when you dress up for a formal event, people should see your face first. So, when you walked into the room, did I notice your face? Or did something distract my eyes to look away from your face? You did an excellent job on that one. With all the dresses, I saw all of you, but especially your face."

"Second, modesty in motion. Third, which of your great qualities did the dress highlight? Fourth, did any of them make me unsure? Ready to hear my thoughts?"

"Yes, I am. Tell me what you think." Relax, I tell myself. I know he wants to help.

"For each category, I chose my favorite." He glances at his notes. "Then I looked at each dress and thought about what a guy sees. I'll state everything positively, except for the last category, where I will mention anything that might be a problem."

I nod. Sometimes, I wish I had brothers. They might give me more insight into things like this.

"First, your face. Which one drew attention best to your face? This is my opinion, remember. Your friends and Aunt Sandi might not agree. For me, it was the green velvet because it brought out your red hair and freckles."

"Second, modesty in motion. The best one for that was the champagne formal. You looked so elegant, and there was no hint of a problem no matter how you moved."

Dad smiles. "The third category was easy. The green was more 'you,' and the black formal seemed to reflect your spunky personality— fashionable and unique."

"You did a great job. Let me tell you what I liked about each one. First, the black formal was so dignified and yet modern at the same time. The champagne formal gave you a classic yet innocent look. The green dress highlighted your beautiful hair, and the red dress made me notice your blue eyes." He stops and looks down at his notes. His knuckles turn white as he grips his pen. He shifts in his chair.

I chuckle. "It's okay, Dad," I encourage. "Go ahead. Tell me the bad part, but please don't be too negative. If you tell me something is wrong with all of them, I'll have to start over."

He finally looks up. "There was one dress that hung a little wrong around the neckline. It might be something you can fix, but let's say that some movements revealed more of your body than you probably want people to see."

The heat rises in my face, and I turn away. I wasn't expecting this. I thought I had been careful. When I get back upstairs, I'll try them all again to see which one it is.

"So that brings me to the other negative." His voice pulls me out of my embarrassment. "Sometimes you tugged on your dress as though you were trying to cover yourself. Nothing wrong with adjusting it after you sit down or stand up, but don't buy it if you need to keep tugging. Or fix it before you wear it. Pulling on it advertises to everyone that you feel uncomfortable and draws attention to what you are trying to cover."

I think back through the dresses. When did I do that? It wasn't the champagne one, but which of the others? He said he wouldn't tell, so I have to figure this out. Maybe the girls will notice?

He scans his notes again. "You did well. They were all beautiful dresses. I think your mother would be proud."

A thought comes to me, and it's out of my mouth before I think twice. "So, Dad. Next time you buy new clothes, will you walk the runway since Mom isn't here to tell you what she likes?"

He laughed. "Maybe. Did you know that Alex sometimes tells me what to wear?"

"She does?"

He nods. "I think my professor-look embarrasses her."

"Well, you do sometimes look like something that the eighties dragged in."

"How would you know what the eighties looked like?"

"I read books?" Laughter bubbles up inside me, lightening my mood.

"One more thing."

Really? I resist the temptation to roll my eyes.

"I don't know what each of those dresses cost. But sometimes a cheaper one is the right choice. After all, no one else has seen the others, so they won't compare them. That way, you will still have a little money left for something else."

"Good idea. I'll remember that."

I turn to walk away when I hear whispering. I stop. He's praying. Does he want me to hear this? He must, or he wouldn't be praying so I can hear.

"Thank you, Father. She's right. I am inclined to see the negative. If she hadn't stopped me, I might have hurt her. Thank you for a daughter who helps me where I am weak. Please keep me from thinking that she needs to be perfect. Only You are perfect. Thank you for guiding us through these waters. I've wanted to talk to her about modesty in motion, but I didn't know how. Carol always took care of things like that, but it's time for her to make her own decisions now. Help her to make wise ones." His whispers fade away, but his mouth is still moving.

My feet make no sound as I cross the soft carpet into the kitchen. Pouring myself a glass of water, I thank God for a dad who loves me enough to risk being uncomfortable to help me. "But Lord," I pray. "I'm glad that's over. It was awkward. Thank You for helping both of us."

CHAPTER 39

Maya, Gemma, and I meet at Gemma's house. We use Dad's runway idea to do our own evaluation of each other's dresses. When Maya sashays through the living room in a too-short and too-tight mini dress, Gemma rolls her eyes at me. But Maya was just testing our honesty, never intending to wear her little sister's dress. And they did find the problem with my red dress. Evidently, I tugged on the hem when I sat down, and they could see clear to my navel when I leaned over to pick up the vase Gemma laid on the floor. Good thing that one was not my favorite.

Every morning before school, I read the two posters hanging on the wall of my bedroom and choose one specific word that God says about me to review on my way to the bus. It's helping. I'm not as tempted to hide as I did before. I'm relying more on God's opinion of me than what others might think.

Last night, I told Dad I was ready for Mom's next challenge, and he gave me number eight. I pick up Mom's letter to read it again.

My dear Cassie,
So you've reached the eighth one. Good for you. I think you'll like this one too.

For this challenge, I want you to go through your closet. As Christians, we are called to represent Christ well. We are His ambassadors to the world. Make sure everything in your closet represents who you are and Whose you are. If something doesn't fit, get rid of it. If you don't like it, give it away. Don't be a hoarder. And, while you are doing this, take time to think about clothes you'll need for college.

This challenge follows the last one because I hope you better understand your identity. Let your clothes show that to others. Represent Jesus well.

Love you to heaven and back,

Mom

Mom, I wish you were here for this one. We would have so much fun going through my overstuffed closet together. A stab of pain runs through me.

Sliding open the closet door, the mix of colors confuses me. A nice, orderly closet would be nice. I don't need this many clothes. Too many choices make it harder to find what I want. And this isn't even all of them. Most of my summer things are in a bin in the basement. A groan escapes as I imagine the work in front of me. I need help. But who?

My phone dings with an incoming text message.

Natalie. *Would you like to go shopping together? I want a new dress, and you have good taste in clothes. I'd love your opinion.*

I do? I text back before I change my mind.
Sure. When?
This weekend?

I send a thumbs up.

Then it hits me. Natalie can help. Not only will she help me stay true to myself, but she's also organized. Maybe together, we can create a wonderful closet for my newly appointed ambassadorship, and it will give me a feel for her style for when we go shopping. I text her.

Can you help me with something?

I explain the challenge, and she agrees to come over right away.

After explaining Mom's request, I open my closet door. "And that's not all. My sweaters and jeans are in the dresser, so I need to think about those too."

"Well, I guess we have our work cut out for us." Natalie reaches into her purse and pulls out a piece of paper. "I was trying to figure out your style. From what I've seen, I'd say it's casual but put together. Am I right?"

"Guess so."

"I found a list of essential pieces needed to build a basic wardrobe. It will get us started. But, before we do that, we need to clear some of these things out." The hangers screech as she pushes them toward one end of the closet. "Now we have a little bit of room on this end. I'm going to hand you one item at a time. You tell me if you LOVE it or not." She holds a dress up to herself and hugs it. "If you adore it, we'll hang it on this end of the closet. If it doesn't fit, you don't wear it much or don't like it, it goes in the giveaway pile. We'll make one more pile for things you're not sure about. Ready?"

I nod, amazed at how good she is at this, and the sorting begins. She hands me something. I hold up to myself in front of the mirror and make my decision. Any time Natalie sees indecision, she points to the "Not sure" pile. By the time we're done, a third of what I had is still hanging in the closet, and a bunch lay in the "not sure" pile.

"Next, we look for matches. Every shirt, skirt, or pair of pants needs something to wear with it. When we find a match, we put them together. First, match the things still in your closet."

I point out the things I wear together, and we hang them next to each other. Some of the matches are in the "not sure" pile. I pick up a top to add it to the brown corduroy pants.

"Are you sure, Cassie?" Natalie raises an eyebrow at me.

"What's wrong with it?"

"Nothing. But why did you put it in the 'not sure' pile? You need to be doubly sure before it goes back into your closet."

I look at the dusty rose turtleneck in my hand. She's right. It's okay. It's comfortable, but it isn't really my color. I wear it on days when I want to hide instead of shine, and I don't want to do that anymore. I add it to the giveaway pile.

Natalie nods. "Good for you. You'll need to do that with everything in the not-sure group, but once you have all your matches, maybe the rest can go away." She yawns and plops down on the bed.

I check my watch. "Wow. We've been at this a long time. I owe you."

"And you get to pay me back next week when we shop for my dress. If I were your size, I'd be scrounging through your discard pile right now."

By the time we're done, I have a large black plastic bag of clothes to drop off at the thrift store.

Natalie organizes my clothes by color. "You may want a different arrangement, but I like seeing the colors together."

I smile at the finished result. My dominant colors are green, orange, and various shades of brown. Jewel tones of purple, red, and teal add a little zest.

Natalie points at a red dress. "I haven't seen you wear this, but it would look great on you." She turns from the closet and looks into my eyes. "You have a great eye for style. That's why I wanted your help."

"Actually, Alex has an eye for style. She helped me with most of my wardrobe." A sigh of satisfaction escapes when I look at my organized closet. "But she taught me a lot, so now I usually shop without her." I turn from the closet. "Thanks for all your help. I still have more to do, but it doesn't feel so overwhelming now."

That night, I pull out my journal.

Thank You, Lord, for Natalie. I knew she was organized, but I had no idea how much help she would be. Tomorrow, when I get ready, an organized closet will greet me. What a gift. Thank you, Mom. Thank you, Natalie.

Days are longer now, and spring is exploding with color. On the night of the banquet, I open the door to the fellowship hall at church to the sound of quiet music muffling the conversations of the teens. I pick up the folds of my long green velvet dress to step inside, where a wall stares me in the face. It looks like a medieval castle. Above my head, white lights glitter, and under my feet is a red carpet leading to an arch on my left. I walk through the arch to see long tables draped with white linens. Wait staff in white shirts and dark pants or skirts fill water glasses and light candles. I smile at Emily as she rushes by, carrying a pitcher full of water. On the other side of the room, Natalie straightens a sagging burgundy cloth napkin that looks like a fan. Around the room, the castle wall looks real. Impressive. Someone knew what they were doing.

I look around at the knots of students gathered around the room. I know most of them from other multi-church events. As usual, Maya is surrounded. They must be from her church because I haven't met them.

Just then, Maya sees me and breaks away from her group. "You look amazing," she says as she wraps her arms around me in a soft hug. "I'm so glad you decided on the green. It fits with this scene, don't you think?" She raises her arms and motions to the castle walls and long tables. "Did you know it was going to be so incredible in here? I think this is the best I've ever seen this room look." When we rejoin her group, she says, "Let me introduce you to everyone." She gives me the names of her three companions and then introduces me.

Stefan is taller than Maya. He bends over in a deep bow. "Pleased to make the acquaintance of such a lovely lady." I giggle and curtsy in return. Everyone laughs, but it sets off a round of bows and curtsies. In the corners of the room, others watch us. Then I see Titus bow to Sophia, and another round of bows and curtsies begins. The decorations have affected our manners.

Titus walks away from his group and joins ours. "May I have the pleasure of escorting you to your seat? I see that they have seated us next to each other." I'm delighted, both with his politeness and being able to sit with him. My heart rate speeds up. He'll be an excellent dinner companion. He's quiet and thoughtful, and he'll have something interesting to offer to our conversation.

As we move to our table, I see Dylan escorting Gemma to her table. He holds out the chair for her and then sits down. A red sparkling comb holds the swirls of loose bun, braids, and curls of her hair in place. Is she trying to impress Dylan? If so, I think she succeeded. He can't take his eyes off her.

Chairs scrape as we find our places. Flowers surround the base of the two-foot candelabras in the center of each table. Pastor Declan clinks his water glass with a fork. When the room quiets, he leads us in prayer. Out of the kitchen, the wait staff stream into the room bearing plates of tossed salad. I look at the array of flatware beside my plate, and I'm glad Hope talked to us girls about what to expect tonight. Laying the cloth napkin on my lap, I pick up the outermost of the three forks and begin eating.

"I wonder if people in medieval castles ever worried about which fork to use." Titus spears a grape tomato and pops it in his mouth.

Across the table, Sophia holds up a finger while she finishes chewing. "Probably not. We ate with our fingers when I went to a medieval reenactment." She pretends to lick every finger. "This is so different from last year's picnic in a rose garden. No one cared about manners then. I wonder what next year's committee will do."

I mix my salad to stir the ranch dressing more evenly. "Who knows? Sophia, will you send us pictures of next year's banquet since we'll be too old?"

"You mighty college students better not forget us," she says with a smirk. "If you don't, then I'll send you photos."

As the meal progresses, our flatware diminishes. Broccoli cheese soup follows the salad. I choose the large spoon on the right side of the plate. Roast chicken, green beans, mashed potatoes and gravy, and sweet corn are served next for our main meal. When the tiramisu arrives with coffee and hot tea for those who want it, we are down to our last utensils. The wait staff rush in and out of the kitchen, clearing plates and refilling glasses. I'm sure I didn't do that well as a freshman. I lean over to Titus. "Are we supposed to leave a tip? They have done better than many professionals."

"Let me ask Pastor Declan." He excuses himself and walks to the head table where Pastor Declan sits with Hope and the Fullers.

Titus' smooth walk as he returns to the table resembles a slow-motion movie. His grace sets him apart on the basketball court and when he walks through any room.

He leans toward me as he sits. 'He's going to recommend donations to the mission trip if anyone wants to do that."

Maybe it's because we've known each other since we were in grade school, but only a few girls have dates tonight. Gemma told me Dylan wants to be in a relationship with her, but she's holding him off since she's going to Juilliard, and he's going to the U next year. Even though Timothy, Titus, and I may end up at the same school, and I like Titus, I don't know what the future holds. Maybe we'll stay good friends. But will he become more than that someday? Only if we both think God is leading us to serve Him together. Right now, we need to focus on the next step—college.

The tinkling of a fork against glass silences the room. Pastor Declan puts down the fork as Gemma steps onto the platform with her violin. I check the program, but it doesn't list what she'll play. Her voice rings out over the microphone. 'For some of us, this is our last year of high school. Some of my friends wanted me to play one of my auditioning pieces tonight, but when Pastor Declan told us that tonight's speaker would talk about the great banquet in heaven, I knew I needed to play something that would let you worship our great King while I play. So I've chosen some worship music. The words will be on the wall behind me so you can follow along as I play."

Her flowing red silk dress catches the light as she puts the bow to her violin. As I watch the words scroll behind her, my heart lifts to praise God.

Soon, light applause tells me she has finished. My mind has been wondering what Mom's doing today. I turn my attention to Pastor Fuller and send up a quick prayer. 'Lord, I have so little time left for this school year. Show me what I should do in the next part of my life."

Pastor Fuller begins, "We're in a castle. Knights in shining armor stand at the gate, in front of the drawbridge, and in the watchtowers on the surrounding walls. Inside the castle, we're safe. We can walk in the garden, eat at the king's table, and sleep without worrying about attack. We're safe here. Or are we?" He waits until everyone is looking at him. "The enemy outside the gates threatens. But enemy spies have infiltrated our safe castle. They are a greater danger than the enemy outside." Beside me, Titus leans forward in his seat, resting his elbows on the table. I have always loved Pastor Fuller's ability to draw us in before he shows us what his focus will be.

Pastor Fuller grabs the microphone off the stand, comes off the platform, and walks among the tables to explain that the castle is the castle of our hearts. "The enemy outside may turn on you, but it is not as dangerous as the ones that slip inside your heart and your head to tell you lies. God has a plan and purpose for you being on this earth. There is danger in our world, but for most of us, what we choose to believe and who we choose to listen to is an even greater danger. What do you believe about God? What do you believe about yourself? Why did God put you on this earth?" As he teaches, we listen intently.

When Pastor Fuller finishes, he passes the microphone to Pastor Declan. The room is quiet enough to hear a mosquito buzz. Pastor Declan looks around the room. "I know most of you. But even if I knew all of you, I would still ask this question. Are you at peace with God? Are you safe inside the castle of salvation where God rules as king? Or have you let the enemy come inside your heart to use his weapons of confusion, fear, and doubt against you?" He closes in prayer, and Gemma's violin fills the room with music again.

I sit quietly in my seat for a minute, thinking. Pastor Fuller is right. Sometimes, I have the audacity to kick God off the throne in my heart and put myself up there. And yes, I sometimes believe the lies that Satan sends my way. Titus sits down next to me with a questioning look in his eyes.

"Just thinking," I say. "Come on, let me introduce you to someone." I walk over to Dylan and introduce him. Soon, they're talking about music like old friends, and I slide away. When she steps down off the platform, I walk over.

Both of my hands reach for hers. "Would you pray with me? Pray that I would quit believing the lies I hear in my head." When she finishes praying, my vision is blurred by tears. She is such a dear friend.

When I get home, the events of the night spill out. "Dad, you should have seen it." I hand him my cell phone. "Here are some pictures. Pastor Declan talked about the castle of our hearts."

As Dad goes through my photos, I lean back into the comfort of the recliner, amazed once again that God met a need I didn't even know I had. Starlight jumps into my lap, and I bury my face in her soft fur. She'll leave fur all over my dress, but it has to be cleaned anyway.

Dad hands me back the phone, his eyes twinkling. "It looks like you had a wonderful time." His smile reaches the deepest part of me that is so thankful I still have my dad and sometimes so scared that something will happen to him. I tamp down that fear, focusing instead on my gratitude that he's still here. "By the way," he continues, "that dress was my favorite of the ones you tried on. I'm glad you chose it."

I lean back in the chair and study him. "Dad, I finished going through my closet and dresser, but I still have the summer stuff in the basement. Do I need to go through that, too, before I get the next letter?"

"What do you think?"

"I knew you would say that." Groaning, I put the footrest down and stand. "If I don't do it now, I might never do it. So, yeah. I think I should."

CHAPTER 41

I sigh. Another last. Sports are over. So is tutoring with Yasmin. During our last few weeks together, she taught me as much as I taught her. And now, the final concert. I'm excited. And nervous. A tiny solo line in the girls' ensemble is loading my stomach with butterflies. Checking myself in the mirror, I add a dash of lipstick before descending the stairs.

Dad walks in from the kitchen, a travel cup in one hand and keys in the other. "Ready?"

"As ready as I can be."

As I buckle myself into the car, I sigh. "This is the season of last things. With April over, everything I've known for four years is ending."

Dad's eyes are on the road, but a smile turns up the corner of his mouth. "I know it's different for you than for me. I'd already met your mom and was excited to move into the next chapter of my life. But you're still finding your way."

I nod.

As we pull into the school parking lot, Dad lets me out. Careful to avoid the puddles from this afternoon's rain, I slide past the crowd at the front of the building and race as fast as my heels will carry me to the choir room. Voices waft out of the room next door, and I stop. Five girls in white blouses and black skirts are already there. Yasmin's skirt brushes the tops of her shoes, and she's wearing a black hijab. Our group makes tight music together.

Maya smiles as I walk in. "I hope you've all warmed up your voices. We only have a few minutes before we join the rest of the choir."

Yasmin pulls out the pitch pipe and gives us a starting note. Low and soft, Yasmin and I begin. Then the second sopranos join us, and the two sopranos. Soon, the song speeds up, and our voices soar on the clouds. Then, suddenly, we stop. After two seconds, Maya starts singing a plaintive solo. I pick up where she leaves off, and then all six of us sing together. As the last note dies into the quiet, all of us are smiling. We are ready.

Maya loops her arm around my shoulders as we head next door. "Nervous?"

"Not yet. A little, but I'll be terrified when we're in front of all those people."

We find our places and run through the songs for tonight. One is about spring, and I love the imagery and music. If flowers and trees could sing, they might sound like this.

I wonder if Alex is in the crowd as we file onto the risers. She said she would try to make it. I scan the audience, but the stage lights blind my view of their faces. After three songs, we step off the risers, and the first group moves to the microphones. Everyone else files into the room behind the stage.

When the guys' large ensemble enters the room, the six of us leave to stand behind the curtain, waiting for Malcolm to finish his solo. His deep voice raises goosebumps on my skin. I had no idea he could sing like that. Even though the audience has been instructed not to clap between pieces, people erupt in applause. I don't blame them. I'd be clapping too. When he ducks behind the curtain, his sparkling smile could embarrass a diamond's attempt to shine. He winks at Yasmin as we head toward the front of the stage, and she averts her eyes.

We step forward. Maya nods. Yasmin gives us our pitch, and we sing. We sing like this is the only moment in history that matters. We sing like no one else is in the room. We blend our voices perfectly. Soft, then strong. Low, then high. Maya's solo easily matches Malcolm's. She sings like heaven is watching. And I sing for Mom. I don't know if she can see me or not. But when I sing, she is the only one I see. And in my mind, she's beaming.

When we finish, the clapping starts, but Mr. Clark puts up his hand to stop them. "I know you'd like to clap for everyone, but it will add time to a long program. So please hold your applause."

When the door to the practice room closes behind us, we hug and slap each other on the back.

"That was amazing." One of Maya's friends stands to hug her. "You would have placed first at state, for sure. Now, if only our trio can do half that well."

One by one, we watch the other groups on the TV monitor. Soon, it's time to file back onto the risers. We sing two more songs and finish with the national anthem. The audience stands with us as we hold our hands over our hearts, facing the flag.

When the song ends, red and black confetti rain down from the ceiling, and I turn to Yasmin. "This is it—our last concert. But the songs will stay in my head for a long time. Whenever I think of them, I'll remember you. I'm glad I had a good friend in choir this year." Confetti rests on her black hijab, like sparks thrown from a campfire into the darkness. Yasmin and I hug each other before she leaves to look for her family.

A tentative voice speaks behind me. "Cassie?"

I turn around. There she is. Stormy. The gray girl. I wondered how this moment would go.

She stares at her hands. Her voice is so quiet I strain to hear. "Cassie, I am so sorry for how I treated you last year. I thought I had this whole Christian thing figured out and wanted to help you be a better Christian. Now I know I was being judgmental and harsh." She looks up. "Please forgive me."

A rush of compassion fills my heart, and I reach out with both arms to give her a quick hug. "I've forgiven you. But I need to ask you to forgive me for cutting you out of my life and holding a grudge against you. Will you forgive me?"

She nods. "I do. Can we be friends again?"

"Of course." I step toward her, and we lean into each other for a quick embrace. The weight I've felt for so long is gone. I should have looked harder for her instead of waiting for her to find me. Behind her, I see her mom.

"How's your family doing with your dad away?" I ask.

"It's been tough. We're looking for a new church."

"Come to ours. We would love to have you."

"I'll ask Mom." Her mom motions to her, and they head for the door while I look for Dad.

"Cassie, over here!" I turn my head to see Alex, Jon, and Dad heading toward me.

"You made it!" I hug Alex.

"We did, and I'm so glad I got to hear you. You were great! Weren't you scared?"

"Of course," I respond.

"You didn't sound like it. You've learned voice control.

Good for you. Have you considered music education as a major?"

"Alexandra Joy, just because I like to sing doesn't mean I like music as well as you do. Music theory would kill me!" I laugh.

"Just a thought since you're still figuring out what's next," Alex says with a wink.

As we enter the night, the smells of damp earth and freshly washed air fill my senses. If I had extremely sensitive ears, would I hear the grass trying to push up through the dirt? Alex joins us in our car, and Jon drives away.

When we get home, Dad pulls me into a hug. "You were amazing tonight, Cassie. And I'm not just saying that because you're my daughter. Even if I didn't know you, I would have been impressed. The blend you girls had. And the strength of your voice and the tone. It was something I didn't think I would ever hear from you."

"Why?"

"Because you've been too timid to try things like that before." He kisses the top of my head.

I smile, squirm out of his grasp, and head upstairs. That night, I pull my journal into my lap to write while Alex gets ready for bed.

Dear God,

Thank You for today. Thank you for the strength and ability You gave to our group and me in tonight's concert. Please help me not to put my abilities in a closet but to use them to honor You.

My pen stops. "Alex, how did you know God wanted you to study music? Was it your abilities, or was it more than that?"

She hangs up her clothes for tomorrow and turns to look at me. "God gives us abilities to fulfill a specific purpose in this world. He gave me my love for music. But I didn't know how everything would fit together. Whenever I prayed about it, songs came into my mind. Most of them were songs I'd known for a long time, but sometimes, they were songs I'd made up. Finally, I asked Him, 'Why do I keep thinking of songs when I ask about my future?

"Then, I realized God gave me a gift and love for music to honor Him. I knew music could take me in many different directions. I thought performance was out of the question, but I told God I would even do that if He wanted me to. I could have gone into music therapy, ethnomusicology, music composition, or even become a music technician. But the more I prayed about it, the more I believed music education was where I belonged."

She sits down on the bed at my feet. "Cassie, you're different from me. Music is the one thing I do well, so it was easier to figure things out. You have lots of different interests, but God will show you, too."

She's right. But sometimes, I get tired of waiting.

May 5. Forever on my mind as the day Mom left us. Tonight, our family and Jon will gather to remember and thank God for her life. With scissors in hand, I trim the stems of the pink and white tulips I've collected from the abundant blooms in our yard and arrange them in a vase. When I put them on the dining room table, the garage door opens, and Dad walks in carrying a large arrangement of white roses.

He gently places the extravagant bouquet on the mantle. "You ready?"

I nod, and he hands me a long-stemmed white rose. On the way, silence shields our thoughts from each other. I'm remembering Mom, and I imagine Dad is too.

When we get out of the car at the cemetery, I grab his trembling arm as we walk across the carpet of green grass. He stumbles and then catches himself. At the grave, he takes a bottle of water from his pocket and fills the vase. Then, kissing the white rose, he puts it in the vase. "I still love you, and I'll never forget you."

Walking away to give him some privacy, I take in the beauty around me. Yellow daffodils and red tulips nod in the gentle breeze. The spring green of the trees lifts my mood, and I try to imagine Mom in heaven. Though God made such a beautiful world for us to enjoy, heaven must be even more magnificent and glorious.

When Dad pulls out his red bandana to wipe his face, I turn back towards the grave. Inhaling the scent of the fragile flower, I place mine in the vase. "I love you, too, Mom." Tears slide down my cheeks. "I'll always miss you." I let the tears fall.

Dad stands to his feet. Silent with our thoughts, we stare at the two roses and Mom's tombstone. Maybe Alex will come by to add a third. Like Dad said, I'm so glad she was the kind of mother that I miss.

That night, Aunt Sandi, Alex, and Jon join us at Mom's favorite restaurant. Every other sentence seems to start with either "Do you remember?" or "She was so..." Tears flow without shame. Smiles and even laughs accompany them. The juicy steak and sweet potato fries are almost forgotten on my plate as I drink in the stories. Aunt Sandi tells stories from their childhood that I'd never heard before.

When I finally crawl into bed that night, I'm exhausted but thankful. Thankful for a wonderful mom. Thankful I still have family and that Jon is now part of it. Thankful that Dad didn't die last fall. But I'm especially thankful God will never leave me.

CHAPTER 43

Our countdown to May 17 began as soon as Alex got engaged. I jump out of bed and go to the window. White, wispy clouds float on a background of deep blue, the color I'd hoped for when I asked God to keep the rain away. In my mind's eye, I can see the sun reflecting off the lake. I'm glad Alex decided on a small outdoor wedding. That was enough to manage without Mom. Alex's bed is empty. Not a surprise.

I wander downstairs to find her in the kitchen eating breakfast at the bar. I grab a bowl and spoon and set them next to her. Pouring myself a cup of coffee, I ask, "Were you able to sleep last night?"

"Until about five this morning. I've been up since then. Too many details are still running around in my head. I sure miss Mom today."

"Me too." My eyes well with tears, and I blink them away. "Do you think she can see us?"

"I hope so, but I don't know." Her eyes mist, and she wipes the tears with her napkins. "Anyway, I'm glad she met Jon and approved of him, so I know our marriage would make her happy."

Four hours later, Alex and I watch through the tinted windows of the parked van as the guests arrive, taking their places under the awning in the white folding chairs.

While someone might catch a glimpse of me, Alex's place in the back seat shields her from prying eyes. Jon's niece, guessing we might be in the van, breaks away from her family and jumps to look in the window before her dad pulls her back. We laugh. Even if she had been successful, she wouldn't have seen much.

Whenever Alex walks into a room, heads turn. Even first thing in the morning, she looks like she's stepped from the pages of a fashion magazine. But today, she's glowing. Aunt Sandi twisted her naturally blond hair in an updo and tucked in sprigs of baby's breath. But the joy and anticipation on her face make her shine.

Alex's roommate settles in at the keyboard, and Bach's "Jesu, Joy of Man's Desiring" soon quiets the small gathering. I draw in a deep breath and check the mirror one more time. Today is Alex's day, and I'm so happy for her. Sliding toward the door, I wait for the song to end. When the last notes reach me, I step out of the van onto the white runner as Dad helps Alex slide out. I spread the train of her gown behind her. The slow, graceful notes of Bach's "Air on the G String" spill from Gemma's violin into the air and move me forward. When I take my place in front, I turn to watch Dad and Alex walk down the aisle together. Poor Dad. His face twitches. His upturned mouth quivers as a tear slides down his face.

Alex's radiant face matches Jon's. His cheeks must hurt from smiling. When Dad relinquishes Alex to Jon, I want to leave my place in front to hug my dad. A single tear runs down his cheek. But he'll be okay, just like I will.

Months of planning went into this day, and now everything is happening so fast. I want to hold on to each moment since it will never happen again. I can almost recite their traditional vows along with them. Tonight, when I'm alone, I'm going to look up the song that Maya and Jon's brother are singing. So beautiful, but I've never heard it before.

As Pastor Fuller leads in the vows and gives a meditation, I force myself to pay attention. "Thank you, Lord," I pray silently, "for a sister who has been there for me through this past horrible year and a brother-in-law who supported our whole family in our grief." I exhale, willing myself to let go even as I realize that this moment will change all our lives.

After the ceremony, I direct the guests toward coolers filled with soda and water and ensure they know the directions to our house for the reception. While the photographer works her magic, the guests catch the day's beauty on their cell phone cameras. Even Dad is beaming now as he watches Alex laugh, her laughter and smile radiating her joy.

When the photo session ends and the guests pile into their cars to caravan to our house, I settle into the front seat of the borrowed van, and Dad drives us home. We walk around the house to the backyard, where tiny white lights sparkle on the hydrangea bushes and the lower branches and trunks of the maple trees. A canopy of white gauze and more lights hover over a small white table with two chairs. Vases filled with fragrant lilacs from Aunt Sandi's yard and glowing oil lamps on the tables invite guests in from the edges. As our guests wander in, I stand back to watch everyone. Our ordinary yard looks so festive, and I'm glad Aunt Sandi took that load off us. Even though I helped, I never could have come up with anything half as nice.

"Introducing Mr. and Mrs. Jonathan Dyer!" Pastor Fuller stands back from the side of the house as Jon and

Alex come around the corner. We applaud, hoot, and whistle as they join us. Alex holds her bouquet of white roses high in the air, but she brings it to me instead of throwing it. "Sorry, everyone! It's unlikely Cassie will be the next one married here, but neither of us likes the tradition, so I'm giving it to my maid of honor."

I grin. "Thanks, sis." I figured she might do something like that.

After she and Jon cut the cake, I walk inside to put the flowers in water. Xavier follows me. "So do you think maybe you and I will be the next ones of this group to get married?" A smirk curls his lip.

"You may be, but not me! I have three years of college in front of me." I laugh.

"Oh, I wondered if you had a secret beau since I didn't notice anyone paying attention to you."

I don't respond. I don't like him probing into my private life. It's none of his business. Besides, if he wants to know, he can ask Jon.

As though he reads my mind, he says, "I asked Jon, and he wouldn't give me an answer."

Filling the dark blue vase with water, I wonder how to get him off my back. "Well, here's your answer. I'm not dating anyone now because my dad says I shouldn't date until I'm ready to get married. I happen to agree with him. Dad told you this when you took me to the concert." I put the flowers in the vase on the counter and wander back outside. He's still following me.

"So, could we be friends?" he asks, moving into my personal space.

I back away. "Friends? Of course. But only if you don't expect anything more than that. And remember. We don't live in the same town, and we aren't going to the same college, so I expect this will be a casual social media friend-ship."

"Can I call you sometime?"

"Wow. You are persistent," I manage to stammer.

He grins at me, one eyebrow going up as he studies me. "Well?"

Gemma slides up next to us and puts her hand on my arm, her eyes on Alex and Jon. "She's so beautiful, don't you think?"

"I do, and so does everyone else. That's all I've been hearing today as I wander around." I'm so glad to turn the conversation another way.

Xavier takes the hint and wanders away. I watch him leave. Even though I enjoyed the concert, I'm not ready for anything other than a brother-sister relationship with him right now.

The rest of the afternoon speeds by. After Jon and Alex leave, the guests linger and then slowly trickle out to their cars. Gemma and Aunt Sandi stay to help Dad and me clean up. Dad brings out the big black trash bags. Soon, the tables are clear, and the bags are bulging. We stack chairs on the rack for the rental company to pick up later.

Aunt Sandi wraps an arm around my waist. "That was a beautiful wedding. Simple. Elegant. Tasteful. You girls did a great job."

"Thanks, Aunt Sandi." I wave at the lights still twin-kling in the bushes. "And thanks for all the decorating you did for the reception."

"You're welcome." She smiles up at me. I feel her arm tighten again as she looks over at Dad. "Adam?" she calls. "I'm leaving." Dad waves, and she's gone.

Gemma's white high heels dangle by their straps from her hand. "The grass feels wonderful on my aching feet. By the way, I need to leave too. Do you want to come over tomorrow after church and eat lunch with us?"

"I think I need to stay with Dad. Even though we're happy for Alex, I don't think he should be alone. Not right now. I'd invite you, but I think it's better if it's just the two of us tomorrow."

She nods and blows me a kiss as she saunters away.

Another table joins the stack as Dad lifts it into place on the rack. When he turns, lines etch his face. I wonder what he's thinking. I join Dad and help him with the last table. "Dad, how are you doing?"

"You mean with Alex?"

Nodding, I search his face for clues. He's relaxed. Even though he didn't say anything to me, I think he wanted this day to be a great one as much as Alex and Jon did.

"I'm okay. We will both miss her, but I'm glad she chose Jon. He's great for her. He loves the Lord, and he loves her. They'll do well together."

I nod. How many times will I want to text her on her honeymoon? Of course, I can't do that, but I already miss her.

As I turn toward the kitchen, tears brim my eyes. How can I be so happy and so sad at the same time? I wipe a tear as it slithers down my cheek.

He lifts my chin so my eyes meet his. "Today, I'm looking right at you. You are not your mom. You are beautiful in your own right. Someday, some guy is going to think so, too. He'll see your freckles, blue eyes, and red hair, and I'll have to beat him away to keep him from carrying you off like Jon did with Alex today."

I lean into his side and put my arms around him. "Thanks, Dad, for believing in me," I say in a choked voice.

He responds with a hug of his own. "I do believe in you, but I believe even more in God, who has wrapped you in His love and will take care of you for all of your days."

CHAPTER 44

At lunchtime on Sunday, Dad and I share our blessings from that morning. Even though it has nothing to do with what happened at church, I add a fifth one. "I was so blessed by Alex's and Jon's wedding yesterday. Not only was it beautiful, but they worked hard to make sure that God got center stage during the ceremony and the reception. If I ever get married, I want to do the same thing."

A smile lights Dad's eyes. "I'm confident that if you do get married, you will make sure of it. I love how much I've seen you grow in your love and admiration for God this year. Last year, you were still an insecure girl, but you are becoming a confident woman, and I love it.

I scrape the last bit of wedding cake from my plate. "By the way, I finished going through the rest of my clothes. I think I'm ready for Mom's next challenge."

"Okay." He starts to clear the table.

"I'll do that." I jump from my seat to help.

A few minutes later, he finds me in the kitchen, loading the dishwasher, and hands me the pink envelope. "This is it. The last challenge."

My shoulders slump. Of course, they have to end eventually. She couldn't keep writing letters forever. But the last one? I stare at the envelope in my hand. Her once bold, curvy handwriting has deteriorated into a weak, shaky scrawl.

Dad closes the dishwasher and starts it. "Aren't you going to open it?"

I grab a knife from the oak block, slit it open, and return the knife. I glance at the note inside and amble toward the couch. Starlight brushes against my ankles. Even though Dad knows what's in these, I want to be alone. Continuing to stare at her handwriting, I trudge up the stairs and collapse on my bed. The void in my heart is transforming into a canyon. These letters have kept me going. How will I do without them? Gingerly, I pull out the last letter.

My dear Cassie,

You made it. You've reached the last of these challenges. Good for you. When you finish this one, Dad will tell you about our surprise.

You have been a joy to me since the day you were born. We didn't expect you to have red hair since Alex wasn't born with it. But God gave you bold, red hair to signify a special purpose in your life. Our bodies, brains, talents, and personalities are all part of God's way of equipping us for the lives He wants us to have. You have been specially designed by God for a particular purpose.

So this is your challenge: Think about your future. Dad has a booklet he'll give you that will help you. Ask God to help you. Dream big. Dream the impossible. We have no idea what the future holds, but God can do more for you than you imagine. (Ephesians 3:20) So don't belittle yourself. Don't hide. Instead, stretch your faith muscles and soar.

> *I wish I could keep writing you these letters so you would have one from me for at least the next few years. But as you can see from my handwriting, it's hard for me to write now. Even typing is hard. But know this: I'll always love you.*
>
> *Love you to heaven and back,*
>
> *Mom*

I clutch the letter to my chest. The scent of her favorite lotion reaches me, and tears spill down my cheeks. How will I go on without her? Then I remember Jesus' promise: He is with me. He will never leave me.

A soft tap on the door alerts me to Dad's presence. "How are you?"

I look up from the bed. He opens his arms, and I walk into them. Safely wrapped, I let the grief pour out of me. When the tears subside, he hands me his red bandana, and I wipe my eyes.

"We grieve when we lose a wonderful thing." His breath swirls through my hair. "It would be terrible if we felt no loss. It would mean she hadn't been a great wife and mother."

I take a step back, and he releases me. "I hadn't thought of it that way. But you're right."

"When you want the booklet, it's in my office."

"I think I need a day or two before I begin. I want to spend some time first thanking God for the great mom I had."

"Say, I wanted to talk to you about something." He motions toward his office, and I follow.

When we get there, he opens his calendar on his computer. "I want to have a gathering to celebrate Mom's life with a few of our friends who have helped us through this year. I wasn't ready on the actual day, but maybe June 14?" The arrow hovers over the date. "What do you think?" When I nod, he types it in and copies it to my calendar. "We'll talk later about who to invite."

CHAPTER 45

On the first Saturday in June, I wait with my classmates for the opening bars of Pomp and Circumstance. "It's all over but the shouting," so the saying goes.

Some of us have extra decorations on our graduation gowns. Nora, our valedictorian, has several extras for being the top in the class. I am comfortable with my gold NHS stole and the honors cord. Nora says I could go to Harvard, but even with the scholarship they might offer, it's too expensive. I'm not going deep into debt for college. I'm staying home to study at Dad's community college for my first year and decide from there. I felt a huge weight come off me when I finally made the decision. Maybe it shouldn't be hard, but it was.

Music filters through the open doors, and the front row of students begin their march toward the front of the gymnasium. Walking through the door, I scan the crowd for Dad, Alex, and Jon. I have no clue where they might be sitting, but at least I know they're here. I'm glad for their support today. Oh, how I miss Mom. She would have loved seeing me graduate. She knows how hard I studied to get here.

I file into my seat. The next hour, I only half-listen to the speeches. A sprinkling of claps accentuates Nora's speech. The main speaker, a professor from some famous university in Australia, is so boring that I'm tempted not to listen except that his accent is charming. I hope I don't have a lot of boring teachers in college.

Ahead of me, the rows of graduates line up to receive their diplomas. Since I'm toward the end of the alphabet, it takes a while for me to get up to join the line and move to the platform. "Cassandra Faith Nelson." The principal's voice draws me forward. I shake the principal's hand and then Mrs. Harding's. Head bowed, I return to my seat.

Finally, we get to the awards section, the part I like the best. It's great when you hear that someone gets an award and no one expected it. I hope it happens again this year.

Students are recognized for various achievements. Then, I hear a name that surprises me. "Yasmin Omar Dalmar." Yasmin goes up to the podium to receive an academic scholarship for children of immigrants. I stand, clap, and stomp my feet in celebration with her. I'm so glad she'll get to go to college. She didn't think she would go because she couldn't figure out how to pay for it, but now she can.

When the ceremony is over, we wave our hats in the hair. Everyone's shouting and hugging each other, but I stay in my seat a little longer. I want this moment to be etched in my memory. When I finally look around, I see Yasmin.

"Yasmin!" I call out when I'm close. "I'm so glad you got that scholarship. Now you can go to college. Where do you think you'll go?"

"I don't know. Maybe the school where you're going?"

"The one where Dad teaches or the U of M? Those two are at the top of my list for next year."

"I don't know. First, I have to find out what the stipulations are." Her smile reaches her eyes. "Then I'll see what I'm going to do. I can hardly wait. I've always wanted to go to college, and now I can." Her mortarboard wobbles on her dark blue hijab as she bounces with excitement.

Maya walks up and pulls me into a strong hug. "I'm glad I get to see you this summer. It would be hard to say goodbye after all we've been through together."

"You know," I say. "Our church has a college group. Just because we're out of youth group doesn't mean you can't come to that now."

"Good to know. I'll keep it in mind." She gives me one more hug and saunters off. I watch her until she disappears into a group of tall people at the other end of the auditorium.

When I walk out the double glass doors for the last time, I turn to look at the familiar building. It's hard to believe I won't be here next year. But I'm anxious to celebrate my high school years with my family at our house this afternoon. Tossing my graduation cap into the air, I catch it and shout, "Woohoo!" and dance my way toward the car.

CHAPTER 46

When I walk through the front door, wet with sweat from my run, Dad emerges from the kitchen, wiping his hands on his "King of the Grill" apron. His dark brown, wavy hair is damp at the temples from sweat, but his blue eyes twinkle with a smile. "Good, you're home," he says. "I really need your help." His eyes survey my appearance. "Hurry up and get ready. Aunt Sandi just pulled in, and the others won't be far behind."

I scramble up the stairs, shoes in hand. After a quick shower, I tie my wet hair into a ponytail, add a smidge of makeup, and run downstairs. In the dining room, Aunt Sandi talks with Dad, and I give her a quick hug. She beams up at me.

"How many are coming?" Aunt Sandi rummages for dinnerware and napkins to set up the buffet.

"Including us, fifteen," Dad says. "Use the paper plates we bought and put on some bowls in case people want them for salad. I need to check on the burgers."

The doorbell chimes. Dad turns to me with his look that commands me to answer, and I open the door. Mrs. Fuller hands me a towel-wrapped casserole dish. "Ian is going to be late. He's stopping at the hospital to visit Mrs. Smith." Bella clings to her mom's skirt. Moriah and her older brothers follow us inside.

"Are there going to be any other kids here?" Zane asks me.

I put the casserole on the table and bend down to hug him. "Sorry." I was about to add that I was still a kid, but to him, I'm not. He frowns like he's unsure and plops down on the couch.

Through the window, I see Gemma coming up the walk, and I run to the door. "Gemma, I'm so glad you could make it."

"Can I help?" she asks.

"Yeah. Just make sure the kids are entertained until we start. All we have to do now is wait for the rest of the people and food to show up."

Gemma heads to the piano bench where Liam is already playing the bottom half of Chopsticks. At first, Gemma plays the top half everyone seems to know and then launches into an original tune that fits the rhythm. I smile. Gemma is so talented and so good with kids too. If I ever have children, I hope I have a bunch that love music as much as I do. I can't play or sing like Alex and Gemma can, but I sure do love to hear it. Alex got Mom's musical abilities, but maybe some of it will pass to my children.

The door opens, and Alexandra and Jon step into the room. I smother Alex with a bear hug, and Jon gives me a high five. Other cars are pulling in.

"It looks like everyone is here, Dad," I call to him.

The screen door slams as Dad comes in from the patio with a platter stacked high with burgers and hot dogs. "Welcome, everyone." He sets the platter on the table. "It looks like we have a table full of food. Thank you for helping me with that." He pauses. "Go ahead and find a seat, and we'll start."

Moriah and Bella fight over who will sit on their mother's lap. Andrew and Zane plop down on the couch next to Jon.

"Boys," Fiona whispers. "Let the adults sit on the chairs first. Why don't you sit on the floor next to Jon until everyone is seated." They nod and slide to the floor.

Dad clears his throat. "Thank you for coming. I invited you because all of you helped us make it through this year." He looks around the room at everyone. His eyes stop when he sees Jon, and he says, "Some of you don't know each other, so let me introduce you, and I'll say why I thought of you when I decided to have this gathering tonight."

"Let me start with Sandi. Sandi is Carol's younger sister. She served as a medical missionary in Indonesia. When she heard about Carol's cancer diagnosis, she came home to help care for her. She has been like a second mother to my girls, and I am grateful for her love for us. Next to her is our youth pastor, Declan, and his wife, Hope. They have..." He sucks in a deep breath. "It will be hard for me to say why each of you is special to us, so I'll leave that until later. Let me just introduce you."

"Next to Hope is my daughter Alex and her husband, Jon. On the floor next to Jon are the pastor's two sons, Zane and Liam. Then we have Fiona, the pastor's wife, and their two daughters, Moriah and Bella. Ah, Pastor Ian just arrived." He nods to the tall man who walks in and sits next to Fiona. "To complete the circle, we have Marcus White, a colleague from work. And standing over by the dining room table is my second daughter, Cassie, and her best friend, Gemma."

"All of you made it possible for me to survive this year. For most of you, I knew you were praying for me. Some of you seemed to know when I was having a bad day. All of you showed me your support in countless ways. Even the pastor's children were a big help to me with their hugs." Liam and Zane sit straighter and smile.

"So, I wanted all of you with me tonight. As you know, Carol died a little over a year ago. This year has been the hardest year of my life." He fights to regain control of his voice. "Tonight, I want to celebrate the gift Carol was to us. Later, after we finish eating together, I hope we can share stories of how Carol made a difference in your lives." His eyes scan the room. "Pastor Ian, would you pray for us?"

Ian's deep voice rings out over the room as he thanks God for the gift of food and friendship. When he finishes, the children jump to their feet and rush toward the table full of food. Fiona calls them back.

"It's okay, Fiona," Dad says. "Carol would have wanted the children to go first." Soon, the house buzzes with conversation.

I'm last through the buffet line. I hear the conversations as they reminisce about Mom. Jon walks over to refill his glass with lemonade. "Are you okay?" he asks.

"Tonight is Dad's night. He needs this, but maybe it will be good for me, too."

Jon puts his free hand on my elbow to steer me to a seat next to Gemma. "You know, Alexandra still worries about you."

I smile. I love how he uses Alex's full name. "Yeah, you can pray with me about that. It's getting better. I'm glad you live nearby."

Across the room, Dad stands to his feet. "Well, it looks like everyone has finished eating. Would anyone be willing to share a story about my wife? I especially need to hear those stories I haven't heard before."

Hope sits up straighter before speaking. "I remember our second Sunday at church. The church had just hired Declan. We had left the only church I'd known when we came. Carol saw my tears, realized I was struggling, and invited us to dinner."

I remember. Mom always seemed to notice when people were sad or lonely. How many Sundays had she invited people over just because she felt they needed some love? We often had guests for Sunday dinner.

Hope wipes tears from her eyes, but her voice is stronger now. "She was the first one to reach out to me. How many of you have shared a meal in this house?" Everyone raises a hand.

I want to be like that. I want to notice when people are hurting and reach out to them. I want to have a home where friends and strangers feel welcome.

Beside me, Gemma clears her throat. "I was always amazed at how she could sing. It wasn't just her nice voice. She drew you into God's presence. Because of her example, it's one of the things I ask God to do through me whenever I'm the one singing or playing. I want my music to draw people to Him."

She's right. Even though she was my mom, her singing sometimes filled my heart with joy. At other times, It made me wonder why I didn't have that kind of adoration in me. Sometimes, it was as though Mom was seeing God as she sang, and she drew me in with her. I asked her how she did it—being in front of a group and all. She said she forgot about the people and worshiped God.

One by one, the rest of the group shares their stories. Andrew is the last one. "She was the best Sunday school teacher I ever had, except for my mom. But she doesn't count because I have to listen to her." Everyone chuckles.

When the laughter dies down, Dad stands to his feet. "Thank you. Carol would appreciate that so many of your stories were of her love for God." He looks around. These stories have quieted us. I would love to hear more, but the evening needs to end sometime.

Alex's soft voice penetrates the silence. "Dad, can we sing a couple of Mom's favorite songs?"

He nods.

"All of you know how musical Mom was and how much she loved praising God." She stands and moves to the piano bench. "One of her favorites was 'Amazing Grace.'"

She turns around on the bench, runs her fingers lightly across the keys in a short introduction, and starts to sing. Pastor Ian's strong voice follows, and the rest of us join in. Gemma and I drop into alto harmony at almost the same time. Around the room, someone adds tenor and bass as the group celebrates God's grace. As the song ends, Alex segues into "You Are My All in All" and then "It is Well with my Soul."

Dad grabs a tissue box and passes it around the room. "Alex, would you do us a favor and sing 'Oh, I Want to Know You More?' The one Mom loved by Steven Fry? The sheet music is on the piano." He points to a piece of music behind the hymn book.

Alex pulls it out, checks it quickly, and begins to play. Starting low and tentative, she gains confidence, and her voice soars into the high notes and swoops down into the low ones, just like a bird catching the air currents, taking off into the sky, and gliding back to earth. A reverent hush falls over our group. We can all remember Mom wooing us into God's presence with her voice. Now Alex is doing it too.

When the song ends, Alex lifts her fingers from the keys and swivels on the bench facing us. "Mom had so many favorites. We could be here all night. But I want to sing one more. On that last night, Dad, Aunt Sandi, Cassie, and I gathered around her bed. Mom had been sleeping most of the day, and we knew the end was near. She awoke and saw us all there and smiled. Then, in a low voice, she said, 'I'm looking forward to seeing Jesus tonight. Would you sing, 'I Shall Know Him'?' As we sang together, she slipped away and was gone. We couldn't finish, and it's been hard to sing that song ever since. Yet Mom loved that song, and I think she would be honored if we would sing it together."

Alex passes out the words she printed out for us. Then, with her leading on the piano, we begin.

When my life's work is ended, and I cross the swelling tide,
And the great and glorious morning I shall see,
I shall know my redeemer when I reach the other side,
And his smile will be the first to welcome me.

The song rises to a crescendo as even the youngest voices join in the chorus. I hear them all singing, but I'm just listening because, in my mind, I still see just the four of us around her bed.

I shall know Him. I shall know Him,
And redeemed by His side, I shall stand.
I shall know Him. I shall know Him
By the print of the nail in His hand.

Then, almost as clearly as if I were seeing it in person, I see Mom stepping across into heaven into Jesus' welcoming arms. Her face beams with delight as she meets the

One she adored here. Just as quickly, the picture fades. It's true. Mom really is happy now. She's where she always wanted to be. Joy and heartbreak argue for dominance in my heart, but then I realize that it's incredible how the verse they're singing now makes sense of what I just saw.

> Oh, the soul-thrilling rapture when I view His blessed face[3]
> And the luster of His kindly beaming eye;
> How my full heart will praise Him for His mercy, love, and grace
> That prepared for me a mansion in the sky.

Then Pastor Fuller lifts his voice. "Father, thank You for Carol and her shining example of a life lived fully for You. Thank You for taking her home where she's safe with You in heaven. Thank You for keeping Adam, Alex, and Cassie through this incredibly difficult time."

He keeps praying, but I'm praying my own prayer now. "Lord, let my life shine as brightly as Mom's. I want to be everything You want me to be."

"Amens" fill the room as Pastor Fuller finishes. Dad wipes his eyes and stands to receive bear hugs from the men.

I throw my arm over Alex's shoulders and smile. "That was intense, but I think it was exactly what we all needed. Thank you for singing those songs, especially that last one."

Pastor Ian is the first to stand. "I hate to be the one to break this up, but we have little ones who need to get to bed if they are going to be happy in church tomorrow. So goodnight all." He heads to the door with his family and

---

[3] *I Shall Know Him, by Fanny Mae Crosby. Public domain.*

turns to Dad. "Thank you, Adam. We all needed to celebrate God's goodness at work in Carol's life. I hope we all live as fully to His glory as she did." Slowly, our guests say goodbye and file out.

Dad looks around at the paper plates, napkins, and cups scattered around the room. "You don't have to help me clean tonight. I need to stay busy for a while to sort through what everyone said. Why don't you head out for a walk? There's still some daylight left, and the lake is always gorgeous at this time of the evening."

"Thanks, Dad." I head for the stairs. "Alex and Jon, you wanna come? Or do you have to leave?"

Jon looks at Alex and nods. "I'm heading out, but if you'll give Alexandra a ride home after you're done, she wants to spend a little more time with you."

She goes with Jon to the car to grab her running shoes. A few minutes later, we walk out together. After the heat of the day, I relish the evening's coolness. The sinking sun leaves long shadows with occasional puddles of sunshine dribbling through the leaves. We jog around a couple holding hands, conversing in hushed tones. On the grass, a woman plays catch with her Golden Retriever. The cool breeze ruffles my hair when we reach the lake, and the low sun casts a rippling golden path across it. Alex stops and points to the little black dots on the other side of the lake. The loons' calls soothe my heart.

We sit near the water's edge. "Alex, how did Mom do it? She was so full of joy and peace even when she was sick. It drew people to her like a magnet. So many have told me their stories about her. I want to be like her, but I don't know if I can."

Alex nods. "Mom would be the first to tell you that you have your own gifts. You are not supposed to try to be like her. You are supposed to be yourself. And if you want to copy someone, copy Jesus, not anyone else."

"But that's even harder," Frustration edges my voice. "Mom was wonderful and godly, but she wasn't perfect like Jesus is. How in the world can I be like that?"

"Well, what do you think?" Alex asks.

"You sound just like Dad. Asking me to think instead of helping me with the answer."

"Well, he's right, especially with spiritual things. I can't tell you how to be like Jesus. I can point you to God's Word, but only the Holy Spirit can help you grow. If you do what I say, you'll follow a pattern of good works instead of growing in loving Jesus. I can't tell you how to be like Him. What works for me may not work for you, and even if it does, it's better if you figure it out yourself."

She turns from staring at the lake and looks at me. "Have you finished Mom's last project yet?"

"Almost. At first, I thought I had to be done by graduation, but Dad said I had one year from when I started, so I'm taking my time with this one. I love dreaming about how God might want to use me. I wish I had one of those booklets for every one of my friends. I think everyone could benefit from it."[4]

"Has Dad given you any hint about the surprise Mom planned for you?"

I shake my head. "I've imagined so many different things that it might be. Maybe it will be something that mattered to Mom? Whatever it is, I know I'll like it because she knew me so well."

---

[4] *For your own download of the booklet Cassie fills out, visit https://www. joanlovestrandfarley.org where you can receive a free copy of "Writing About My Future."*

CHAPTER 47

I kick down my bicycle stand and walk across the green grass to where a white rose sits proudly in a pewter vase. Dad has been here already, even though it's still early morning. Before gently placing my rose in the vase, I inhale its scent. The memory of the first time we came here together comes roaring back. A month after Mom died, Dad, Alex, and I came with three white roses. I put mine in the vase and immediately sobbed, wrapping my arms around Dad.

School's been over for a couple of weeks, and I only come once in a while. Dad still comes a lot. Sitting on the soft grass in front of her headstone, I cross my legs and stare at the white roses. They remind me of her life—short-lived but beautiful, pure, and gentle.

Memories flood back. Christmases baking cookies. Birthday parties. Thanksgiving dinners. Sundays at church. Bedtime stories when I was little. But mostly, just her presence, constantly reassuring me that she loved me. Even when she was dying, her frequent words were, "Cassie, I'm so glad God made you my daughter. He has great things in store for you."

I'm starting to believe her. Even though my insecurity still visits me frequently, this past year proves that God has been working in me. If Mom were still here, she'd tell me again she was proud of me. I have a long way to go, but with God's help, I'm learning and growing. It's hard to believe everything that happened during this last year of high school. Our cross-country team won a medal at the state competition. I played in the starting lineup for basketball several times and didn't mess it up. I sang a solo line in an ensemble. I got good grades. I gave and received forgiveness. Best of all, I made a new friend.

I look around the cemetery again. The tall oaks murmur in the gentle breeze. "God," I say aloud. "You brought me through this year. Life is still scary sometimes. I have so many questions about the future. Dad, Alex, Gemma, and Aunt Sandi will be there for me. Maybe even Maya and Yasmin. But no one is like Mom."

Tears pool in my eyes and drip down my cheeks, and I wipe them away, drying my damp hands on my green t-shirt. "I'm claiming Isaiah 41:10 as my verse this year." I recite it in my mind, and then I put the words in my own words as a prayer. "Lord, don't let insecurity and fear stop me because You are with me. Don't let me be so dismayed or intimidated that I forget to stand for what's right. You are the Almighty God whom I claim as mine. You will strengthen me. You will help me. You will keep your hands under me to hold me up. I still have so many questions, God. It's good that Alex and Jon are nearby. If I go to the community college, I'll get to live at home and see them. But I still need Your guidance. What will I do after that? I wish Mom were still here."

A whisper of a reminder comes to my heart from Matthew 28:20. "I am with you always."

The hurting hole in my heart where Mom was may never go away. But God will never leave me. He will help me.

When I finished the booklet Mom left me, I felt peaceful. I may not know the twists and turns of the future, but I now have a better idea of who I am and how I might be able to live my life for God. I'm starting to get excited to move into the future.

The night I told Dad I'd finished Mom's ninth challenge, he grinned. "See? I knew you would. It's a good thing, too. I don't know what I would have done with your surprise if you had decided you didn't want to do them anymore."

Hmm. I wonder what my prize is. Sometimes, I think the real prize is all her handwritten letters and what I learned from them.

Moving from sitting to kneeling, I sniff the roses again. Then, looking up and stretching my arms to the sky, I stand. I'm glad no one was in the cemetery with me today. It's nice to talk to God out loud. I swing my leg over the bike and turn back to look at the two roses. Even though she's not here, God is. And one day, I'll see her again and tell her about all the amazing things God did while I was alive.

Moving the kickstand back with my heel, I put my feet on the pedals and roll down the narrow lane to the paved road. A song bubbles up in my heart — one of Mom's favorites that Alex wrote.

You're my rock in shifting sands,
Holding me with powerful hands,
Leading me through unknown lands.
You are God. Yes, You're my God.

As I pick up speed, the wind lifts my hair, and it streams behind me. My voice grows more assured, and I belt out the second verse.

You are stronger than my fear.
When I pray, You draw me near,
Helping me to persevere.
You are God. Yes, You're my God.

The wind carries my voice through the empty cemetery. No one can hear me but God. He's my only audience, and I sense His smile. When I turn my bicycle onto the busy road toward home, my smile stretches across my face. His strength and love will be there for me. Deep down, I know this.

When I walk back into the house, a suitcase sits by the door. Whose is that? Did someone just arrive, or is Dad going somewhere? After I remove my shoes and put them on the boot tray, Dad comes down the stairs with a big grin on his face. "Pack a suitcase for eight days. The flight's tomorrow."

What?

He sees my expression. "Your surprise from us is a trip. But you won't know where until we get to the airport."

Airport? I've never flown before. I feel like a kid on Christmas Eve. "What do I pack?"

"The nights are about the same as here, but the days are cooler, so pack a sweater or light jacket. Oh, and take a swimsuit in case you need it."

"Jogging clothes?"

"If you want." He smiles again. "Now get going. It may take you a while to figure out what to take. I left a packing guide on your bed."

At the airport, Dad and I roll our suitcases to one of the long lines in the lobby. I look up, and the board reads Dublin.

"Dublin? Seriously? I mean, I love the idea of going there, but why?"

"Mom always wanted to see the land of her ancestors, so she wanted you to go in her stead. That way, you can pass along more information about your heritage to your children someday."

Although Mom and I talked about Ireland, this isn't what I was expecting. But I don't know what I was expecting. I thought it might be a small gift, like a necklace, but this is a thousand times better than that. What fun!

Someone taps me on the shoulder. Turning around, I see Gemma and her dad.

"Surprised?" she asks me.

I give her a quick hug and stand back, confused. I shake my head. "Did you come to say goodbye? I'll only be gone a week or so. Why didn't you tell me you were coming when I texted you last night about my trip?"

She looks at my dad, and a smile passes between them.

"Wait a minute," I say. "Something's going on. You're in cahoots about something. Spill it."

"Well," Dad says slowly. "I'm not the one going with you." He points to the suitcase beside him. "This is Gemma's bag. She brought it over yesterday while you were gone. She's going with you."

"What? Really? So you knew about this?" I give her a quick hug and start bouncing on my toes. Dublin was great when I thought I was going with Dad, but this is even better. Is he sorry he's not going? From the huge smile on his face, I guess not.

Dad hands me my passport and an envelope. "You will be met at the airport. Here is your itinerary for the week—hotels, things to see in each place, and your transportation around the island. In addition to the tourist spots, there are two colleges I want you and Gemma to check out together. Since you haven't decided what you are going to do next year, I want you to see if you want to spend a semester or even a year abroad at one of these schools. You'll also stop for two days in London on your way home. If you like the idea of studying abroad, but the two schools in Ireland aren't for you, there are others in London you might like. Or you can just spend those days sightseeing."

I can't believe it! I'm going to Ireland with Gemma. And then to London. On a plane. For more than a week. I want to squeal or shout, but I squash it down and try to act like an adult instead of a five-year-old with a brand-new toy.

After we check in and say goodbye to our dads, we head through security. While we wait for the plane, Gemma takes out her tablet to read a book, and I grab my journal.

God,

This is amazing. Here I am at the MSP airport waiting to fly to Dublin with Gemma!!! I've never been on a plane before, let alone abroad. And Gemma going with me makes it the best gift ever. After we head our separate ways for college, we won't spend a lot of time together. And now I get to think about one more option—studying abroad. Maybe I'll do that. Thank you so much for giving Mom this idea as my surprise gift.

I close the journal and watch the people swirl around me. Different languages filter through the air as people pass. I still can't believe it.

We take off, and eight hours later, when the plane descends into Ireland, I understand why they call it the "Emerald Isle." I marvel at the many shades of green. After the long flight, finding our bags and the driver, we settle into our hotel for the night. The next morning, we are ready to explore.

At breakfast, Gemma and I talk over the itinerary. We'll start in Dublin, but we'll also get to visit the Cliffs of Moher, Killarney National Park, and the Ring of Kerry. In Galway, we'll attend the International Arts Festival to learn about local culture. What fun! We'll also stop at the grave site near where Mom's ancestors lived to see what Kelly names we find there from the 1850s. Today, we'll visit the first college, and when we return, we'll go to the second, sandwiching our tourist visits between the opportunities to study here.

Six days later, Gemma and I sit on a big rock on a green hill where small cliffs fall straight into the sea, the spot Mom wanted to see at sunrise. Here on this rise overlooking the ocean, her ancestors would have watched the sun rise and set every day until they made the journey across the ocean in hopes of a life without famine. Around us, the birds begin to take flight as we watch the eastern sky turn the darkness into gold.

Gemma sits with her knees drawn up to her chin, her warm sweater tucked around her, and her eyes follow the birds through the air. "Did you know that some composers have tried to make bird songs with instruments? It doesn't even come close to the music they sing." She smiles as we listen to them. "I wish I had my violin here so I could accompany them."

I marvel at God's providence in taking my ancestors from here and Gemma from China so that we could become good friends. Sitting close on the rock so that our body heat helps ward off the morning chill, we both watch as the sun crests over the horizon and lays a glittering golden path on the water. The birds grow more ecstatic in their praise, and a light breeze lifts the leaves of the trees nearby so that they, too, seem to be applauding God's gift of light.

I have no idea what the future holds. It's an open book yet to be read, but for today, I know two things: God loves me, and I am His girl.

Precious Heavenly Father,

Thank You for the many people who helped make this book a reality. I could not have done it without them. My critique partners in Word Weavers helped me improve my writing with their loving and critical analysis of my work. The beta readers (Jenny, Laurie, Kat, Makenna, Sarah, and Trish) gave me helpful feedback. My mom did one last read-through to look for typos and other editing issues. The hard workers at Hope Books coached me through the entire process to get it onto shelves. Many people along the way encouraged me to finish it, and the teen girls at Anchor of Hope Baptist Church even asked for a sequel. My husband lovingly listened to me talk way too much about this book, especially in the past year when I used so much energy and time to finish it.

But mostly, my dear God, I am thankful for You. Thank you for this idea and for the people who made it possible. You have blessed me with so many people whose lives have touched mine and, therefore, these pages. Thank You. You are in control of what happens to it.

So, I pray for every person who reads it. Would you use it to encourage them? Would you strengthen the weak, heal the broken, and lead people into your warm embrace? Would You enable them to rejoice, like Cassie does, that they, too, belong to God?

For the honor and glory of Your Son, Jesus,

Amen.